Jeff Noon is the author of fiv[...]
Automated Alice, Nymphomatio[...]
two collections of short fiction [...]
lives in Brighton.

Acclaim for *Falling Out of Car*s:

'If *Needle in the Groove* was a novel written to be sung, then
Falling Out of Cars is fragments of a diary as ambient music
. . . One of Noon's strengths in this book is the way he
presents the impossible as ordinary . . . *Falling Out of Cars*
is part of Noon's continuing revolt out of genre and into
creative resistance against all traditional forms of fiction,
as if he believes that the ultimate incomprehensibility of
narrative. This is a road novel, stripped of plot and meaning.
What you get is what you read. Anything else might risk
making life comprehensible; and one gets the feeling that, for
Noon, this would be to collude with his readers'
Guardian

'Though one is loathe to resort to the old "like X on acid"
trope, this inexplicably titled novel really does recreate the
woozy weightlessness of a bad (road) trip, or at least a severe
hangover . . . Clever'
The Times

'Jeff Noon has an unsurpassable talent for creating worlds
both recognisable and utterly removed from our own . . . This
is classic Noon – strange, compelling and disturbing'
The List

'To his fans Jeff Noon is a punk Aldous Huxley stringing
together images and oddities to assemble an apocalyptic
dreamworld . . . [*Falling Out of Cars*] is a futuristic road trip in
which Marlene, a journalist, narrates how she and a bunch of
groupies drive around the UK searching for fragments of a
mirror in a bid to tame a bizarre wasting disease that
manifests itself as noise and makes photos lethal'
Arena

'*Falling Out of Cars* is described as a road novel . . . The virtue
of the narrative is that it keeps on going, like the road itself.
We don't know where – road atlases seem scarce – but go it
does and the reader feels compelled to go with it. There are
moments of grace and beauty, such as, in the surprising
Museum of Fragile Things, a room devoted to books whose
text disappears as you read it. It's one of many tantalising,

www.**books**at**transworld**.co.uk/jeffnoon

Also by Jeff Noon

Vurt
Pollen
Automated Alice
Nymphomation
Pixel Juice
Needle in the Groove
Cobralingus

FALLING OUT
OF CARS
>
JEFF NOON

BLACK SWAN

FALLING OUT OF CARS
A BLACK SWAN BOOK : 0 552 99970 9

Originally published in Great Britain by Doubleday,
a division of Transworld Publishers

PRINTING HISTORY
Doubleday edition published 2002
Black Swan edition published 2003

1 3 5 7 9 10 8 6 4 2

Typeset in 10/14pt Clarendon Light by
Kestrel Data, Exeter, Devon.

Black Swan Books are published by Transworld Publishers,
61–63 Uxbridge Road, London W5 5SA,
a division of The Random House Group Ltd,
in Australia by Random House Australia (Pty) Ltd,
20 Alfred Street, Milsons Point, Sydney, NSW 2061, Australia,
in New Zealand by Random House New Zealand Ltd,
18 Poland Road, Glenfield, Auckland 10, New Zealand
and in South Africa by Random House (Pty) Ltd,
Endulini, 5a Jubilee Road, Parktown 2193, South Africa.

Printed and bound in Great Britain by
Cox & Wyman Ltd, Reading, Berkshire.

For Jack

With many thanks to
Julie
Michelle
Hayley
Bill
Grant

Edgar Allan Poe
George Eliot
Michael Bracewell
Samuel Pepys

Transmission

Where do you come from?
And where are you going?

Reception

\>

It was bad last night. Very bad. The worst yet. There were too many of them, a family, and all of them crazed. We had to leave empty-handed. Henderson took a knock to the skull. She's blaming me. Finally, we holed up in a bed and breakfast outside the city. A dark and nasty place it was, with people stumbling up and down the corridors all night long, moaning, lamenting. Difficult to sleep. Blood in the toilet bowl, shit on the walls. All the mirrors, and even the screen of the television, all covered over with black paint. But it was cheap, and safe. No questions asked, even at the three of us wanting to share the one tiny room. And then a late start this morning, and many miles yet to cover. Another job. What good will it bring us? I feel confused, dispirited, after last night. We all do. Nobody's talking.

\>

We made a stop for lunch. The best we could find was a mobile kitchen parked in a lay-by, a few tables set out around it. The food was OK. Afterwards, we took our medicine. Peacock said that we had to keep it sweet from now on, no matter what might happen. He's got a thing about rules. Henderson made a face.

A young kid wandered over from the next table. She was six or seven years old, with dirty brown hair, and a slightly dazed look in her eyes. She asked me if I wanted to play with her doll. I pulled the little string, as directed, and the doll spoke to me in a sick, miserable drawl. Not a single word could be heard properly, but the girl was delighted, as though the toy had declared its undying love. She jumped up and down, squealing.

And then, watching the girl laugh, and listening to the broken voice, I felt a pain steal up on me, this sudden cold yearning. My heart closed up against it, but too late, far too late. What can I do?

Where can I go?

>

Hours of travelling. No real problems, until we saw the roadblock ahead. Police lights whirled and fluttered in the soft twilight. Intrigue, danger, lives lost or being lost. The crying of a siren. Cars were being channelled into a single lane, a uniformed officer giving us hand signals as we passed along.

I looked at him through the side window.

He was young, nervous, his white-gloved hands moving themselves through a series of repeated patterns, one for each vehicle. It should have been simple enough; an order to pull over, to let the ambulance through. Instead, it looked as though some complex ritual was being performed, or else a primitive tribal dance. The officer's mouth was covered by a surgical mask.

His two hands becoming tender, caressing the air, and turned towards me directly. A lover's hands. But still, I couldn't make any sense of the shapes he was making.

I would have to be careful.

We moved along the line of cars, slowly now, towards the trouble. A large articulated truck had fallen over onto its side. It must have come from the opposite

13

direction, driven at speed to break through the central barrier, and then to climb halfway up the steep grassy incline. I imagined the vehicle teetering at this highest point, and then falling, and sliding down to where it now rested, jack-knifed, the long container on the slope of grass, the driver's cabin blocking a good part of the motorway.

'Close your window,' said Peacock.

'Why?'

'That's what they want.'

Police officers moved around the site. The day was only just touched with darkness, but they were already setting up a small floodlight, or trying to. The light was pulsing to a strange rhythm; shining brightly for a second, and then dying, fading, coming bright again, over and over. And then the beam swung upwards suddenly, into the sky. The purple sky, the first of the stars.

Cold blue Venus had only just arisen.

And now, the crashed lorry reared above us; it looked enormous from this close up, like the side of a house. An angry noise started, sparks flew through the air. A fireman was holding the blade of a cutting device against the one exposed door of the cabin. Nearby, the ambulance crew was standing ready, with their medical kits and stretcher.

The poor driver trapped inside there, dead or alive. What had gone wrong?

We had ground to a halt in the line, near enough to see that one part of the lorry had spilled its contents onto the road. Wooden boxes lay scattered about, glass sparkled from the tarmac. A cloud of dust hung in the air. My head was swimming with the detail of it all. There was too much to take in, too much information. I felt the noise taking me over.

The beam of light circled around, and the crackle of sparks was caught in its pathway; a cascade flower, in violet and gold, bloomed behind my eyelids. There was a smell of burning. A dry metallic taste filled my mouth. My ears were buzzing.

The sound of the blade.

'What the fuck?'

It was Henderson, speaking to me. She had twisted round in the passenger seat. Her face, with its tangled mass of hair, was painted with colour as the floodlight bathed the car.

'Marlene?'

The voice was slurred, and too distant. The light swung away from us, but now the trail of sparks appeared to dance around the car's interior.

'Marlene, you OK?'

'Yeah . . . yeah. I'm fine.'

I used the technique that Peacock had taught me; not to shut the eyes, but rather to concentrate on just one tiny aspect of the world. I had my notebook in my lap, and I looked down, focusing all my attention on the cover image. For some reason, I felt embarrassed; I mustn't let them know I'm suffering, not this much. And so I kept my eyes tight on the notebook, closing out all other images, to let the picture form in my head.

Holding it there, holding . . .

It seemed to work. The feelings passed through me; the sparks, the light, the blade's fire. And I looked up again as a policeman banged on the side of the car, telling us to move on.

There was a heavy security presence, more than I'd seen in a long while. All of the officers wore the white masks. Some of them were armed. I was puzzled by this, until we saw the floodlight sweep over the company logo painted on the lorry's side.

'Ah shit,' said Peacock. 'Will you look at that.'

'I'm looking,' said Henderson.

It was a large open eye, blue, surrounded by a swirl of gold. And I knew then just what the cloud of dust promised. Speckles of the stuff collected on the windows as we drove along, a bright yellow glitter. The police were there to stop us from stealing the fallen load. But I just wanted to climb out of the car right there and then, even as we gathered speed. This crazy urge came over me, to taste the powder fully for once. To run through the particles of it, open-mouthed and breathing the dust in deeply, overdosing.

>

My name is Marlene Moore. This is my book.

It's the kind of notebook a teenager might buy, with the picture of a tiger on the cover. A tiger with blue stripes. Inside, the paper is thin, almost translucent; the ink from my pen seeps through. All these lines of writing. Shadows, glances.

This is the story. These are all the various things that have happened to me in the last few weeks. But now, as I flick through the book, I see only the mess I have made. Words, sentences, paragraphs, whole pages, scoured with black marks. Mistakes. The noise gets in everywhere. Pages are ripped, or torn out completely; some discarded, others taped into new positions. There are smudges of dirt, of food, of blood. The marks where once a pressed flower lay; stains of chlorophyll, pollen, the tiny fragments of a petal.

This is the story.

I've decided to make a new start. I will begin again from what I'm sure of, the events of this day, this night just gone. Many times before I have done this, and always each time the confusion takes over. I can bring to mind scattered details, emotions, overall moods; it's just that something gets lost along the way. The noise is a dark hand, a soft hold, slow poison, sickness, it will not leave me go. And yet I will have such moments of lucidity, a sudden pain of memory, whole and vibrant; a fleeting glimpse that must be caught hold of immediately, or else be lost for ever. I must be strong. I have to keep writing. There is no other escape, especially now that I seem to be getting worse.

This is the book.

I have taken the photograph from its pocket on the inside front cover.

Perhaps the light is flickering. There is a slight fuzziness to the image. The faces are smeared. Only by holding the photograph at one precise angle can I make out clearly the gentle smile.

Angela.

These words . . .

\>

Moving south, trying to reach the new town by night-fall. We have passed through a cloud of gold. Beyond this, the roads empty out once more. Most of the traffic seems to be avoiding this area, and what there is moves slowly.

There are too many accidents.

Every few miles we see another car, abandoned at the roadside. Some of them with evident damage, of a crash or a fire. But mostly the vehicles stand there forlorn, unmarked, as though the driver had simply stepped out for a moment, and then decided to walk away. This is the kind of image that would turn up in the science fiction books I read when I was a teenager.

The abandoned car.

I thought it a supremely romantic image, the symbol of a dying civilization. I suppose that most teenagers have this strange desire, to be alive during the end of days. But now, becoming commonplace, the image has lost its poetic allure. The cars have been vacated, simply because the drivers can no longer trust themselves.

Can there be any other reason?

Peacock and Henderson were talking about the

crashed lorry, and the cloud. They were arguing. Peacock had wanted to stop, to watch the containment operation a while longer, maybe even to pick up a few stray supplies. The drug. Our daily salvation, he calls it. But Henderson had said no, we drive on. She's more or less taken control of the mission.

I've travelled around the country with this couple for a little over a week now. Not long. They found me in the public gardens that night, digging at the soil with my bare hands. That was a low point. The black flowers that grew there, with their overpowering scent. I had followed the clues to this place, this small patch of ground, and yet my hands pulled up only dirt, roots, worms, stones. Where was it? Where the fuck was it?

I was on the edge of giving up, when I heard Peacock's voice saying, 'Now there's a sight.' And they helped me then. We pulled the treasure from the earth, the shining treasure. It was odd, them helping me, and I'm still not sure what they're looking for, beyond a share in the takings. Certainly, I wouldn't have got this far without them.

Peacock's a big ugly brute. He wears a brown leather porkpie hat, a suede carcoat. I've seen him without the hat only a few times, revealing the butchered razor-cut left over from active service. He can turn his hand to most things. He does most of the driving for instance, and even when he's suffering. It's all a question of using the drugs properly, but I'm getting worried about him. Easy enough to get along with, except that sometimes his face will shut down hard. It's a wounded face, and the hardness held there like a mask, not to hide the wounds but to show them off. I've seen a good few times already the violence of the man. The war, his time overseas, the cold distance that will come into his eyes. But there's something behind the toughness, I'm sure there is. I want there to be. Something being kept at bay. I don't know his first name.

He's got a gun.

Henderson, or Bev, as Peacock calls her in their friendlier moments, is even more of a mystery. In many ways she's tougher than Peacock, more volatile, I mean. More prone to anger, and sometimes this is useful, and sometimes it isn't. Dressed in green tracksuit bottoms, a sports top, flashy trainers, she's always ready to leap into action. She doesn't drink much, she doesn't smoke. Every morning she goes through a complex t'ai chi routine. She's in her mid-twenties, a couple of years younger than Peacock. She's the least affected of us. I haven't a clue what she did, before this journey. Just wandering around, I imagine. Because I know it's not easy finding direction these days; we're all lost together, all of us, all the people. Along these tangled pathways, briefly meeting, and then to part. Strangers, only strangers . . .

Sometimes, I can't help suspecting that Henderson actually enjoys the chaos. The sickness allows her character to be revealed, without need of excuse. And then I think back to what I was doing at her age. Ten years ago? I was just married, pregnant. My career on hold. We had moved to Oxford, a new house. Everything seemed perfect. Well, normal, I suppose. The start of a proper life. But now, all of that feels like a mirage; a story of mist.

The truth is, and despite all the things we've been

through together this last week, I still can't bring myself to trust Henderson, nor Peacock, neither of them, not completely.

There is no easy decision.

We have not yet talked about last night, except for a few comments from Henderson about the pain in her head. It wasn't our first failure, and perhaps we can make it up later on, I don't know. I feel like I'm coming to the end of something, to the end of what I can give. A few more days perhaps, a few more collections, and then I want to get the case back to Kingsley, and get the money for it. Just to make a living. But it's not that, it's not just the money.

I don't know what it is.

I keep returning to Angela. That last time, that one last time at the hospital. Watching her there through the screens, I wanted to go in, to get in the room with her, to hold her. Even though I knew the dangers, the dangers of contact, of touching, of letting her see me there, of talking to her even, still I wanted to. Maybe I knew already, this would be the last time. I don't know. And I let the doctors warn me off, as always.

It was shameful, turning away.

My only child . . .

Perhaps these feelings affected my decision earlier tonight. We were approaching the turnoff that would lead us towards the new town, when Henderson said:

'Look now. Here's a sad one.'

It was a hitchhiker, standing by the side of the road. A young woman.

'Keep driving,' I said.

'What does the card say?' asked Peacock.

22

I watched the hitcher as we passed. She was holding a piece of card with some letters scrawled on it. It was nearly dark by now, and the woman was shining the beam of a small torch onto the card, but still I couldn't make out what was written there. She made a rude gesture with her fingers as we drove by.

'Fucking cheek,' said Peacock.

'Wherever,' said Henderson.

'What?'

'That's what it says, the sign. Wherever. Can you believe that?'

We had seen a lot of these hitchhikers, during the last week. All of them seemed young, a lot of them women. Very often they were walking along the motorway shoulder, far from any slip road or service station, as though they had simply dropped from the sky. I don't know what they were running from, and it was best to just ignore them, I thought. Just keep to the job in hand, no distractions.

I turned to look through the back window; the woman was already lost in the dark air. And then, and for some reason I'm still trying to work out, I said:

'No, wait. Turn round.'

Last night, when we shared that one room, that dreadful B and B. There were only two beds, two singles. I was constantly being woken up by people moving along the corridor, but at one point I came awake to realize that the sounds were coming this time from the room itself, from the other bed.

A soft moaning, tiny cries, gasps of breath.

Of course, I'd realized early on that Henderson and Peacock were an item, even if they hardly showed much affection in public. But still, it was uncomfortable, being there in the same room.

They were surprisingly gentle, given their outward natures. Perhaps they were restraining themselves on my behalf, I don't know.

What could they be feeling; how would the sickness affect their pleasure? What would it turn into? The noise would surely be overwhelming at such moments; a touch might drag like a blade, or fall like dust blown across the skin.

All those broken messages . . .

And then I tried to think about the last time I'd made love. When was that? I just couldn't bring it to mind.

There seems to be no ruling to how my memory works; certain events will stay with me, free as yet from infection, but lately, and more and more, I can feel the past drifting away. Beyond hold. The weeks, the years gone by, one by one, all drawn over by confusion.

Love? Where was love? The last time? Had it really been with my husband? Has there been nobody since then? Oh, but where has the closeness gone to?

Where has it gone?

Henderson was all against it, of course. She was calling me some bad names, and saying how she was in charge. I agreed that she was, but that I had started this, and I would finish it how I pleased. I told her it was my car, and above all I had the key to the suitcase.

'Fine,' she said. 'Whatever.'

'It's only till the next stop,' said Peacock.

'Fine.'

The road was completely empty. We did a wide U-turn, and then travelled back until we passed the young woman once more. She wasn't even looking at us now, but just standing there with her head lowered. The sign had fallen to the ground. And then we made another turn, to bring us round to the proper direction.

'She's trouble,' said Henderson. 'Look at her.'

I could see that she was even younger than I had first imagined. A teenager. Peacock stopped the car, but the girl made no move towards us. She just stood there, looking at the car. I wound down my side window, asked her where she was going. I thought the girl might give me a smile, at the least. Instead, she just repeated the word on the sign.

'Wherever.'

So then I told her our destination, and she said, 'The new town?'

'That's the one.'

'It's not far enough.'

Henderson spoke to her. 'Girl. If you want it, get in. Otherwise, we're out of here.'

The teenager looked down the road, as though another car might appear at any moment. But nothing did, not even the hint of a distant headlight. The moon had followed Venus into the sky. Everything was quite still.

'OK.'

I opened the door for her, and then moved along the seat so that she could slide in beside me.

'You want to move that?' she said.

It was the suitcase. I pulled it off the seat, down to the floor of the car. And then we set off once more. I introduced the three of us, but the girl made no reply, and we travelled in silence for a while.

'Well, this is fun,' said Henderson.

The sodium lamps passed by, some alight, some dark, and I caught repeated glimpses of the new passenger.

She was a neat, serious looking young woman, perhaps sixteen or seventeen years old. A girl, really. Her black hair was all knotted together at the back of her neck, and she was dressed simply, a well-worn denim jacket, a scarf, a pair of jeans. She kept a large grey bag slung around her body, her only possession. I don't think she'd been travelling for very long. There was a softness to her face, set off by a smear of purple on her lips, and a cosmetic beauty spot on her right cheek. It was a fashion thing, I remembered, amongst the young. It was the last good fashion in place when the trouble began. The girl had kept it going, for some reason, when all the mirrors had sickened, and been turned aside.

Applied in the dark . . .

And she looked at me then, with her dark eyes held tight behind a pair of rimmed spectacles.

What did she want? It wasn't a thing that people did much any more, maintaining eye contact. It was too much like a bad reflection; unlawful, dangerous even. Peacock, Henderson and myself were for ever avoiding each other's gaze, and yet here was this young woman staring at me, intently. I had to turn away.

'So then, girl,' said Peacock. 'What's your name?'

'Tupelo.'

'Tupelo? What kind of name is that?'

'It's a town, in the States.'

'You're American?'

'No.'

'Where do you come from?' I asked.

But the girl would not answer, and that was the end of that, and we drove on in silence once again. We had left the motorway now. Peacock started to explain about how the new town would maybe have some kind of security around it. A border zone, walls, gates, maybe a guard or two. 'We need to be careful,' he said. 'After last night. We can't let Kingsley down.'

'What are you people up to?' asked the girl. 'Who's Kingsley?'

'Never you mind,' said Henderson.

Tupelo picked up my notebook from the seat. I'd been working on it, during the day.

'Is this yours?'

I told her it was, and she flipped through the pages, here and there. 'You're a writer?'

'A journalist.'

She looked through the book for a while longer. What could be seen there, in the fading light?

'You're working on a story now?'

'Yes.'

'About the sickness?'

Again, her eyes met mine.

'About the sickness,' I answered.

That seemed to satisfy her, and nothing much else was said.

>

Peacock stopped the car, right there on the roadside. He got out. We all wondered what the problem was. There was a wrenching sound, and a curse, as Peacock pulled at the driver's mirror. Eventually, he raised up one booted foot and kicked the mirror loose. More cursing then, with Peacock saying how he kept getting glances of himself, whenever he leaned out. The other wing mirror, and the rear-view, they went ages ago. Likewise, the dashboard clock; long since broken, the two hands held still behind the cracked glass.

'No more looking back,' said Henderson.

We're losing ourselves. We're losing all the traces, all the moments of the world, one by one.

I have to keep writing.

>

A terrible sight. Peacock pulled into a petrol station to get the tank filled up, and to buy some cigarettes, some chocolate. I went with him to the little shop, only to find that a small boy had been taken ill there. He was lying on the floor in front of a video game, his arms reaching out wildly to push away some invisible object, and a dreadful wailing noise coming from him. His parents were standing off to one side, helpless, scared, as the garage staff tried to hold the boy still. I felt a cold grey numbness, thinking only of Angela, and her first real attack. And then I stepped forward, bringing Peacock with me. Peacock held the mouth and the tongue in the correct position whilst I broke open three capsules one after the other, releasing the powder direct to the boy's throat. And then . . . and then we bought our cigarettes and our chocolate bars and paid for our petrol and we left that place behind us.

\>

We moved through a series of complex road junctions and roundabouts. There seemed to be too many signs erected here, too many traffic signals, a glut of bill-boards and panels where images danced. Neon shapes were flickering, overly bright in all their colours, and each of them demanding my whole attention. But the more I looked, the less I could see.

The noise levels were too high.

Dominating the landscape was a large visual display advertising the Lucidity drug. It was the same eye we had seen painted on the side of the crashed lorry; but this time the logo was constructed from many hundreds of tiny bulbs, which flashed on and off in sequence, to give the impression that the eye was opening and closing.

'Dear sweet Lucy,' said Peacock.

'Fucking bastard company,' said Henderson, 'the money they're making from this.'

The eye was a sharp electric blue, with the golden swirls of dust spiralling outwards from the centre. I felt I was being hypnotized by the effect.

Below this image, a line of copy was moving across

the board. I thought I saw the phrase, 'If you can read this . . .' just briefly, but the letters kept dissolving into each other.

'What does it say?' I asked.

'Can't you read it?' said Henderson.

'No.'

There was a silence then, inside the car.

'What does it say?'

It was the girl, Tupelo, who finally answered me.

'If you can read this,' she said, 'it means you're alive.'

>

I was looking through the earlier pages of my journal, the ones abandoned. Sitting in the car, using the torch that Tupelo had brought with her, trying to find where I described my last telephone call to the hospital. It would be somewhere near the beginning. When this journey first started, and before I met Henderson and Peacock, I would spend long nights in hotel rooms alone, writing, just writing. Remembering, as I could, all the details.

They seemed important, back then, the details . . .

The words slid by under the beam of light, manic and scarred. Where was it? Where were the lines detailing the doctor's response?

I tried to remember the call itself.

Where was I? Away on some job somewhere, that would be it. There was that final visit, and I was tired. Weary and numb from staring at the video screens all day and all night, hoping for some sign from my daughter, and seeing only the poor girl wandering her bare, white room, or else immersing herself in the isolation tank.

The soft liquid enfolding her body.

There was nothing I could do there, and I had to admit that to myself finally. There was only the waiting, which took for ever, and so, running from that into work, some petty writing job no doubt. But where exactly? I couldn't think, just that somehow I had managed to find a telephone that worked. In those days the sickness had not yet found its way completely into the network, but calls were already plagued with interference, with hiss and crackle, ghosts on the line. But still, I tried to call every day that went by, to see how Angela was doing. Whispers at the other end, or many people talking all at once. It's all a question of chance, but just sometimes a stray signal would get through. I called the hospital.

What was said?

What did the doctor say to me, that time, before the line went dead? Again, I searched through the book, the pages moving quickly under my fingers, back and forth. It must be here somewhere. I wrote it down. I can remember writing it down, I'm sure I did, I would've done.

Condition: stable.

That must be it. Was that it? An unexpected white page in the notebook, with just those two words, centre field, and underlined.

'Are you all right?'

'What?'

It's the girl, Tupelo. She was asking after me.

'Are you OK? You look . . .'

'Leave me alone.'

Condition stable. The road headed down through a tunnel. Lights were strung along the ceiling, leading the way, flickering in beauty. A bird was flying ahead of us through the dark and golden light, and my eyes were set to burning with the splendour of it all, suddenly, and filled with tears.

>

The new town seemed to have a climate all its very own. Peacock had been wrong; there were no walls around the place, no security guards. It just turned gradually warmer as we drove through the outskirts; and quieter, more serene, the closer we came to the centre. The sky was held low, trapping the night's heat in the leafy boulevards.

We were late. Not for the job itself, which would have to take place well after dark anyway; Kingsley had given specific instructions about that, in his last communication. However, he had also arranged that we stay overnight at the house of one of his friends, an old woman. 'Lady Iris', he called her. This would be our first destination.

Peacock stopped to ask directions. The young man he spoke to replied in a slow, hesitant manner, as though afraid of his own tongue. During this conversation, the girl, Tupelo, got out of the car.

There were no goodbyes.

'Miserable cow,' said Henderson.

The house, when we found it, was slightly apart from the main town, and set on the rise of a hill. It was a large, old-fashioned place, built many years before the prefabricated units of the new community. The stonework was covered in grime.

It was around eight, I suppose. Two hours or so later than expected. Kingsley, for some reason, insisted that we get there in the early evening. But I'm not very good with time, these days. My watch has long since been discarded, and now the days slip by in vague periods; such and such, just gone, late morning, almost, around about, early evening, and so on. Only the taking of the medicine gives any real structure to our lives.

We were shown around by a man, Edward, who seems to be the servant of Lady Iris. Nothing was said about our late arrival. There was an antique grandfather clock in the hallway; the hands had been removed from the face. Edward told us, politely, that the lady of the house had already retired for the night, and that she would speak with us in the morning. It all feels quite odd, but at least I will have my own room tonight.

And this is where I am now. I have caught up with myself. Soon, we will go in search of the next precious item. I feel calm enough, a lull in my sickness has allowed these thoughts to be written down. But once again, the doubts creep in. I can only hope tonight turns out better than last night did. Peacock has a phrase he likes to use, about keeping your head closed down. I will try.

This is a strange household. There are no electric lights, only candles. Shadows, whisperings. Something scratching behind the walls. I write, sitting at an antique dressing table. An empty cradle of wood rises from the worktop. I can see the tiny sockets, where the glass should be held. On one wall of the room, there is a carved ebony frame, with nothing inside it. I have noticed similar empty frames, downstairs, and along the quiet, candlelit corridors. Or else a sudden rectangular patch, where the wallpaper is cleaner.

The official guidelines were clear on this matter: do not look at yourself whilst suffering the effects, or the after-effects, of the new condition. Madness takes hold of your image. Most people simply turn the mirrors over to face the wall, or cover them with cloth. In this house, however, they have all been removed.

I have a sudden vision now, of the mysterious Lady Iris ordering dear faithful Edward in this curious task. The mirrors. Perhaps they are keeping them all in storage, somewhere, until the sickness has died down, or a proper cure is found.

I imagine a dark cellar, filled with reflections.

Reflections. Spirits in the glass. Images, the human expression. Our personal appearance. The face. Oh, the face; this strange object that daily we examined, for marks, creases, evidence of time's passing, for beauty, ugliness. All hidden now, turned away from. And when was the last time I looked at myself, truly?

I have been thinking of the moment when Kingsley first mentioned the task, the proposition, as he called it, and the possibility of my involvement. We were sitting at a small table in his garden, drinking tea brought to us by his maid, the interview just over. This was, we had agreed, the last of our sessions. It was the spring of this year, some while ago now. Angela was not yet ill, or not that I knew of; the noise levels slowly increasing all around us, unnoticed, a phrase misheard, a sign misread, a quiet buzzing in the ear. I had been coming to this house of shadows twice a week to interview Kingsley, to capture on disc his varied adventures; each night I would play back the recording, hardly considering why certain words could not be made out clearly.

It was a job that had already gone over its official bounds. The magazine had gladly allowed me this project for one of its human interest articles, but I now had the vague idea that Kingsley's story might be expanded into a book of some kind.

A curious man, a curious life.

But for all the material he had given me, and for all the tours around his collection of Victorian oddities, I still felt I was no nearer to understanding Kingsley; the dull cloud of sadness that always hung over him, the cold pain in his eyes. And now, as we sat there in the falling light, and he asked me to switch off that 'infernal machine' for the final time, he turned those cold eyes upon me. 'My dear Marlene,' he said, 'soon I will not be able to do this. To let my eyes hold themselves thus, directly upon your own.' I asked him what he meant by this, and in reply he only smiled, a rare occurrence.

Music drifted through the open French windows, as the keys of an old mechanical piano moved through their ghostly patterns. Kingsley raised himself from his chair and extended his hand to mine. He wore his years gracefully; how handsome he looked, with his linen suit, his pomaded hair, his mahogany cane. He said, 'I have lived a sorry life all told, in search of rare objects. Really, they are the fragments of a dream, nothing more.' And together then, we strolled along the pathways of the garden. The sun touched the tops of the trees; the day lost a little of its colour.

Kingsley's house was a grand, rambling place set in the countryside outside Oxford. Its tended grounds merged into the surrounding forest, without fence or marking, and, as we walked the narrow scented lanes between the trees, I realized I was now quite lost. This was a labyrinth, but not one planned by human hand; rather, nature had folded itself, over and over, creating this tangle of avenues. Kingsley led the way forward, taking each turn seemingly at random, and presently we came to a small, shaded clearing.

Here, within a circle of trees whose long branches intertwined above our heads, an upright structure could be seen. It was waist-high, old, made of black stone, with flowering vines growing around it.

A church font.

A mournful light gathered, beneath the canopy of leaves. I could hear a lone wood pigeon cooing; apart from that, all was quiet. Kingsley urged me to step closer. He made a wordless gesture. A wooden lid covered the top of the font, and this I now removed. I leaned over to peer into the hollowed bowl.

There was a pool of water inside, which glowed with a faint violet sheen. A flickering image played upon the surface, as though a film was being projected into the liquid. Was this yet another item from Kingsley's prized collection, I wondered, some strange optical contraption designed to both delight and educate, rather like the magic lanterns we had looked at earlier in the day?

Gradually, the image took shape. It was a face. An old man's face, briefly seen; his mouth opened wide to take in air, before being pulled back into the water. Another face took its place, and another. A multitude of faces appeared one by one, each of them different from the last; all of them rising for a moment with their silent gasping for breath, and then being drowned once more. And then, leaning further over to better see the images,

I saw myself, my own face, held within the water. Tears fell from my eyes, drawn forth without reason. I moved back slightly, but the water would not let my reflection go. I was captured there, enthralled, taken over. And even as I watched in horror, in a dreamlike trance, my image was pulled down beneath the surface. The breath caught in my throat.

Something had been taken from me . . .

Kingsley made a noise, a gentle cough. He stepped forward to meet me, and, without a word, he put his hand into the water. A shiver went through him, and he brought his hand back out, with something held now between his fingers. A silvery light flashed around the clearing, cast by this small triangular object. It was a broken piece of mirrored glass. A violet glow floated around the shape, creating a slight halo effect.

'Nothing is lost. Reflections cannot make their escape.' Kingsley spoke quietly, calmly, and yet once again I was aware of his underlying sadness. 'Can you imagine, Marlene? That every face that ever gazed into this glass is kept there, alive, seduced.' His eyes were half-closed, and he moved the piece of glass slowly from side to side. 'I first glanced into the mirror many years ago. I was a young man. And always I come back here, to gaze again. I have seen many a stranger's image. But never have I seen my younger face return. No, never.' Finally, he let the mirror slide back into the shallow pool of the font. 'Well then, still we await . . .'

The air seemed darker now. The hushed trees bowed towards us, releasing their scents. Kingsley took hold of my hand. 'I have a proposition,' he said. 'It may be of interest to you.' Turning about, we followed a different pathway back towards the garden, with Kingsley speaking along the way. As we drew near to the house, the lonely, melancholic sound of the piano could be heard through the leaves.

We took the Lucy just before setting out. Really, it should be taken last thing at night, to stop the bad dreams coming. First thing in the morning, the middle of the day, and then just before sleep; this is the schedule. But Henderson insisted, given last night's stupidity, I guess, and the possible nature of what lay ahead.

It's so easy, making mistakes.

Taking too much, taking too little; taking the right amount, but at the wrong time. Taking the right amount, but then overloading the senses, beyond control. There is no simple measure.

We were gathered in the kitchen, the three of us, and Peacock gave out the capsules, one for each. I turned mine over and over in my hand.

The tiny blue eye on the yellow casing.

What would I be, without Lucidity? I would not be able to write. I would have no real understanding of words, as they are spoken. The world would fill up with noise and I would be lost, completely.

'Keep it sweet,' said Henderson.

She popped the capsule into her mouth, with a sip of

cold water. And she watched then, as Peacock repeated the mantra, as was necessary.

'Keeping it sweet. Nothing but.'

And he swallowed his share.

I was thinking about what had happened, earlier that day, at the crash. The details, again and again. I had suffered a mild attack, even though the drug was inside me. And then seeing that beautiful cloud of dust. That sudden urge I had felt, to just run through it, the powder, breathing it in. Taking far too much, all at once. What would that do to me?

I had heard stories, from the doctors looking after my daughter. They said an overdose brought a veil down, between yourself and the world, a veil so black that nothing could be truly experienced; nothing touched, nothing seen or heard, nothing tasted. They said it closed up the body, sealed it. And this is what they did to Angela, towards the end. Encircled her with darkness. Is this what I now desire, for myself?

Peacock and Henderson were looking at me.

And so I did what I had to do, what I was supposed to do. The rules. But what exactly was I keeping so sweet? I could no longer remember.

The travel agent's premises were easy to find, following Kingsley's instructions. It was a dismal building, bland, clean, identical to all the others on the street. The shop was called TRAVEL, the single word in scarlet letters. There was a window display with a few tatty posters on show: a white hotel block, a tropical beach, a lonely swimming pool. Above these, a sign asked the question, 'Where are you going?' The floor of the window was filled with sand, and littered with cigarette butts, crisp packets, holiday snapshots, a child's bucket and spade, a beach ball. An old box camera was propped up on a tripod. The place was dark, the upper windows draped with cloth.

'Do we go in now?' said Peacock.

'No,' said Henderson. 'Later. And Marlene stays out of it. Last night was bad enough. You hear me?'

I nodded, and we split up then, with Peacock and Henderson going off together, arguing about which bar they would visit. It was good to be alone. I walked the streets for a time, without aim. Nobody would look at me, not directly, and nor at each other, not properly. I listened to people talking; conversations were being remembered, quoted, not created there and then.

'My wife and I were wondering, would you be free to take supper with us, tomorrow evening?'

'I should be delighted.'

'No. The delight is ours.'

'Oh, most charmed, I'm sure.'

Emotions were scarce. All the public telephones were closed down for the evening.

Only the most important road signs could be seen, and these limited to half a dozen basic symbols. LEFT, RIGHT, GO, STOP, YES, NO. Very few of the stores had proper names to them. They were called things like BUTCHER, or else BAKER, or even PRODUCT. There was more than one shop called, quite simply, SHOP. This was safety, of a kind; information held at bay.

The town hall clock was hidden behind tarpaulin. From the shade of a doorway, a young woman was singing. It was a tuneless drone, a cold lament. And then, standing near a glass-fronted booth called DRUG, I watched an orderly queue of people having their night's supply issued to them. A card was stamped, the single capsule handed over.

The company's eye beamed down.

I bought something to eat; something green and soft, that the street vendor squeezed into a piece of dough. He asked me what flavour I wanted. I chose the Spicy option, and a single squirt of juice came out of a nozzle.

With this damp creation in hand, I continued my walk. Most of the buildings were built to the same pattern, using the same few materials: grey steel, fawn coloured blocks of stone. Blue glass, non-reflective. I'd heard stories about this new invention, but had never seen it before and now I couldn't stop myself from looking in the windows as I passed.

A few places were still open. Public houses, late-night cafés, and the like. PUB, CAFÉ, DRINK. In one such place, a young couple were sitting in a window seat. They were playing chess. Neither of them spoke to the other; perhaps they were mannequins, or robots even. And then, on one of the darker streets, I found a place that gave out its full title, proudly.

It drew me forward.

The Museum of Fragile Things.

It was a tall thin building, the only one in its street that was still lit up. I thought this strange, a museum being open at this hour. The window was empty, a clean, white space. There was a kind of shimmering effect in the space. I looked more closely. My eyes were drawn to a different focus, and then, slowly, finally, I made out the singular device that created the effect.

A spider's web.

A vast silken web, that stretched from the four corners of the window, from floor to ceiling. It was a thing of terrifying complexity. A small electric fan placed in the back wall of the display caused the structure to tremble; in places, the connections were already broken. And there, repairing one of these damaged areas, hung the maker of the pattern.

The spider was a tiny mechanical creature, finely made, delicate, constructed from glass. The transparent body was half filled with a silver fluid. It was crawling along the strands, quickly now, towards the site of another breakage.

How could I not want to see more?

There were four storeys to the museum, with the most prized exhibits kept on the top floor. The woman on the desk gave me this information. 'As the visitor ascends,' she said, 'the objects become more fragile.' Her voice was measured, quiet, tightly scripted. 'Upon reaching the highest level, we gently urge that care be taken.'

I paid the entrance fee gladly, and then wandered upwards, past sculptures made from tissue paper, plastic animals suspended on water jets, a pendulum made of ice. There were many exhibits. A cloud of trapped butterflies landed as one on the branch of a tree, forming there, briefly, an array of beautiful flowers all with petals made of wings. I saw a dead man's final breaths, caught in a glass jar. I heard music, made from the weight of water falling drop by drop onto the various keys of a xylophone. Only by bending down close to the instrument could the music be heard. I thought I recognized the melody, but the name of it escaped me. On the next to last floor, a young girl's face was crafted in the flames of a gas burner.

She was smiling, this child of fire.

I closed my eyes for a second, and when I looked again, the face had vanished.

>

Condition stable. What did he mean, the doctor? Why did he say that? Was she really stable, was there something wrong with the equipment? Or was the doctor lying to me? Why would he lie? Condition stable. What was being hidden behind the words? Stable? The word, what did it mean? Caught suspended, on some kind of balance, on the edge of something, on the edge of falling. Falling. Condition stable. The next day I called again, or tried to. It was the same telephone I used, I remember now. But this time there was no connection made, none.

Condition stable.

And by the end of that day, during the night of that day, as I learned, as I later came to know, my Angela died. She died. I felt that a great, cold wave had moved through me; cold, so cold, and terribly slow as it closed around my heart. And I let it happen, I let the coldness happen. I should've been there, oh why wasn't I there? Only the coldness . . .

Nine years old. She died away.

\>

A single exhibition space occupied the whole top floor of the museum. It was a brightly lit room filled with books. And there, reading one of the volumes, I saw the young hitchhiker, Tupelo.

'Oh, it's you,' she said. 'Henderson, right?'

'No. That's the other woman. I'm Marlene.'

'Marlene, yeah.'

'You like reading?' I asked.

'This is great. It's just perfect.'

I looked around. All four walls were lined with shelves, and every shelf tightly packed. The books were old, clothbound or hardback, with a few modern paperbacks tucked in between. There was one other person in the room, a man sitting in the corner, the museum attendant. He seemed to be sleeping.

I walked over to the nearest shelf, and ran my finger along the spines. It was curious. I pulled a book off the shelf, and then another one, looking at the covers. I moved along the shelf a little way, doing the same with further volumes.

'None of them have titles.'

'No,' said Tupelo. 'Not now.'

'What do you mean, not now?'

'Take a look inside.'

I opened the one book I was holding.

'Please be careful,' said the attendant. His head nodded dreamily.

The book looked normal enough, except that a few lines of the text were missing, here and there, from the page I had turned to.

'Read to me,' said Tupelo. 'Out loud.'

So, I did. I started to read.

'Surrounded by phantoms in the noonday, trembling under a breeze when the leaves were still . . .'

I can remember them. I can bring the words to mind, quite easily, as I now write. But then, at the moment I read them out loud, I felt a coldness come over me. I was shaking. I had to stop reading.

'I don't understand.'

'No,' said Tupelo. 'It's weird, isn't it? A strange feeling.'

I looked down at the page. I thought I might have imagined it. But no. Those few words I had just read out, they had now vanished from the book.

'What's happening here?'

'Carry on,' said Tupelo. 'Keep reading.'

I looked at the girl. Her eyes, when they met mine, had a gentleness to them.

'Go on. Read.'

Again, I turned to the page . . .

'Without appetite for the common objects of human desire, but pining after the moonbeams.'

And one by one, as my eye scanned them, as my tongue pronounced them, each word faded slowly from the page of the book.

53

What surprises me is that I have seen many strange things during this trip, and no doubt I will see some strangeness yet, but this one particular effect really got to me for some reason. Perhaps because I have made my living from words, up to now. Or else because I have prized books, over the years, collected them, reading and rereading my favourites. The stories that my father used to read to me; the stories that I read in turn to Angela, before the sickness came; and very often the one same story, night after night.

All gone now. All gone . . .

The books in this room could not be read, not a second time.

I chose another volume from the shelf. Again, there was no title to the book, and even more of the pages had words missing from them. Some of the pages were almost completely blank.

'Please, do be careful,' said the attendant.

I turned to a page where most of the words were still present, and then started to read.

'Hence the potency of Bowie's impact on England: the marriage of alien and dandy giving birth to the ultimate outsider figure for the modern age, the queer messiah from space . . .'

Again, I had to stop. Seeing the words disappear from the page like this, it brought only a sadness.

'I can't do it. I can't.'

'It's beautiful,' said Tupelo.

'No.'

'All books should be made like this. I saw one at college. The fragile narrative, destroyed by the very act of reading. It's like . . . it's like the most perfect love, like one that's only grasped for a moment, you know, and then lost, for ever. What do you think?'

I couldn't answer.

'Marlene, one day all the books in this room will be blank. Empty. They will be filled with emptiness.'

'Where do the words go to?'

'Please be careful,' said the attendant. 'We are closing now.'

And there, in the fading light, Tupelo was moving from shelf to shelf, pulling down books and opening them, and reading a few lines, and moving on. 'Look here now,' she said. 'This page has one line left upon it. Just the one line. *All the broken children learn to dance.* That's it. And there, it's gone.'

'Where do they go?'

'What?'

'When the words disappear, where do they go to?'

I needed to know this.

I needed to know if the words sank back into the paper's fabric, or whether they were drawn upwards, into the reader's brain. Or perhaps the words floated through the air of the room, invisible, but present all around. I needed to know this, but the girl wouldn't answer me. She was reading. She was reading the words.

The sound of pages being turned, the girl whispering. The room growing dark.

\>

And maybe, in remembering the words that I read earlier tonight, I have saved them in some way. Maybe by writing them down, here, in my own book, I have saved these words from being lost.

I don't know.

Of course, I cannot recall the exact words used, the exact structure of every sentence. I don't recognize the passages from any book previously read. I can only try my best to give the words this second life. And even within these few examples I have given, from my visit to the museum, there will be mistakes.

But then again, this book of mine is filled with similar errors. Half-remembered conversations; things seen in shadow, magnified. Words that disappear from the tongue, even as they are being said.

But that first sentence, it will never leave me.

Surrounded by phantoms in the noonday, trembling under a breeze when the leaves were still . . .

>

The windows would softly flare with a yellow light. The curtains would bleed with this light, momentarily, and then return to darkness. It was against all the rules of the new town; all the other buildings, even the few houses I had passed, none of them showed any light at all. Peacock had explained it, that all non-essential systems were switched off, after a certain hour. But now, here was this one place, this travel agent's, with some kind of power being used, some random generation.

'What's going on in there?' asked the girl.

'I don't know.'

'What are you doing, you people? What's the game?'

'Look, you should go.'

'Should I?'

We were standing in the shadows, just down from where the car was parked. The streetlights had a shrouded effect to them; there was no sound to be heard. The roads were deserted. The whole town had been turned low for the night. Even the moon, although nearly full, was muted by thin clouds.

'Just go. This isn't for you.'

'Go where?'

She'd followed me, this Tupelo, back from the museum. Peacock and Henderson had already gone ahead.

'Do they always leave you alone?'

'What?'

'Your friends? The big guy, the funny woman. What is it, they do all the work, you just write it down?'

'Something like that.'

'But you're the start of all this, right? You're the problem?'

'The problem?'

'I mean, you started it?'

'Yeah, I started it.'

'So, what is it then? You're too sick? You're too sick to do the job? Is that it?'

I looked at her.

'We're all sick, girl.'

'Yeah, we're all sick. But you're the worst.'

The girl was leaning against the wall, smoking a cigarette. There was an obvious pose about her, I felt, in the way she stood, the way she blew the smoke, her nonchalance. But she's of that age, I guess.

'Where will you sleep tonight?'

'Around,' she answered.

'But you're used to this?'

'Oh sure. Been travelling.'

'For how long?'

'A while.'

'How long a while?'

'A fair while.'

She was lying. I felt sure she was lying, and I was

just about to ask if she wanted to stay with us tonight, when she directed my attention over towards the building. The lights were burning now, brighter each time, pulsing on and off without any pattern to the flashes.

'Is that good or bad?'

'I don't know.'

It might have been a half-hour or so since we'd got there, and there was no way of knowing how long it was since Peacock and Henderson had gone in. But however much time had passed, it was too long a time. I went to get a torch from the car.

'Where are you going?'

'After them.'

'Right. OK. I'll come with you.'

'No.'

'Maybe I can help.'

'Oh please.' I turned back to the girl. 'Will you just . . .'

'What?'

'Look, Tupelo . . .'

'Yeah?'

'Piss off. OK? Just piss off.'

'Oh.'

I'd hurt her. Immediately I saw that, and I regretted the way I'd said it, and the language used, but there was no alternative, not now.

'Go on.'

And then I turned away from her, and I walked across the street towards the travel agent's.

I took the alley that led down the side of the building, to where a wooden gate in the wall opened onto a small yard. The back door of the shop had been left unlocked and I walked through into a storage area. The slow swing of the torch; cardboard boxes, stacks of brochures, a pair of computer terminals, both with broken screens. The floor was wet, sticky, and lines of the same liquid, dark red in colour, ran down the walls; it seeped down from the ceiling, from the light fitting. There seemed to be too much air in the room, too many molecules packed into the one small space. Hot, sweaty, humid. The beam of the torch was sluggish, a sick yellow that clung to objects as it passed.

A dreadful silence, made more so by a slight ringing in the ears, a distant sparkle of sound.

I was curious about the lack of security, until I went through into the shop itself. A woman was sitting in the dark. Alone, shivering, she was slumped down in the corner, making a continuous gesture with her hands, a constant sweeping of the body.

Well then, she has taken it too far.

This was the big temptation, and we'd seen it already

more than a few times on our way around the country. The damage. People hold the treasure in their possession, thinking it to be their saviour; instead, and far too late, they find that only pain can ensue, only sadness. But this looked a very bad case. The woman was lost to the world, completely. Perhaps she saw me there, staring at her, I don't know.

A flight of stairs took me up to the next floor. The thick red liquid covered the stairwell, giving off a perfume, sweet and cloying. I thought I recognized the smell, something that lingered over from my former life, and just out of reach. The tiny sounds were louder now, hypnotic. Two doors, one of them leading to the front of the building; carefully, quietly . . .

It's always different, every time.

Kingsley is working from his own set of clues, and sometimes he knows a little of the circumstances; more usually, he knows only the location of the various pieces of glass. But for my own part, and despite any of the clues given, always, I have to go through this moment of doubt, of disbelief almost. And this despite what I have seen already these last few weeks.

And so, I was standing there at the doorway, looking through, and I found myself suddenly unable to move. The feelings contained me, holding me fast. Here was the upper front room of the building, the one the girl and I had been watching from the street below. The torch beam flitted here and there, trying to make out the figures in the darkness. Vaguely seen, I thought at first that they might be statues. They were standing at various points of the room, about a dozen people, and all caught in some twisted, final position. I could see arms raised up, heads thrown back, or forward. Everything was locked into place, frozen. Spellbound. The closest to me, a young man, had fallen to his knees, with his hands covering his face; a perverse kind of prayer.

There was no movement; and no sound, except for the noises in my head, which became now the quiet faraway strains of an old-time waltz.

I stepped forward, cautiously, walking from figure to figure. My torch held onto faces for a second, each coloured with flecks of the red liquid. The floor also was covered with the stuff; each step I took had to be pulled from the floor, slowing me down.

From face to twisted face . . .

Some wore hard expressions of pain, with their eyes screwed tight, teeth bared. Others looked almost wistful, bemused. One, a little old woman with grey hair, was laughing, her mouth split wide with the joy of whatever she was experiencing.

I had the distinct and eerie feeling I was walking through a piece of art, a living sculpture, or even a kind of three-dimensional image. It was the strange heady perfume bringing this to me. Memories; back at the magazine's offices, going to see if a photograph had come out OK. It was the same smell. Developing fluid. Time had been stolen here, in this room, and held captive. And always, at these moments of discovery, I have to bring Kingsley's words to mind, that people are paying for the effect, whatever it might be. In pain, or in pleasure. The payment might not be in money, necessarily, and not always so willingly given; but paid for nonetheless.

There was Peacock, perfectly still.

Henderson was standing next to him, some few feet away. Her face was a blank; all traces of emotion had drained away. But Peacock's expression was frightening. His eyes were opened out in shock, or fear, his mouth halfway through a scream. His body was curved over to one side, with his two arms coming up to grab at empty air. I had never seen him display such feeling, not in the normal, waking life, and that was the thing that really filled me with dread. The mask was broken.

I reached out to touch Peacock's face.

It was warm, hard with muscle, old scar tissue, but pliable. Alive. The torch beam set the face afire, and his pupils suddenly widened out, hungry to pull the light from the air. And he was moving, I could see that now. I could feel Peacock's body shifting slowly, slowly, along some pathway of sleep, unreachable.

My fingers, his skin. It was the first time I had been this close to him. And did he see me there, I wondered. Did he know it was me? Was there any comprehension?

I went back to the landing, the second door. This, when opened, led to a small room filled with a thick red light. Here it was, the darkroom. A single bench covered with equipment. Photographs were pinned to the walls, all around the space. My torch picked them out; pictures of people, of people caught in their final moments, wounded, sick, fearful. Cold. People falling, or reposing, in the various positions of death, and I felt my skin crawl.

Journey's end.

Kingsley's words: people will pay for the effect, no matter. But who would want to know this, truly?

One woman's photograph appeared more than once, many times, as though the subject could not believe her own demise. Over and over I saw this one repeated image, the female body licked with flame.

A drift of colour drew my attention. It was coming from the workbench; a slight movement, a flicker of soft violet in the blood-red room. I moved closer, shining the torch that way. The beam swirled.

It was the colour. The signal tone.

I moved towards the bench. It was slow going; I had to consciously push myself across the room, the weighted air clutching at me every step of the way. The violet cloud was hovering above one of the developing trays, above the liquid contained within the tray. A number of photographs were floating in the liquid. They filled the tray completely, and there, lying on top of all the other images, I saw the photographs of Peacock and Henderson.

I pulled them free.

The prints were warm to the touch, sticky, and still not fully developed. What had I effected, by pulling them clean from the fluid, by shining the torch on them? Would this release my friends from their trance? Was this really the truth of their lives, being shown to me? What could I do?

I slipped the two photographs into my bag.

Using a pair of tongs, I removed most of the other pictures from the tray. And then, submerged, catching only a glimpse, I saw the sudden, violet sparkle of another world. This was it. The mirror. Another piece.

Lying face upwards at the bottom of the tray, the source of the spell.

The fragments of a dream, nothing more . . .

I must not look. I must not look at the surface of the glass. Always approach from an angle. Kingsley was insistent on this rule, saying that the effect of it was far worse than any normal mirror. Far worse. And so, using the tongs to get a good hold on the jagged edges, I raised the mirror from the fluid, carefully, to keep the reflective surface away from my direction.

It was a small piece, the size of a playing card, nothing more, and irregular in its shape as always. Some broken fragment of a larger, impossible object. Trembling now, I placed the mirror face down on the workbench. I needed to get Peacock's bag from the other room, the special covering. But when I turned round, there she was, the woman. The woman I had seen downstairs. She was standing in the doorway, still making the same continual gestures, but now with a more determined manner.

Was this the artist, the photographer?

She tried to speak, but only a broken mumble of words came from her lips. The woman was brushing at her clothes repeatedly. She was trying to put out the imagined flames on her body, I saw that now. And the terrible sadness I had witnessed so many times already; the sadness that the pieces of the mirror always bring with them.

'Please . . .'

This one word, it was all she could manage, and she came forward then. She was looking at the mirror where it lay beside the developing tray. Her body brushed against mine, and I moved aside to let her pass.

I just wanted to get this over and done with. I went back into the front room. Here, some of the people were coming round, slowly moving their limbs, their heads. One of them fell to the floor, groaning. Another man stepped forward, hesitantly; it looked like he was emerging from another room into this one. Peacock and Henderson were stirring themselves, coming awake. I felt that everything might work out now, and that together we would take control of the situation.

And then I saw the girl, Tupelo, standing just inside the doorway. 'What is this?' she said, her eyes moving from me on to some other figure.

A voice called out.

I turned, and there was the woman. She had a camera raised to her face, and, in that one long moment, I felt certain that I could actually see the lens open, slowly, to gather me into its secret chamber. It was a feeling of being held, quite sweetly. Flashbulbs popped in sequence, and they made soft yellow unfoldings in my skull, with the woman etched in black against the yellow, and then I was turning or trying to, trying to turn away before the lens closed again and caught me there for ever, but the world was too far away and I could not move myself, not properly, I could not make it happen.

>

I was floating, suspended in some strange fluid, that's all I know. A pool of silver. I was floating, trying to push myself forward through the liquid, and then falling, not sinking, but falling through the liquid.

Into darkness.

That's all I know. That's all.

>

Movement, noise. Scatters of light. Stumbling, being dragged down the flight of stairs, with the long cry of a woman's voice, howling. Somebody had me now by the hand. It was Tupelo, and she was pulling me all the way down and out, and through, into the back yard.

'Come on, Marlene. Come on!'

'Where are they? The others, where are they?'

'Right behind. Now come on.'

My eyes were still on fire from the flashbulb's hot, chemical gleam, and there was a dark shape printed on my retina. I could not see, not clearly, until Henderson came up close from nowhere, breaking the image.

'Where . . .'

'It's here.' Henderson held up a bit of rag, some small object wrapped inside it.

'What is it?' said Tupelo. 'Let me see.'

Peacock came out. He was holding the gun in one hand, holding it just so, pointed.

'Shit,' the girl said.

'Let's go.'

Following Peacock, we moved down the alleyway, onto the street, and Tupelo came with us. Even to the car, the girl came with us, and she was getting into the car alongside.

'What's she doing?' said Henderson.

'I—'

'Get the fuck out.'

'Hey, but come on, I helped. I helped you.'

And then Henderson came round to grab at the girl. She had the girl by the lapels of her jacket, pushing her back against the wall.

'Hey!'

'Go home.'

'What?'

'Fuck off home.'

I wanted to do something, I really did. I wanted to offer the girl something but what could it be? How could I fight with Henderson, when she was all fired up like this?

'Leave her now,' said Peacock.

It was that simple. Henderson left the girl alone, and she moved back to the car, saying, 'OK. Fuck, we're doing this. Fuck, yes!' That was it.

I looked at the girl for a second, and then away from her. I had to turn away. Peacock was placing the mirror in the boot of the car. This is what we had come for, the job was done, and yet . . .

The windows of the building opposite were flashing nonstop with the yellow light, and the light in my eyes still, mixing in with it, and the dark figure of the woman trapped there, inside me, and only this moment starting to fade away.

The woman, the photographer.

I do not know just where she found the fragment of

glass, nor the price she paid for it, the real price. Oh but the sadness. The terrible sadness of the woman, and what we did to her, and what we were doing, all over.

And then I climbed into the car.

Peacock started the engine. The girl was standing alone on the pavement, watching us leave, but we did not stop, no. Not for anything could we stop, not now.

\>

Drifting through silence, through the empty streets. All the road signs had folded themselves over; *Sleep*, they murmured, *only sleep*. The closing of so many eyes. To speak one word, in a whisper even, would wake the town from its slumber.

But what was really being left unsaid?

We were stopped by a police car. Had the woman dared to make a complaint? Nobody had ever done this before; there were too many laws broken. But the officer only wanted to know what we were doing out after the curfew. Peacock handled it, just fine. He explained how we were new in town, visiting friends that day, and we were just leaving, that's all. And how we didn't really know the rules that well, this is what he said.

We did not know the rules.

>

We could not wake the old woman, and there was no sign of the servant, Edward, who had let us in earlier. It was very late, past midnight. I rang the bell a few more times and then Henderson made a curse and she broke open a window.

The house was quiet. We lit a few candles in the kitchen. Henderson washed the red liquid off Peacock's face, and then he did the same for her. No words passed between them during this procedure.

Peacock was hungry, but the cupboards were filled only with tins of cat food, the larder with tinned cream. There were no cats, not to be seen; only shadows that moved with gentle noises, and with flickers of green light. Henderson found a bottle of Scotch and we drank some of that.

Then we sorted out the mirror.

With all the proper care and attention, in silence, we wrapped the fragment in one of the pieces of velvet that Kingsley had provided. The red liquid was still dripping slowly from the glass, from the hole it made in the world. I was conscious of being close to some infinite wonder, something not of this realm. My hands trembled. We had to place the fragment tight against the side of the case, hoping to stem the flow. None of us would look at the mirror, not directly. It was a question of working at certain well-practised angles, away from the lines of sight; to not see ourselves reflected there, or even a glimpse of anybody else.

These were the measures taken.

And then, it was done. The mirror was in the case, alongside those pieces previously found.

'There you go,' said Henderson. 'There you go.'

'What's wrong?'

'Nothing. Just, a bit tired.'

'I'm the same,' said Peacock.

Six pieces in total, each with their own particular spell. One lost the night before, and a few more before that, so really there should be seven or eight or nine by now, according to the schedule. I was losing count. But this would do, this would suffice. I was thinking that maybe one more would do it, all told, to locate and secure just one more piece of the broken mirror, no matter what Kingsley might demand, and then all this would be finished.

I think the house itself, its atmosphere, the dust settling, the smoke rising from the candles, all this, and the night's events just over, all of these together made it difficult to speak. We sat round the table for a while, drinking, with Peacock taking more than we were. The candlelight danced around his face.

'Well then,' he said, finally.

'Don't start now,' said Henderson.

'What about that girl?'

'What?'

73

'That girl, she did all right.'

'What did she do?' I asked.

'You didn't see it, Marlene? Oh, the girl was good.'

'Was she?'

'Sure thing. She went for that woman. Knocked the camera right out of her hands, and then down, onto the floor, the both of them, mind. Rolling around the floor, they were. You should have seen it.'

'Fuck,' said Henderson.

'What?'

'Piss off about the girl, please.'

'What's up with you?'

'Nothing.'

'Bev?'

Henderson looked away. 'What happened tonight?' she asked. 'Marlene?'

'I don't know. I'm not sure.'

'You're not sure?'

'No.'

She turned to Peacock. 'What happened? Did you go dancing?'

'Did I what?'

'Did you dance, tonight? Did we dance, together, in each other's arms? When the flashbulb went off. What happened? I need to know.'

Peacock poured himself another drink.

'No,' he said. 'No.'

'You're sure?'

'No dancing.'

'OK. That's fine.'

'Why do you ask?'

'Never mind that.'

'OK. Fuck, I'm tired.' He downed the whisky in one mouthful. 'You coming to bed now?'

'I'll be there.'

'Good.' Peacock picked up his bag. 'Good.'

And then it was just myself and Henderson, sitting alone at opposite sides of the table. A few moments went by, with Henderson taking little sips from her drink. And then she spoke.

'It was a tropical beach. A lovely place, just golden sands all the way, you know. Like a paradise, and Peacock and I were dancing on the sand. Did you see us?'

'Dancing? No, I didn't see that.'

'But you saw us there, right? In the room?'

'Yes.'

'And what did we look like?'

'Well, you were just, you were just standing there. Frozen.'

'The both of us?'

'You and Peacock, next to each other.'

'We weren't touching?'

'No.'

'And what about my face? What did it look like? Was I happy? Did I look happy? Was I smiling?'

She still had on her brow a single spot of red.

'Yes, nearly,' I said. 'It was nearly a smile.'

'Good. That will do. It was an old-fashioned dance, you know? I mean, it's not something we've ever done before. A waltz. That's it. That's all.'

'That's all?'

'I don't know. I couldn't help feeling that this was our last time together . . .'

'There's no need to feel that. You will dance. Many times, you will dance.'

'And Peacock, he was smiling as well, wasn't he?'

'Yes,' I answered. 'He was smiling.'

There was nothing else I could say.

Henderson went to bed. I sat there for a while on my own, looking at the candle that Peacock had placed on the table. I let the flames play in my eyes. And then I took the photographs from out of my bag.

They had been pulled from the fluid too soon, and they were not yet fully formed. Crackles of noise floated above the images. But I could see enough.

In truth, I would rather I had never seen them at all. These final moments.

The first showed an old woman, her crumpled body lying on the floor of a dirty room. It was a shot taken from above. A green cardigan, lank hair, a well-used face. Around the body I could see pages torn from a book, a vodka bottle, stains on the carpet, something that looked like a pool of vomit. A small hand mirror.

Oh god. It seemed a terrible conclusion for a person like Henderson. A dreadfully sad ending.

The second photograph showed Peacock.

He was leaning against a red brick wall, holding his hands over his stomach, and his face held tight with some pain he was trying to keep hidden. There was blood coming through his fingers.

He looked to be not much older than he was now.

I looked at the photographs, one after the other, and over and over. I thought about the woman in the travel agent's, taking these pictures.

Where are you going?

And I thought then about how my own photograph had been taken this same night, and what would it show there? What story would the image give to me? That fall I had taken, just momentarily, in the strange, silvery liquid. And was there any other destination?

Where the fuck are you going?

I held the photographs in the flame of the candle, watching them burn away. The paper curled, blackened, caught, the chemicals melted. The man and the woman, their two images, now turned to some few flakes of ash and sent drifting on the air.

I climbed the tall staircase. I wasn't really that tired, not yet, but I wanted to feel the soft sheets around me, the comfort of a good bed, and maybe to write a little more. Walking the long dark corridor that led to my room, I heard my name being spoken.

'Marlene . . .'

Was this the old lady, calling me?

'Marlene? Is that you, dear?'

Kingsley must have mentioned my name to her. Yes, that must be it.

'Marlene . . .'

There was a door, slightly ajar.

'Lady Iris?'

'Come in. Let me see you.'

It was a medium-sized bedroom, nothing grand, and simply furnished. Lady Iris was sitting in a high-backed chair next to the window. A single candle stood nearby, and a small book lay closed upon her lap.

'We thought you were asleep.'

'I was,' she answered. 'The bell was ringing.'

'I'm sorry. We woke you . . .'

'I don't understand. I thought I had told Edward that the door be kept unlocked.'

I had not seen the woman until this moment. It was impossible to guess her true age. There were deep creases in her face, and her skin and her hair were grey and covered with powder.

'Yes, you did. Thank you.'

The flame of the candle was held in the lenses of her spectacles; the woman's eyes could not be seen.

'Did you have a successful evening?' she asked.

'Tonight? Well, yes. I think so.'

'You got what you wanted?'

'Yes.'

'Mr Kingsley will be pleased.'

She was gazing out of the window now, and I joined her there. The sparkles of a distant city could be made out; closer by, only a single light revealed the presence of the new town. One careful eye left awake.

'A monstrous place,' she said. 'They have built their contraption around me.'

'Have you known Mr Kingsley long?'

'We were lovers.'

I turned to her. 'You were?'

'Of course, I was younger then; and Mr Kingsley was younger still.'

I tried to imagine a more youthful version of Lady Iris, but whatever beauty there might once have been was now hidden away, or else dissolved.

'Please, do sit down.'

There were no other chairs in the room, only the bed. Feeling a little awkward, I sat down on the edge of it. A name was embroidered in the folded corner of the sheet, in a fine gold stitching.

Iris White . . .

The old woman did not turn round. 'Mr Kingsley is a good man, at heart,' she said. 'He does not however quite know where his heart exists.'

'No.'

There was a silence then, and I thought she was falling back into sleep. I could not see her face from where I was sitting, only the back of her head, her silvery hair.

'Would you like me to go?'

Lady Iris breathed, heavily, and she said, 'Bring me that box. Would you?'

'Which box?'

'Under the bed there.'

I bent down. There was a porcelain chamber pot and beside it a small wooden box. Two eyes were peering out from the darkness.

'Uh.'

'What? What is it, my dear?'

'Nothing. Nothing, I . . .'

Green eyes. It was a cat. A black cat was sitting under the bed, staring at me.

'The box? Do you see it?'

'Yes.'

I pulled the box out from the bed. It was a simple thing, without a lid, without any decoration, filled with envelopes and other documents. Pressed down between the first of the letters and the front of the box, I saw two plastic syringes. They were still sealed in their see-through wrappers and printed with the brand, the little eye symbol. Only in my visits to the hospital had I seen the drug in its liquid form. I remembered, suddenly, one of the doctors pushing the needle into Angela's flesh. The most potent application.

'Quickly now. Bring it to me.'

I carried the box over and Lady Iris placed it on her lap, on top of the book that was still lying there.

'Let me see now.'

Her eyes were cast straight ahead, whilst her fingers searched through the contents, the envelopes and papers. She pulled out some photographs.

'Do you have children?'

The question took me by such surprise that I couldn't answer it, not at first.

'Do you?'

'Yes. Just the one.'

I couldn't bring myself to say any more than that.

'These are my children.'

I took the photographs from the woman's hands. The noise levels were particularly high around the images; they could only be seen when held at one precise angle, a certain distance from the eye. The first of them was a hand-tinted picture of a cottage garden. The next showed a bicycle, leaning against a wall. The third was actually a postcard of an oil painting: a bowl of fruit, a pipe, a French newspaper. The last photograph showed a black dog, lying on a rug.

'They are very beautiful, don't you think?'

I looked at the woman. Her eyes were still hidden by the flames, with no clear signal.

'Yes. They are beautiful children.'

'Why are you lying to me?'

'I . . .'

'Oh, if the world could be pure again, and sweet again. This is for you, I believe.' She had taken one of the envelopes from the box. 'It came this morning, by special envoy.'

It was a letter from Kingsley. The latest batch of money, for expenses. And then two sheets of paper, the first of which detailed our next few assignments.

'Where shall you go?'

I told her, mentioning only the first location.

'Oh the seaside, how lovely. And the theatre as well. Of course, I was myself an actress. They called me the most divine presence on the London stage. Did Mr Kingsley mention?'

'No, I don't think so.'

'Ah well. So forgetful.'

I had by then already seen the second page of the letter. It contained only a few scrawled lines, reading, 'I was most sorrowful to hear of the death of Lady Iris. I trust her servant is looking after you.'

'Is there anything wrong, Marlene?'

'What? No, no. It's fine.'

'So very forgetful. Please, forgive me.'

There was a tear, moving down the lined face. She wiped it away gently with a silk handkerchief.

'I am tired now. Would you stay with me?'

'You want me to sleep here?'

'Well, you shall have the bed, of course.'

I have brought my things from the other room. The old lady was already asleep in the chair when I came back. I can see her there now; the back of the head, the powdery hair. I am lying on the bed, fully clothed. There are two candles on a bedside cabinet, which I have lit, and by their twin flames I have been lying here on my side, writing this.

I have been writing.

I wonder what Kingsley's letter could mean? He must have received some false information, perhaps, regarding Lady Iris. Well, that is easy enough; we spend our whole lives these days moving through falsehoods. Between transmission and reception, the pathway is clouded with static, with shadows, and the noise is rising daily.

Clouded with static, and with shadows . . .

I can remember writing those words, for an article once. Some weeks ago, a month ago?

Another lifetime, another person.

And I think then of Peacock and Henderson in their own room down the corridor. Are they asleep at this hour? Have they made love another time? Perhaps they lie awake as I do, and they are talking of what they saw this evening, when the camera's flash caught them. I wonder if Peacock knows anything, about the fate I saw for him in the photograph? And if he does know, what would he admit, even to himself?

And then I think about the young hitchhiker. Where is she now? Has she found a room somewhere? Perhaps Tupelo has met a boy, and they sleep together close and warm in some darkened bedroom. Perhaps she has taken another lift, in some more expensive vehicle, and with kinder passengers. Or else the girl is sleeping rough on the streets. What must that be like?

And then Kingsley. I picture him now, wandering his house of mirrors, alone, sleepless. He would never cover their surfaces; a covered mirror, he once told me, is the place where reflections die. And so, in these days of the sickness, only at night dare he enter the rooms where his collection is housed. In the darkness, I picture him: Kingsley, haunted by his own ghost as it moves with him, slowly, from mirror to mirror.

All these people, their lives, their various forms of sleep. Their dreams.

My father . . .

I do not think of him very often, and when I do it is only as an absence, an unknown object, a shape in the mist. He left home when I was very young. I can hardly remember him, his face, his gestures. Sitting on my bed, reading to me. Only this. I don't know what took him away. One night, woken by a noise, I looked out through my window, to see a car pull up outside the house. I don't know who the driver was, I could not see that far, but my father was there, and he spoke with the driver, before getting inside the car. They drove away together. I used to think that I was to blame in some way, that I forced my father to leave.

I think about him now; this blurred figure. He would not be asleep, I cannot imagine him being asleep; in my mind he is always on the move, always with his back to me, walking away, and all the time draped in shadow.

From some other room, I can hear a clock striking the hour. The chimes drift by like blossoms, they cannot be caught or measured. The air closes upon them.

Tomorrow, I will call Kingsley if I can; tell him I'm coming back early.

The old lady stirs, just slightly, and then her head settles once more against the back of the chair. There is a sound of breathing in the room. It might be mine alone, so gentle it seems. It might be myself, breathing alone and quiet in this night that gathers around me.

\>

I have taken out the photograph of Angela.

It is a picture of myself, and my daughter, taken when Angela was only seven years old. I know the captured moment, so well. The young girl standing close to the camera, head held at an angle, just about smiling. The bobbed hair, the clear eyes. One blue, the other brown. That one sweet glance. Myself behind, sitting on the grass, looking away slightly. High summer, shadows on the lawn, the cat curled up nearby. All the details perfectly known in the heart, but just now as I look at the image, only a soft haze can be seen. Figures lost. The sun has been turned up too high.

Oh my darling, my sweet.

What can I do? Days go by. So much has been lost, and the days go by and each day takes me further from the moment when I could have saved you. And the noise that took you from me, even now it will not leave you alone. It burns away your traces . . .

I must find sleep.

>

There you are now, afloat in your chamber of black water. Fed by tubing, made blind and deaf to the world. No taste will come to your tongue, no perfumes will float over your body. I cannot remember the last time I touched you, actually touched your skin. For fear of arousing some message too painful to bear.

The cradle.

This was your life at the end, controlled, held in a delicate, fine system. Fragile. Condition stable. A life that I watch now, sleeping, dreaming, only as a series of readouts, panel displays.

Flickering lights, in darkness.

Nothing more.

Isolated even from love, the most painful of all messages.

>

I don't know. Something happened. I can barely remember this. At some point in the early hours, I woke up. I think I did. There was a figure in the room. It was very dark by then. The candles had burned down and the figure could not be made out clearly, but I knew it to be the manservant we had seen earlier. Edward. He was standing by the side of the chair. The head of the woman could not be seen. She must have slumped down in the seat. And the servant turned to look at me.

'What are you doing?' I asked

'Attending,' he said.

That's all I remember.

>

In the morning, Lady Iris was nowhere to be seen. Neither could the servant be found. The house belonged now to the cats. They had come out from their hiding places, too many to count, and all of different colours.

I searched all over for a telephone, without luck.

A scent of talcum drew me back along the up-stairs corridor. Traces of powder covered the chair, the window, the small bed where I had slept. I felt cold, shivery. The wooden box had fallen to the floor. The various envelopes and other documents were scattered around.

The two syringes. Lucidity.

I decided I would take them with me. Bending down, I saw the book lying under the chair. It was a volume of English poetry, with, below the written title, a series of black dots, a pattern. A code. I turned to a middle page. My fingers moved over one poem, a few lines only, and all the patterns unyielding.

The book was printed in Braille.

>

We came out from the house, and the girl was waiting for us. She was leaning against the car, looking just as neat and tidy as before. The scarf round her neck, bag across the shoulder. Hair still tied in the knot.

'You're up late,' she said. 'Are you going my way?'

'No,' said Henderson.

'Which way are you going?'

'The opposite way.'

'That will do.'

'What is this please? How come she knows where we are?'

'Search me,' said Peacock.

'She was in the car,' I said. 'Last night, when we asked for directions.'

'Come on, Marlene,' said the girl. 'Just to the next place, wherever you're going.'

'It's a long way.'

'Wherever. Look, I can drive, if you like.'

'Drive?' said Henderson. 'Are you old enough?'

'I can drive. I'm a good driver.'

Henderson turned to me. 'Marlene, get rid of her.'

'Well. It might be all right.'

'What?'

'It might be,' I said.

'She's not driving,' said Peacock. 'I'm the driver.'

'Just get in the car,' said Henderson.

'Sure.'

Peacock climbed in behind the steering wheel.

'OK,' said Henderson. 'This is what happens. We're gonna get out of this new town shit. We're gonna find a café somewhere and have us some breakfast, some proper food. And the girl stays there, right? We leave her there, at the café, no messing. OK? Marlene?'

'Yeah, that's good.'

'I'm just all heart this morning, I really am.'

And the day begins.

\>

Heading west, towards the London circular. The sun is pale, barely seen, almost the same colour as the sky. I think we must have taken a wrong turning somewhere. We have passed through a small village, still being built. The houses were painted bright primary shades. There were no fences, no proper gardens; only blank stretches of lawn, and gravel paths. Security cameras followed our progress. A show home contained the one sign of life: a young couple, their two children, they all looked up and waved as we drove past.

'What are they smiling about?' asked Henderson.

'They'll have all the latest gadgets,' said Peacock. 'Electronic Lucy, and all that.'

'You reckon?'

'Sure. Check the cameras, the satellite aerials.'

'It's an outrage, isn't it? Us lot suffering like we are.'

'Where are we anyway?'

'Fuck knows.' Henderson was turning the pages of a road atlas. 'This place isn't even listed.'

'Are we lost?' asked Tupelo.

'I don't know.'

'You don't know?'

'Where I've been,' said Peacock, 'they don't have maps. They have holes in the ground.'

'Why? Where have you been?'

A small orange car passed by, moving in the opposite direction.

'Oh right,' said Tupelo. 'You were in the war?'

'For a while.'

'Wow. Is that where you got the gun?'

'Never mind that.'

'How many people have you killed?'

'Too fucking many. Now shut up.'

'OK.'

'This is making my brain hurt,' said Henderson.

'Why is that?' said Tupelo. 'Didn't you take your Lucy this morning?'

'Cheeky slut. I know your kind. Taking the sweeties all day long, think you can do anything.'

'I'm not like that.'

'Dangerous business. You ever seen a person in a black trance?'

'I took the usual. That's all.'

'Yeah well, keep it sweet. Why don't you?'

'I'm hungry. I thought we were finding a café.'

'Ask the navigator,' said Peacock.

'Fuck. Just keep driving.' Henderson threw the atlas over her shoulder. It landed on the seat beside me.

'Perhaps we'll never eat,' said Tupelo, 'not ever again. Maybe, you know, we'll just be stuck in this car until the day we die, just travelling the same roads over and over, and eventually we'll run out of food and water, and we'll die, right here in the car whilst it's still moving along. Yeah, that's it. And the car will carry on without anybody driving it. It'll be like our very own funeral carriage.'

Henderson turned round one more time. She looked at the girl, and then shook her head, and turned back.

'We'll run out of petrol first,' said Peacock.

We drove in silence for a while, and then the girl pulled a black box out of her bag. There was a little clasp, which she undid, and then the box unfolded, and inside there was a half-size chessboard and pieces, a traveller's set.

'You want to play?' she said.

'It doesn't work, does it?'

The girl just smiled.

We had seen people playing chess, here and there on our travels. It was becoming popular, especially amongst the young. It was strange. No one can explain why the noise affects some things, some activities, more than others, just like some people suffer more than others. But the game of chess had been one of the first to lose all sense of its rules. Clocks, mirrors, chess . . .

'What is it? How can you play?'

The girl shrugged, and started to move the pieces on her own, taking both sides, the red and the white. I couldn't work out what rules she was playing by, but I watched her for a while, and then took to gazing through the window.

We had moved into a lightly wooded area, with the road shaded by trees. Many of the traffic signs, at crossroads and side junctions, were obscured by leaves, moss, by mud, graffiti, by strange clouds of dust, or else covered over entirely with black tarpaulin. Those few I could make out properly seemed to be written in some foreign language I could not recognize. Another class of sign was completely blank, just the white ground, the coloured border, and no message or symbol held within.

I felt sure we passed the same small country church twice. Perhaps they all looked more or less the same. At one point, a dog ran across the road and Peacock had to swerve away from it. He stopped the car.

'Are you OK?' asked Henderson.

'Yeah, yeah. Shit.'

He was shaken by it, I could tell.

'You want me to drive?' said Tupelo.

'I'll drive,' said Henderson.

'I said I'm fine. Leave it.'

We moved on with Peacock still at the wheel, and nothing much seemed to change; no matter which way we turned, the same landscape unrolled ahead of the vehicle, the same dull features came and went.

A small orange car passed by, moving in the opposite direction.

'You know', said Tupelo, 'that some places are more affected than others?'

'We know that,' said Henderson.

'I'm just saying.'

'About bloody time,' said Peacock.

'What is it?'

'Houses. Some kind of village.'

'Let's hope they have a café.'

But as we drove along the one tiny main street, with the houses resplendent in their bright colourings, it became obvious that we had made a mistake; we had circled round, back to where we started.

'It's the same fucking place,' said Henderson.

The houses seemed even more vibrant this time around. The colours were vibrating in the air; I could hear a buzzing noise in my head.

'Look,' said Peacock, 'there's the show house.'

The young family was still there in the garden, and once again they waved to us as we passed.

'It's not them,' said Tupelo.

'What?' said Henderson.

'It's another family. Look, now the wife's got blonde hair; before it was dark, dark hair.'

'No way.'

'It's a different village.'

'Shit, the girl's right,' said Peacock. 'Where the hell are we?'

'Oh, I've had enough of this,' said Tupelo.

The girl closed up her portable chess set, and she went to place it in her bag. As she did so, some other items fell out onto the seat. I saw a paperback book, some coins, cigarettes, and a small plastic object. It took me a moment to realize what it was. Rectangular, coloured a pastel green, with a symbol printed on it.

It was a mirror.

It was a small vanity mirror, still folded in its green plastic case. The symbol belonged to a famous cosmetics company.

Tupelo saw me staring. She pushed the illicit item back into the bag, keeping her eyes tight on mine. And then she brought a finger to her lips, asking me to keep silent.

'What's going on back there?' asked Henderson.

The girl looked at me, shaking her head.

'Nothing,' I answered.

Tupelo smiled, just briefly, and then she picked up the road atlas from where it had fallen. She turned to a certain page, and studied the map for a second or two. She was making comparisons between the world outside and the map, her fingers tracing shapes along the roads.

Tupelo closed her eyes, gently.

'Take the next left,' she said. 'And then the second right.'

'What?' said Henderson.

'You sure?' said Peacock.

'Just do it.'

>

The forest gave way to a more built-up area, the traffic signs began to make sense. We passed a lay-by where an old couple had set up a little market stall. It was just a couple of folding tables, some chairs, a canvas sheet to keep the wind at bay.

The woman was selling flowers.

The man was sitting at an artist's easel. He had a large printed notice in front of him. We slowed down, and Tupelo read out the words on the notice.

'Portraits in oil. Genuine likeness, guaranteed.'

Examples of the artist's work were on display; a series of fierce, darkly coloured swirls of paint, with lines of a brighter colour slashed across them.

I could see no trace at all of any human face.

>

At a table close to ours, some teenage boys were making fun of each other. Every so often one or the other of them would glance at Tupelo.

'What are you looking at?' said Henderson.

The boys returned to their game.

We were taking breakfast at a greasy spoon. The girl's directions had turned out just fine in the end, and now Henderson would not leave her alone.

'Best make your plans, girl.'

'You're not really leaving me here?'

'Sure, chat up the boys. They'll take you places. Go on, you can have a laugh.'

'I wonder what this tastes like,' said Peacock. 'I mean, really?'

He was on his second full meal, the works.

'Who cares,' said Henderson. 'Eat the stuff.'

'Girl . . .'

'Me?' said Tupelo. 'What're you asking me for?'

'What does this taste like, to you?'

'Jesus,' said Henderson. 'It tastes like breakfast.'

'Come on then,' said Tupelo.

Peacock filled his fork with food, and the girl took

this into her mouth. She chewed it. She was taking her time, moving the food around, and making a real show of working out the flavours.

'I feel sick,' said Henderson.

And all the time the girl was looking at me; the secret shared between us.

'It tastes', she said, 'of eggs, and of bacon.'

'Oh my,' said Henderson.

'Funny that,' said Peacock. 'I'm getting custard. I'm getting severe custard from this egg.'

'What about the bacon?' said Tupelo.

'Prunes. Yeah, that's it. Prunes and custard.'

I went off then, to call Kingsley. The man behind the counter directed me down a short corridor. He wished me the best of luck. The telephone was lying on the floor, outside the gents lavatory. I bent down, picked up the receiver. There was static on the line, nothing else. No dialling tone, no response to the buttons being pressed. And then I noticed that the flex had been cut.

Where was the static coming from?

When I got back to the table, Henderson and Tupelo were arguing once again.

'When we get to the seaside,' said the girl.

'What?'

'We can go to the beach, right? I mean, we can walk on the beach.'

'You're not going.'

'But I'm good for you. Last night—'

'Never mind last night. That's done with now.'

'And what about this morning then? I mean, you'd still be lost if it wasn't for me.'

'You know, girl, there's no escaping it. The sickness just grows in the world, it creeps up on you.'

'I know that.'

'You see the trouble with the girl? Just because she's suffering the least . . .'

'Oh fuck. What do I have to do?'

'Baby, the noise is coming.' Henderson turned away from her. 'Now listen. Marlene, Peacock. Listen to me. I want this day to slide on by real easy. I want to get down there, find the kid. What's his name?'

'Jamie.'

I had already shown them Kingsley's letter.

'Jamie. Yeah. The theatre guy.'

'What's all this about?' said Tupelo.

'No trouble,' said Henderson. 'That's all I'm after.'

I gave my assent. 'No trouble.'

'That's it, Marlene. No messing. Peacock? You hearing this? Peacock? What are you doing?'

'What?'

'What are you doing?'

'I'm looking at myself.'

'Right. In a spoon?'

'In a spoon,' said Peacock. 'That's OK, isn't it? I mean, there's nothing in the guidelines about spoons.'

'He's right there,' said Tupelo.

'Well fuck me,' said Henderson.

Peacock was holding the spoon in front of his face. He was looking into the bowl of it.

'What do you see?' I asked him.

'Well then?' said Tupelo.

Peacock's eyes would not shift from the image in the spoon. We were all sitting there, staring at him, right there in that dingy café, waiting for Peacock to speak. But Peacock could not lift his gaze from the spoon and he did not speak, not at all.

'Well?' said Henderson. 'What is it?'

But Peacock did not speak.

'Give me that,' said Henderson.

Peacock held the spoon more tightly.

'You've got your own spoon,' said Tupelo.

'I want that spoon.'

Henderson touched Peacock's hand, quite gently, and only then did Peacock let the spoon go. Henderson took the spoon for herself and she looked into it. Henderson looked into the bowl, into the silvered reflection of herself and she did not speak. She bowed her head, away from the tiny curved mirror of the spoon, and Peacock also was staring down at the table now, and they kept like that, the two of them, for a while, and Peacock was speaking some words to himself. They could not be heard, these words. And then Peacock looked up and he said the words, more plainly.

'I don't know,' he said. 'I don't know what I look like. I don't know.'

His face turned away.

'I don't know. I just don't fucking know.'

The girl made a noise, a tiny sound which seemed to come from deep within her. And then she spoke.

'I can do it,' she said. 'I can tell you.'

'What?' said Henderson.

'I can tell you.'

I tried to catch the girl's eye, but she would not look at me.

'Tupelo . . .' I said. 'You shouldn't . . .'

'I can do it.'

'What's she saying?' said Henderson.

'Believe me.' The girl unwrapped the scarf from her neck. 'Do you see this?' She moved her fingers along the exposed skin. 'Just here.'

Henderson leaned round. 'What is it? You've been bitten? A love bite.'

'Look closely.'

Tupelo turned her head for all to see, and Henderson moved in close. Marks. The tiny marks where the skin had been punctured.

'Shit,' said Henderson. 'Oh fuck . . .'

The girl replaced the scarf. She was smiling the whole time. 'You see now?'

Peacock had been quiet during all this, but now he turned to Tupelo, and he said:

'Girl, what do I look like? Tell me that.'

Tupelo looked at Peacock's face just briefly. 'Well now, you look like shit.'

'No, really. Give it to me.'

'OK. Warm shit.'

'Really,' said Peacock. 'Really . . .'

Henderson grabbed hold of Tupelo's wrist. 'Tell him, girl.'

'OK. I'm doing it.'

Tupelo looked at Peacock. She touched his rough face with her fingers. She traced the scars on his face, his great, stone slab of a face.

'You're a handsome devil, no problem.'

'Am I? Really?'

'Really.'

'Now me,' said Henderson. 'What do I look like?'

Tupelo studied the face of Henderson.

'Beautiful,' she said. 'You look beautiful.'

'How beautiful? Stupid beautiful?'

'No. Not that. But beautiful, like something that's about to burn up. Like a gun. Yeah. Like a gun that's just about to be fired.'

'Good,' said Henderson. 'That's good. Now Marlene.'

'No. Not me.'

'Now Marlene. Be Marlene's mirror.'

'I don't want it. I don't want to know.'

'Tell her. The truth now.'

Tupelo looked at me then, and I tried to turn away from the look, but I couldn't do it. I could not turn away from being looked at.

'Say it, girl,' said Henderson.

And Tupelo told me.

She told me what I looked like.

>

Looking bad? Looking good? I don't know any more. Why did the girl say that? I bring my hands up to my face, I run them through my hair. These have been my only touchstone, these fingers, and even here I wonder about how much truth there is, contained. Perhaps some small element of noise affects the signal, between the fingertip, and the message of the skin, the dirty tangle of hair. I don't know. And I know I've never been a beauty, not by any standards, and that these last few months can only have made me worse. But why did the girl have to say that? Fucked up, terrible. A mess. Damaged. Her final word. Of course, of course I'm fucking damaged. Jesus. I curse all mirrors, and hope they never get well again.

>

Circling round London, a wide orbit. The traffic is
more pronounced here, and we have to be careful. Even
with the speed restrictions in place, the police vehicles
prowling the motorway, there's still lots of crazies
around. All these people desperate to carry on with
their work, even with the noise levels rising. Or else
the fallen, who just don't care any more. We've already
had one near miss, and a couple of scary moments.
It wouldn't be so bad, but Peacock keeps on with
the driving. He's trying to prove something; trying
to deny that he's succumbing, getting worse, losing
control.

The sickness creeps up on you. No escaping . . .

Henderson's sitting beside him. She's been very quiet
since breakfast. I know she's worried.

The girl, Tupelo, is with me in the back.

There wasn't any real decision about this, about her
coming along further. 'Girl could be useful.' Peacock's
words. To which Henderson nodded her head, just the
once, and then went outside to the car. For myself, I
simply feel the pull of events. The pull, the pulling.
Things are happening to me, one by one, and if only

I could grab hold of them, as they happen, make something of them, if only . . .

And now, we travel.

Tupelo is reading a book, a paperback edition of Edgar Allan Poe. *Selected Tales of the Grotesque.*

I remember, the talk of being in college. She must have given up on the course. Left some family behind, a mother, a father, some friends. A boyfriend, perhaps. Everything.

That one conclusion, made in haste.

To set yourself free.

I can't even imagine what it must be like, to be immune. I've never met one before. There's not many of them, and I know they have a lot of trouble. Stories of violence. One terrible case, where a man was found dead with his neck cut open. The blood sucked out. I remember another writer at the magazine was working on a piece about these people. Every week, they're supposed to report to a designated hospital, to have the extraction made. Some quality in the hormones, which forms the base element of the Lucidity drug. They say that just one tiny droplet will calm a million or more bad signals.

Tupelo has removed the scarf. She seems quite relaxed now, self-contained. She's a girl who lives in her own world, that's for certain. And maybe we're all like that, these days. We all move through the noise, bound by our limits. The flesh, the hairs on the skin, the small circle we set round us; scared of a touch, a word out of place, the sudden desire we can hardly dare to trust.

And yet . . .

And yet, this connection. I can't help but think of the

juice being drawn out from Tupelo's body. And how that juice, diluted, will find its way into so many batches of the drug. And how that drug is then made into powder, coloured, held within capsules; or else in liquid form, poured into syringes. Loaded up, transported around the country, consumed, who can tell where each drop begins, and each finds an end. And perhaps, even in this morning's one capsule, some tiny part of Tupelo was present.

The most precious part.

And then I have to think of Angela, and all the many needles, tablets, the slow-motion flow of the drip-feed unit. The liquid in the pool. The constant supply, just to keep her precious, stable, in suspension.

Clouded.

That's all. No more. Pointless, a few extra months of life, and then weeks of life. Days of life.

Hours, minutes, moments. Passing . . .

And yet, whatever good there is, all of it comes from people like Tupelo, these few lonely people.

I reached over, to touch the girl's arm.

'What?'

'Listen now . . .'

'What's going on back there?' said Henderson.

'I'm telling her.'

Henderson didn't turn round. She made a noise, her head moved just slightly.

'Telling me what?' asked Tupelo.

'It's your business, Marlene,' said Henderson. 'We're only along for the ride, the money.'

'What, there's money involved?'

'Like you've never seen, girl.'

The motorway rose up then, to pass over a sprawling industrial estate; windowless buildings, parking lots and storage units. Drifts of smoke. And all things painted the same flat colour. In the distance, a glass-fronted office block held the sky in a cold embrace.

'What's the story?' said Tupelo.

I looked at the girl. 'There's a man. Kingsley.'

'Yeah, I got that.'

'I did an interview with him, for a magazine. That's how we met.'

'And Kingsley is . . .'

'A collector.'

Tupelo thought about this for a moment. 'OK. What does he collect?'

'Many things. Objects, contraptions. Mirrors . . .'

'What is he, good-looking?'

'It's not . . .'

'He's a madman then?'

'Mad?'

'Sure,' said Tupelo. 'He's a good-looking madman, who just can't stop looking at himself all day long, all night long.'

'No. Not mad . . .'

'For fuck's sake,' said Henderson. 'What's to tell? We've got a job to do, we're doing it.'

'Come on, Bev,' said Peacock. 'This isn't easy.'

He was slowing the car right down to let a delivery lorry overtake. Ahead of us, the motorway was filling with traffic coming in from a slip road. Car horns were sounding as vehicles jostled for position. The smoke drifts were closing in.

'I think I missed the exit,' said Peacock.

'What?' said Henderson.

'I don't know . . .'

The whole scene was a dull yellow flame, somewhere to the forefront of my skull.

'And what we did last night,' said the girl, 'that mirror . . .'

'That's a part of it,' said Henderson.

'It's a special mirror, right?'

'Oh sure. Special is the word. Ask Marlene.'

The girl touched me then, I'm sure that she did. She reached out her hand and touched me, and maybe a question was asked. The road was all I could really focus on, the cars and the smoke trails which clustered over them, the warning lights flashing on the overhead gantries. The yellow flame in my head which pulsed to its own rhythm.

'Watch yourself,' said Henderson.

'I'm watching,' said Peacock.

Cars were weaving in and out of the lanes, some of them moving far too quickly. Others were dragging back like we were, and I had this sudden, strange insight just then that nobody was travelling at a normal speed. And the fast and the slow did not cancel each other out; they jarred and crackled against each other.

'Fuck.'

'Peacock . . .'

I was losing moments here and there, as though my eyes were opening and closing of their own accord. Cars jumped into new positions without travelling.

'Look now!'

There was no smooth pathway, only the grain of the

world, which was exposed and magnified and brutal, and the car veered wildly across two whole lanes as Peacock's hands slipped on the wheel, and we were spinning away from ourselves.

>

Angela's body, her lovely coffin, her hair and skin and bones and flesh, all sent to the flames. The little church. My mother's face all creased with pain, beyond reach; and the space beside her where my father should have stood. And my husband across the aisle from me, distant. The black curtain moving aside, and back again. Closing. Beyond reach. And what it was precisely I do not know, but I really did feel something of myself burning alongside.

Closing. In the smoke, the ashes, myself.

Alongside . . .

I cannot recollect a single moment from the days that followed. Nothing. Darkness. Lost to the noise. And then, about a week or so after the funeral, I found myself standing outside Kingsley's house, without any knowledge of travelling there. I was thinking of my last visit, and the walk through the garden, the tree-lined pathways. The church font, the mirror that sparkled beneath the water. I had turned down the offer of work, those months before, with some regret I think, but fearful of what had been shown to me in the pool, revealed to me. The face in the water, and the subsequent truth of that image, with the long weeks of sickness, and with Angela, her passing away beyond my reach, all reach . . .

My face, my face of tears.

Now, I stood with Kingsley in one of his inner rooms. The curtains were drawn, all was dark. All was quiet. A large wooden frame rested on the table. The few extant pieces of glass had been brought from their various resting places; now they lay within the frame, awaiting their neighbours. And Kingsley's voice in the shadows, whispering his love of what was held there, the mystery, the promise.

Henderson does not know the truth of it, and neither does Peacock. Not really. The girl knows even less. I've told them a little, enough to keep them from asking for more, I hope. And what more could I tell them, in truth, when the truth is still moving away from me?

Shards of glass, silver nitrate, reflections half seen from strange angles. A broken mirror, the fragments of it stolen, separated, sold off, fought over, lost, found again, and lost once more, and now scattered around the country. The one hundred shivers, as Kingsley calls them, with each fragment having a different quality, a quite specific, individual effect. I should think of it, he told me, as a magical spell, broken down into its various components. Many, tiny treasures, which people would not easily give up, despite the sadness they brought with them. The sadness, which lingers over from the moment the glass was shattered. Kingsley spoke of the mirror as though it had been injured, wounded, a living thing. In need of healing. And all I have to do is find the various pieces as directed, and return them to this house, this room, this simple wooden frame where the shadows move now, tinged with violet.

This will be my task, my scent, my substance.

And this has been my one good purpose in life these last few weeks, and I'm still not sure, even this far along, that I can believe all the claims Kingsley made. Finally that day, with his voice a bare murmur, he spoke of what he hoped would take place once the pieces of the mirror were brought together. The spell, the one spell, as he called it, the dreaming spell.

A melting of the way . . .

We were parked on the hard shoulder with the car resting at a bad angle, and the traffic streaming by regardless. Peacock was sitting on the grass verge, his head in his hands. Tupelo and I were leaning on the car, watching him. We didn't know what to do. Henderson was pacing up and down, muttering to herself, and then she came up close to Peacock.

'You crazy fuck. What's wrong with you?'

'Nothing. I'm tired.'

'Tired? We nearly got killed.'

'We didn't,' said Tupelo. 'We're all right.'

'What's it to you?'

'What's it to me? I'm in the car with you. It's me getting killed as well, except I didn't. We didn't get killed. We're all right.'

Henderson turned away from the girl. 'Peacock,' she said.

'What?'

'You want the Lucy now?'

'No.'

'No?'

'It's too early.'

He had taken the gun from his belt for some reason, and now he let it hang from his fingers.

'Fine,' said Henderson. 'Fine.'

Peacock kept silent.

Henderson looked at the road, at the road and the traffic, and the long distance still to go was caught there, in her eyes. And then she turned my way, with the distance gathered in the look she gave me.

'OK,' she said. 'The girl drives.'

The road curved away between the sides of a valley, where, on either side of us, along the tops of the hills, radio antennae crackled with noise, with sparks of blue light. Peacock kept spinning the dial around, searching through the channels. He was catching at signals, transmissions, all of them broken in some way or else covered in static, or else hardly there at all, only whispers in the ether. The car was passing through the sparks; it was passing through the moments, the hiss, the whispers. It was moving through the scatter and the drag of data, through the remnants of songs, prayers and lullabies, the human voice, a weeping voice. Cries in the daytime, cries in the air. And then Peacock found a clear and strong signal right at the end of the dial.

'That will do,' said Tupelo. 'Radio Lucy.'

It was a complex mathematical shape, turned into some kind of melody. Waveforms. A slow, quiet pulse along the spectrum.

'Oh come on,' said Peacock.

'No. Leave it.'

'Put some music on,' said Henderson. 'Something loud and murderous.'

'There's nothing else,' said Peacock. 'Nothing that works.'

'This is music,' said Tupelo.

'Put a tape on. Put my Blood Bucket tape on.'

'Blood Bucket? That's not music.'

'Blood Bucket got busted,' said Peacock.

'When? When did the Blood Bucket get busted? Who busted it?'

'You did, Bev. You stood on it. Back in Manchester.'

'Shit. Did I?'

'Did I ever mention that I can play the piano?'

'Shut up, Peacock,' said Henderson.

'Radio Lucy is music,' said Tupelo. 'It is.'

And there was a kind of beauty, I suppose, within the government test signal. A well-coded elegance, a mystery; lulling, hypnotic.

'Fucking computers,' said Peacock. 'I don't know what they hope to find.'

'Stop the car,' said Henderson. 'I need a piss.'

'Put a squeeze on it.'

'I'm hungry,' said Tupelo.

The girl had taken the wheel gladly, found us the exit route without any problem and now we were driving down along the motorway, away from London.

Down to the coast.

There were a few cars using the opposite carriageway, but the road south was more or less empty. Peacock was cracking jokes and making inane comments. 'Nothing can stop us now,' he said. Sometimes the line of a song would come from his lips, and every so often he'd turn his big face round to flash a grin at Henderson sitting in the back. I don't know what it was, but everything had changed since the girl took over. Peacock's mishap had been put aside, the road was easy.

'I had a computer,' said Henderson. 'Once.'

'What happened to it?'

'I threw it away, over a bridge. Mercy killing.'

Tupelo started to explain about Radio Lucy. 'They're just sending out signals, measuring responses. Trying to find some meaning in the chaos. Some pattern or other. That's the plan of it.'

'Oh my,' said Peacock. 'Now there's a good plan.'

'It is good,' said Tupelo.

'And have they?' I asked.

'What?'

'Have they found any meaning in it?'

'Well, they proved once and for all that the effect isn't constant. It changes from place to place, and from time to time.'

'We know that,' said Henderson. 'We live that.'

'And that within the chaos, there are various fixed points. It's like how certain images keep turning up, for each person suffering.'

'Apart from that?' Peacock asked. 'Any good pattern?'

'Not that I know of.'

'You hear that, Bev?'

'What now?' said Henderson.

'What I'm saying is this. Listen to me. That the big guys might well have the good-time Lucy, they might even have the cold shit like the girl here.'

'The what shit?' said Tupelo.

122

'The cold shit, you know? Turned off. Turned down. Whatever it is you people have.'

'It's not like that.'

'Whatever. But what I'm saying, these lab boys, they ain't got what we've got. No. They ain't got the magic. They ain't got a case full. Right, Bev?'

'Yeah, sure,' said Henderson. 'That's the way.'

'Oh look now,' said Tupelo. 'A stroller, coming up.'

It was a young man standing by the side of the road. Tupelo slowed the car.

'Fuck off,' said Henderson. 'There's no room.'

'But he's lonely,' said Tupelo. 'Look at him.'

'Check out the sign,' said Peacock.

I had to concentrate all my attention on the figure, on the piece of card he was holding.

'What does it say?' I asked.

'It's blank,' said Tupelo. 'A blank piece of card.'

'You still want to stop, girl?' said Peacock. 'I mean, the guy's young, good-looking. He's going nowhere. Blanktown. What more could you want?'

'We drive on,' said Tupelo.

There was quiet then, for a while, and I was glad of it. I was working on my notes, the recollections of the day up to the moment just passing.

'Don't you ever stop that?' said Henderson. 'That writing thing?'

'No.'

But now, as I looked at the last few pages, already the meaning was being lost to me. Usually, it took a good number of days for this to happen.

'Once,' said Peacock, 'I saw a road sign, and guess what it said?'

'What?' said Tupelo.

'Danger. Damaged road sign ahead.'

'Yeah?'

'Damn right. And a little further on, there it was, the damaged sign.'

'What did that one say?'

'Well, it was damaged, wasn't it? There was a haze around the words, the usual, but I could just about make out the message.'

'Go on.'

'Danger, it said. Damaged road sign ahead.'

'You're making this up.'

'It's true, listen to me.'

'Let me guess. Another sign came along.'

'Oh yeah. There it was, coming right up.'

'And?'

'And what?'

'Could you read it?'

'Oh sure, completely. No damage at all.'

'What did it say?'

'Ignore all previous signs.'

'Jesus,' said Tupelo. 'Why do I bother?'

'I don't know, why do you bother?'

The motorway moved slowly through the levels, flat and lonely, endless. We passed a radio telescope, its huge bowl upturned to collect the sky. A cloud of noise danced around it. A few miles further on a kind of mirage effect took over the road.

'What is that?' said Peacock.

It was a blue shimmering in the distance, in liquid waves of air that rose from the tarmac. There was another car some way ahead of us, which passed

through this wall of heat, the mirage folding softly
around the vehicle's sides, and then we moved along
ourselves, and through. The temperature rose, and we
seemed to slow down without any real knowledge of
slowing down. I could hear sounds, voices, breathing
noises, all of them barely heard, as we made our way
through the mirage. Henderson turned to look at me,
her face unknown, never seen before, a stranger's face.
I lost all sense of movement. The car was suspended in
space, held there, vibrant, and then to emerge finally on
the other side, travelling now at our proper speed and
filled with a sudden cold, and Henderson's face back to
normal.

'What the hell was that?' said Peacock.

Tupelo shook her head. 'I don't know.'

'Where's that other car gone?'

The road ahead was long and straight and clear, with
no visible turnings. The vehicle we had seen but a few
moments earlier was no longer visible.

'Shit,' said Peacock. 'It really is nasty around here.'

We drove on. I found that I could no longer write; the
episode had made me feel nauseous. The words were
reeling on the page.

'Oh, fuck,' said Henderson. 'Will you . . . ?'

'What is it?' said Peacock.

'Jesus.'

'What?'

'A mirror.'

'Hey,' said Tupelo. 'That's mine. Get out of my bag.'

'Christ,' said Henderson. 'I nearly looked in it then. I
nearly saw myself.'

'Leave it alone.'

'What's this? A watch. A fucking wristwatch.'

'I'm warning you.'

'What time is it?' said Peacock.

'How the fuck would I know? Marlene . . .'

Henderson handed the watch to me. The fingers were a blur, a triple image, superimposed.

'What's this book?' said Henderson.

'It's a book,' said Tupelo. 'What's the problem?'

Henderson had found the girl's bag on the floor of the car. She had pulled first the mirror out of it, then the wristwatch, and now the book. It was the copy of Poe's stories the girl had been looking at earlier in the day. Henderson flicked through the pages.

'I don't know what you see in these things. Reading, and all that.'

'Try it, why don't you?'

'Steady now,' said Peacock. 'A crawler.'

There was a slow-moving vehicle ahead of us, a small car, sky-blue in colour, the first we'd seen since the mirage. And there were so many crazies about, we had to be careful. Tupelo gave the vehicle a wide berth; as we passed by, I looked over at the driver.

'Trance job,' said Henderson.

The driver's hands were clutched hard on the steering wheel, and his head rocked slowly from side to side. He turned to look at us, with his face all empty, drained of all expression.

'Jesus,' said Peacock. 'There you go. It should not be allowed.'

We moved on, leaving the blue car behind.

'Now then,' said Peacock. 'Where were we?'

'This is seriously weird,' said Henderson. 'This here book. Seriously weird.'

'What is it?' asked Peacock.

'The Tell-Tale Heart.'

'That's the title?'

'That's it.'

'What, like a romance, is it? Like a romance book?'

'No. Not that.'

'Bev, there ain't no good story but this one. Me and you, babe. Listen to me. I'm your love story.'

'Object there was none,' said Henderson. 'Passion there was none. I loved the old man. He had never wronged me. He had never given me insult.'

'What are you saying?' said Peacock.

'I'm reading from the story.'

'Oh.'

'For his gold I had no desire.'

'I'd like his gold,' said Peacock.

'For his gold I had no desire. I think it was his eye! Yes, it was this! One of his eyes resembled that of a vulture. A pale blue eye with a film over it. Whenever it fell upon me, my blood ran cold.'

Henderson's long hair fell ragged over her face, all ragged and matted and dirty and crawling with life and the hair was shielding her eyes but I felt sure she was looking my way as she read.

'And so by degrees, very gradually, I made up my mind to take the life of the old man, and thus to rid myself of the eye for ever.'

'That's it?' said Peacock.

'That's the way of it,' said Henderson. 'He's going to kill the old guy.'

127

'It wasn't the old man he was killing,' said Tupelo.

'What?'

'He was killing the eye. He had to kill the eye.'

'He's a mad fucker, that's for sure,' said Peacock.

'No,' said Henderson. 'He reckons he isn't mad. It says here that the disease has sharpened his senses, not dulled them.'

'The disease?'

'He doesn't explain it. Not yet, anyway.'

'So why does he kill the old man's eye then?' said Peacock. 'Do you get it, Marlene?'

'I think so.'

'He doesn't like being looked at,' said Tupelo.

'What's that?' said Henderson.

'He can't stand being looked at. He hates it.'

'Yeah well,' said Peacock. 'I know that feeling.'

'But he's still telling the story to somebody, isn't he? I mean, somebody's looking at him still.'

'Who's looking at him?' said Henderson.

'The reader,' said Tupelo.

Henderson shook her head. 'Don't start that stuff on me. It's messing me up.'

'This is the plan. He's going to gouge the reader's eyes out. The storyteller, he's going to tear out the eye of the reader!'

'Shit, yeah,' said Peacock. 'I like it.'

'Fucking books,' said Henderson. 'There should be a law against them.'

'There is,' said Tupelo. 'In your mind.'

'Right. That's it.'

'What?'

'Stop the car.'

'I—'

'Stop the fucking car!'

Tupelo brought us to a standstill. The sound of the engine died away, leaving only the quiet, electronic melody still coming from the radio. Nobody spoke for a moment, and then Peacock said, 'Best apologize, girl.'

'Me?'

'You.'

'What have I done?'

Peacock sighed.

'I want her out of here,' said Henderson. 'Go on, get out of the car.'

'You can't—'

'Get the fuck out.'

Something was lost in Tupelo then. She lowered her head, resting her brow against the steering wheel. I thought I could maybe plead with Henderson, for whatever good it would do, but then the girl spoke some words, quietly, into her folded arms.

'I didn't hear you,' said Henderson.

Tupelo lifted up her head. 'I'm sorry.'

'Turn around. Let me see your face.'

'What?'

'Turn around.'

Tupelo twisted round in her seat. Henderson had the little vanity mirror ready, folded open, and now she held it out so that only the girl's face was caught there.

'What did you say?'

Tupelo looked into the mirror, directly, and once again she said the necessary words.

'I'm sorry.'

'Good.'

We drove on in silence. Peacock busied himself with the road atlas. Henderson rested her head against the seat, her eyes closed. I spent the time just looking out of the window, with no clear thoughts in my mind. It felt awkward to speak. Finally, it was the girl herself who broke the mood.

'You know where we're going?' she said.

Peacock looked at her. 'What of it?'

'The places around the coast, they're the worst hit. You do know that? The most sick. Which explains, you see, why nobody's going our way. Oh sure, we're the lonely ones.'

'Why is it?' asked Peacock. 'Why the coast?'

'It's like a cloth, unravelling. That's the theory, anyway. The whole country's fraying at the edges.'

Peacock nodded. 'A bit like me.'

'Everyone wants to stay in the middle. It's safer like that.'

Henderson opened her eyes. 'Is there a place coming up?'

'Motorway services,' said Tupelo. 'A few miles.'

'Good. I really do need the toilet.'

A large sign was suspended over the road, the slogan flashing on and off in gold letters; and the words so clear and so bright that even I could read them as we passed beneath.

Drivers! Have you taken your Lucidity?

'You know what I heard?' said Peacock. 'There's more than enough special juice flowing through one of them signs, one of them newfangled signs, to keep a guy like me sane for a year, a year and a half, more even. Is that fair? I mean, is that fair?'

'It's a crime,' said Tupelo.

'I sure would love to get my hands on some of that special. Some of that Electronic Lucy, as they call it. Shit, yeah. What I could do then.'

'What would you do then?' said Henderson.

'Stuff.'

'Right. Of course. Stuff.'

'You know what else they have? They have a lucidity engine. No, listen. It's a machine. You can put whatever you want in one end, anything that's broken or mixed up or fucked up whatever, anything that's got the noise in it, and it comes out the other end, all mended.'

'There's no such thing,' said Tupelo.

'No. I heard this. The government's working on it, in secret. It's a black box, and inside the box there's a little piece of space that ain't got the disease. That's it. A little piece of the world where all the signs come clean. Imagine getting your hands on that thing. Shit. The black box. The things I could do.'

'What would you do?' said Henderson.

'Why do you keep saying that, Bev? What would I do?'

'I'm asking. What would you do?'

'What would I do? I'd jack you lot in. Yeah, the lot of you. I would be gone. You wouldn't see me.'

'You know what,' said Henderson. 'When I first found Peacock, you know what he was doing?'

'Oh, here we go.'

'He was lying drunk in a dark alley, with a shopping bag over his head.'

'Really?' said Tupelo. 'A plastic bag?'

'No. A lady's shopping bag.'

'Fuck off please,' said Peacock. He turned round in

his seat to face Henderson, and then his eyes locked on something through the back window. 'Oh shit!'

'What?' said Tupelo.

'A crazy. Coming up fast.'

'Where? I can't see it.'

I looked behind. There was a vehicle approaching, a bright red car taking up the whole second lane. Big, powerful. It was moving at speed directly towards us, gaining easily.

'Pull over,' said Henderson.

'What?' said Tupelo.

'Pull over!'

And suddenly then, I could not move. I could not take my eyes away from the vehicle. It was a limousine, the windows all blacked out. Closer now, closer. It was scarred and dented all around the front bumpers and the bonnet. The driver could not be seen. There was a molten wave of heat flowing around the vehicle and I lost sight of it for a second. When the limousine emerged from the heat, it was almost upon us and a screaming noise came with it. It was coming from the inside of my own skull, the noise.

'Come on!' cried Peacock.

We swerved onto the hard shoulder, and the limousine followed our direction. We hit the crash barrier with a terrible screeching that coursed all the way through my body. The limousine pressed against us. It was burning the side of our car and the day was dark, and then filled with colour, with sparks of colour.

I had the sudden clear thought that I was going to die here, in this place, this moment.

Time was being held back, drawn out.

Melted down.

Henderson was thrown across the seat and I took hold of her, I took hold of Henderson quite easily, I don't know how. Voices, murmurs. The hazy bump and blur of something that was jumping around in Peacock's grip.

'Girl, move back!'

Peacock's voice, lost, crying out as we scraped along the barrier, burning up with noise. Something was thrown from his hand. Whatever it was that Peacock had been struggling with, now it was lost and thrown away, and it landed on Henderson's body where she was crouched down on the back seat, and I reached down to pick up the object.

It was the gun.

I felt that another person's hand had taken hold of mine, to pick up the gun, to move it slowly through the air, through the colours, the sparks.

Scatter and drag.

Whispers of song, static hiss. Stupid prayers and lullabies, and all of the tears not yet fallen, where do they come from, where do they gather in the eye, waiting? And here's me now, just looking for the one good thing that was clear and pure and strong, a blessed fucking signal, alive, dancing, at the far end of the dial. And somebody somewhere was shouting at me to stop but no, I could not stop.

I couldn't stop myself. This one small action that had now been started; I pulled my finger tight against the trigger of the gun.

How long did it take, this whole thing? From the moment the limousine made contact, to the shot being fired; a few seconds maybe, a minute or even more? I don't know. There was a popping sound behind my eyelids, which had closed shut at some point, and the sound was made from little flecks of colour bursting open in the darkness. I did not hear the gun firing, but the kick of it sent me back against the door with a dull soft roaring in the brain and the body bouncing back off the door, and then the car coming to rest at last.

The report of the gun seemed to catch up with me, many seconds after it had happened, the sudden noise of it. Painful. My eyes came open. Thin trails of smoke curled before me, giving off a burnt, powdery smell.

I looked around. The car had come to rest across the motorway, facing the central barrier. There was another car passing along the opposite carriageway, but it did not stop, it did not even slow down, and then we were alone once more.

'Jesus fucking Christ.'

It seemed that Peacock was the only one of us who could speak. And I saw then what I had done. The noise

of the gun had died to a strange high sound and I saw
what I had done clearly now as though a light had
suddenly been turned on. The side window opposite me
was smashed. There was nothing left of it except for a
few ragged teeth around the edges where some glass
remained in the frame. There were little pieces of
glass all over the seat, and some of them had landed on
Henderson, who was lying curled up on the seat with
both her arms tight round her head, protecting herself.

'Is everybody OK?' said Peacock.

The gun fell loose from my hand. There was a dust in
the air, a bright dry dust which floated inside my
mouth and I could not speak, not at all.

'What's that noise?' said Peacock. 'What is it?'

'It's the radio,' said Tupelo.

'Turn it off.'

Tupelo turned off the radio, and the quiet closed in.

'Well then,' said Peacock, and he turned round in his
seat. 'Bev? You OK?'

I watched Henderson pulling herself up, slowly.

'Shit. Where's the limo?'

'Gone. Long gone.' Peacock laughed.

'What?'

'She missed. Marlene missed the fucker.'

'What happened?'

Peacock looked at Henderson. 'What happened, Bev,
is that you just pissed yourself.'

'What? Oh fuck. Christ.'

Henderson looked at me, a bad look, but I was
seeing beyond that now. I was looking out through the
window. I was looking through the broken window
where the bullet had flown. I was wondering just how

far the bullet had travelled from there and towards what possible target.

Henderson was making a noise about something.

I looked past her voice, and out, to the flat open landscape beyond the motorway. There was a field of wind generators close by, their bright shining blades turning in drowsy circles.

I pictured the bullet.

I imagined the bullet passing easily between the moment of each turning blade and the bullet floating onwards through the clean empty air. I imagined the bullet simply reaching the end of its pathway and slowing down now, and falling in a lazy curve some-where to the ground, the earth. Or else the bullet never did stop at all but rather carried on and on and broke open a small hole in the sky.

And I pictured the bullet.

Beyond the sky even, as it travelled.

Slowly now, slowly, with the damaged car more or less dragging itself along the road. Patches of blue paint stained the tarmac. All the signs were covered over by the same colour. I felt we were entering another world, by degrees. And then, in the distance, we saw the elevated walkway of the service station. There seemed to be some kind of activity going on, near to the exit road. As we drew closer, I saw that whole sections of the central barrier had been removed. A group of people were crossing the motorway on foot.

'Fuck me,' said Peacock. 'Do you see that?'

These were the first words spoken in the car for the last mile or so.

'A horse. A fucking horse.'

Tupelo stopped the car. The people held the horse back, some few feet away from us. They stood there, three men dressed in blue overalls, and all of them watching us calmly. But the horse was troubled, this old, dusty white creature stretching the reins tight. And then one of the men broke into a smile, and he nodded our way.

'What's happening?' said Tupelo.

'He wants us to go first,' said Peacock.

'Are you sure?'

'Come on.'

But the horse was scared, I could see that. The animal reared up suddenly, onto its back legs, and a terrible noise came from its peeled-back gums.

'Shit,' said Tupelo.

The horse broke loose; it broke loose of the reins, lurching forward, its two forelegs crashing down onto the bonnet of the car. The whole vehicle shook with the impact, and Tupelo and even Peacock, they both jerked back in their seats, shielding their faces and crying out.

'Fuck . . .'

I was shaken myself of course, but when I looked over at Henderson, she had the same expression she had worn these last few miles. The same hard-set look around the mouth, the eyes, and her fingers holding tight onto the handle of the suitcase.

And the horse rose up once more, in fever.

>

Tupelo steered the car down a small neat road that turned lazily between rows of trees. There was nothing much to distinguish this particular road, these particular trees, but I couldn't help feeling that I'd been here before. It was many years ago, when Angela was still a small child. It was myself and my husband and Angela, on holiday. We had stopped at this same place, to get some food, some rest. That was it, I was sure.

The only sign we passed had been painted over, the same sky-blue we had seen on the way down, but now with the simple image of a white dove added, and some new words.

'The People's Republic of Leisure,' said Tupelo. 'What's all that about?'

'Cheeseville,' said Peacock.

'But we can get fixed up here, right? Bev, you hear that?'

'Leave her be.'

Henderson was hunched up in the seat with her hands squeezed in her lap, and her face was turned away and I felt awkward looking at her, and also somewhat ashamed and there was a bad taste in my mouth.

'We can stay here awhile.'

'No, Marlene,' said Peacock. 'Not here.'

'I need to rest.'

'We get the car mended, and then we get going.'

'Marlene needs her medicine,' said Tupelo.

'We all do,' said Peacock. 'We all fucking do. Jesus, what a day.'

Tupelo slowed the car. 'What's this?'

There was a barrier lowered across the road, with a young man standing close by, dressed in a blue uniform. Tupelo brought the car to a halt, and Peacock spoke through his open window.

'Hi there.'

'Hello. My name's Paul. How are we doing today?'

'We're doing fine.'

'What's happened to your vehicle?'

'Been through the shit, Paul. The whole shit.'

The young man did not respond, not properly. Instead, he kept his stare overly bright, and his voice cheerful and well-mannered. 'Anything to declare?'

'Fuck all,' said Peacock.

'Oh . . .'

The man blinked his eyes, just the once, and then wrote something on his clipboard. 'May I remind you,' he said, 'that this is a leisure complex. We permit only the finest of leisure activities to take place.'

'No trouble,' said Peacock. 'What's the damage?'

'I'm sorry, sir?'

'How much is it?'

'Will you be wanting overnight leisure, or short-term leisure?'

'Short.'

The young man told Peacock the price.

'What?' said Tupelo. 'We have to pay to get in?'

'That's OK,' said Peacock. 'That's just fine.'

He reached down to the floor of the car, and when he came back up, a chocolate bar wrapper was in his hand.

'There you go, Paul. That should cover it.'

A frown came to the man's face. He looked from the wrapper to Peacock, and then back again. And then, once again, the young man's lips found the lovely smile.

'That will do nicely, sir. Please enjoy your stay.'

'We will,' said Peacock.

'What's wrong with him?' whispered Tupelo.

'Too much Lucy. The way it goes.'

The barrier was raised up before us, and the car slid through.

>

We moved slowly through the ranks of a large, crowded car park, which curved around the main building of the complex. The people's flag of leisure could be seen everywhere, strung overhead or fixed to poles; the white dove on blue ground, barely stirred by a low breeze. All about us, canvas awnings decorated with the same colours stretched from one vehicle to the next.

Market stalls had been set up between the cars, with all kinds of goods and provisions on sale. Men and women walked between these stalls; others sat in deck-chairs, reading, or talking to their neighbours. Children played amongst the stalls, running wild. Dogs wandered around. A fight was going on between two middle-aged men and nobody paid it much mind. It was a tired and lazy fight without any real violence to it.

We could hear music being played, coming in through the broken window of the car. A few people were dancing to this, moving through the crowd with their partners held closely to them. Others danced alone; truly alone, or else with ghostly companions.

'I don't get it,' said Tupelo. 'Who are these people? What are they doing here?'

'They live here,' said Peacock. 'They've taken over.'

Something struck the side of the car. A young boy was pressing his face against the window, right next to me. And then Henderson made a noise, an angry noise; another boy was at her window, and it was the same face, the same boy's face on each side of the car. The same face, twice over. Twin boys. And everywhere I looked, these boys, the man at the gate, and all the people around, everybody held the same bright, glazed expression.

'Sleepwalkers,' said Peacock. 'Cheap powder.'

The cold trance; too much bad Lucidity. The mind just lifted up and sharpened so much, it could do nothing more than contemplate some far-off realm, and the world became a place that other people lived in.

Tupelo drove the car into a garage area, where a smiling mechanic told us the price for the check-up, the fix, and a full tank.

'Patch it,' said Peacock. 'Quick job.'

I paid for the work, real money this time.

Peacock shifted round in his seat. 'Beverly. We're here now.' But when Henderson just looked at him, without replying, he said, 'Please yourself.' He turned back to Tupelo. 'What time is it, girl?'

'Right. The time, sure. Marlene . . .'

I handed the bag over, and Tupelo took her watch out and looked at it. 'Just gone two,' she said.

'No,' said Peacock. 'Exactly.'

'Four minutes past.'

'More.'

'Four minutes past two, and twenty-five seconds.'

'Good.'

This was the first real, precise knowledge of the time we'd had in these last few weeks. It was a strange feeling, for me; painful, as though somebody had jabbed a needle into my face.

'Good,' said Peacock. 'Four past two, and how many seconds, just now?'

'Thirty-seven.'

'Good.'

'Thirty-eight, thirty-nine . . .'

Peacock took the medical kit and a water bottle out of his bag. He put a Lucy into his mouth and he took a drink to swallow it. 'Keep it sweet.' He threw the kit onto the back seat. 'Don't forget your own.'

'Can I have some money?' said Tupelo.

'Whatever,' said Peacock.

I gave some money to the girl, and she looked at it, and then said, 'Is this all?'

'That's it,' said Peacock.

'You're not really going to leave us, are you?'

'Us?'

'Because you said that if you ever got what you wanted, you said you'd leave us, all of us.'

'Us? I don't know you, girl. I don't know who the fuck you are.'

'I know that. I know it. But you're not really going to leave?'

'One day,' said Peacock. 'Sure.'

'OK, fine,' said Tupelo. 'One day.'

Peacock opened his door. 'We're not staying here too long. You people got that?' He climbed out.

'Got it,' said Tupelo.

Peacock bent down at my window. 'Marlene, you stay with the car, the suitcase.'

'Right.'

The driver's door wouldn't open, there was too much damage. Tupelo climbed over the seats, to get out through the passenger door. Peacock walked off towards the main complex, and Tupelo went racing her own way, into the market area.

And then it was just Henderson and me, in the car together, a silence between us.

'Right then,' I said, finally.

'Let me out,' said Henderson.

'What?'

'Let me out.'

'Right.'

Henderson's door was also jammed shut and I had to get out of the car first, and then she clambered over to my side and she got out herself. She took the suitcase with her, and her own bag.

'What shall we do?' I asked.

Henderson ignored me. Instead she walked round to where the mechanic was working on the engine of the car.

'Where are the toilets?'

The mechanic looked at the mess she was in.

'Where are they?'

The mechanic pointed, and then Henderson went off that way.

I leant inside the car, cleaning the remains of the glass off the seats and the floor of the car. The glass was broken into tiny cubes and I really felt I was scooping up some bad luck jewels just then. Oh why had I been so stupid? Why so foolish?

A small line of blood appeared on my index finger.

Taking my shoulder bag with me, I climbed back out of the car. It was looking bad; the broken window, the white bodywork all scarred and buckled inward. The mechanic looked up from where he was working on the driver's door. He was smiling to himself, whistling a little tune. I felt tired already, as though the day was closing down too quickly.

'Is there a phone?' I asked. 'A telephone?'

The mechanic looked at me, blankly. 'Yes. But only to the other side.'

'The other side?'

For a second I actually thought he meant that I would be able to contact the dead, to telephone the dead, but no, no; the mechanic was looking over towards the motorway and the buildings on the opposite side.

'There's no outside line?'

'None that work.'

He went back to the car, banging at the panels with a hammer.

'How long have you been here?' I asked.

'How long?'

'How long working here?'

There was a lost expression on his face. 'I don't rightly know, madam.'

'You don't know?'

'I don't have a replacement.'

'What?'

'For the window, madam. Shall I provide a temporary covering?'

'Please,' I said. 'Please do that.'

There was a small lawn beyond the garage forecourt, a low brick wall around it. I took the water bottle and the medical kit, and went to sit there. The mechanic was at his work and I watched him for a while. I could hear the music playing; they must have loudspeakers all over. It was a soft-hearted mechanical sound with no tonal centre, no melody, no place for the sickness to inhabit.

My head dropped down, slowly. I needed some time. I wanted to let the bad day grow steady, inside. And the idea came to me then. Maybe I could just walk away? Maybe I could just walk into the crowd here at this place and take all the cheap Lucy I could find. That would be good. Memories would die. Maybe I could lose myself this way, become folded and bound and lost for ever.

'She was putting make-up on.'

I looked up. Henderson was standing there, looking down at me. She was holding the suitcase.

'Who was?'

'This woman in the loo.'

Henderson had changed her trousers. Her bleached hair was combed back from her face, held in place by a scarf. Her face was shining. As far as I could tell, this is what Henderson looked like, just then, and I thought she looked very beautiful. I'd always thought that, ever since our first meeting, in the darkness of the public gardens. She saw me there, digging in the dirt before she even knew just what it was I was searching for, and she said, 'Bury yourself slowly. It's more fun.' Her first ever words to me. And the way that she said the words, and the look in her eye, the way that she held herself, the way that she reached out her hand towards me, all this allowed me to see the beauty in the woman. A strange beauty, far beyond the usual kind.

'She was putting on lipstick, Marlene. Lipstick and powder. You hear me?'

'In a mirror?'

Henderson sat down next to me.

'They have mirrors here, Marlene. They have mirrors in the toilets and lights and everything and this woman, she was standing there by the glass and she was loving herself no trouble. She was singing away to herself, you know, some stupid tune and she turns to me.'

'What did she say?'

'Nothing. She just kept on smiling. Well then, you know me. I'm not taking that sort of thing. I'm not. I'm not having people smile at me for no good reason. It's inhuman. It's freaky. And more than anything else, it's distasteful. Here's her bag.'

Henderson handed me a lady's handbag made of a shiny blue material.

'You stole it?'

'The silly cow handed it over.'

The bag was filled with capsules, sky-blue, with the white dove symbol inscribed on each one. Many of them, far too many. I pulled out a handful, let them fall.

'Shit. This what I think it is?'

'Have a taste.'

Henderson opened one up for me, just pulled apart the two halves of it and then poured the contents onto my palm. The little pile of dust. I took some on my finger, licked the end of it. A sweetness, like caramel.

'Bootleg version,' said Henderson. 'Ah, there'll be a touch in there. A drop of the good juice, nothing much.'

'I wonder where they get it from.'

'It's chemicals.'

'The good bit, I mean. The real stuff.'

'Like who gives a fuck.'

'I suppose.'

Henderson turned the bag upside down, spilling the contents onto the ground.

'Is this really the future, Marlene? Really? People doped up, all the hours of every day of the year.'

There were some items of make-up amongst the fallen capsules. I picked up a lipstick.

'You going to put some on?'

'Perhaps later.'

'Yeah, perhaps later.' Henderson took one of our own capsules. 'Keep it sweet.'

'You're not mad at me, Bev?'

'Come on.' She drank some water. 'Your turn.'

'You're not angry? I thought you would be.'

'Marlene, I fucking hate you.'

'Yes.'

'But I can't carry on without you.'

'Can't you?'

'You heard me. Marlene, meeting up with you, and all that, well listen now . . . listen . . . how can I say this, but Peacock and I, we were just wandering around before, with no real direction, you know?'

'I know.'

'And now, searching for the mirrors, and all that,

well now we do have, we have a direction. That's it. You do see that?'

'I see it. Beverly . . .'

'What?'

'Nothing. I was . . . well then. Never mind.'

'You want to stay here, right?'

I looked over at the car. The mechanic was stretching a sheet of clear plastic over the broken window, fixing it there with black tape.

'Marlene. We're so close now.'

'I know that.'

'It's easy. We find this Jamie guy, the theatre kid. OK? We get the dealer's name off him. One more piece, there you go.'

'No, there's more. Kingsley's asking for more.'

'Fuck him then. Yeah. One piece, and that's it.'

'I was thinking that.'

'There you go then.'

'One more . . .'

'So then. We get back to Kingsley. We get paid for the job. It's simple. It's over.'

I closed my eyes.

'What can I do?' said Henderson. 'We need this.'

Still, I didn't say anything. And Henderson's voice came softer now.

'Shit. It's not you. It's . . . look, Peacock's to blame. Sure he is. That gun, that fucking gun. He got it out, right. The catch was off. He was gonna fire it, I don't know. Marlene, I don't know.'

She was quiet for a moment. And then:

'Peacock's in trouble. Old debts. You don't know, you can't know. Marlene, we need this money.'

I opened my eyes. Henderson must have seen something, in my face. Something cold, turned off.

'Fine then,' she said. 'Forget the world. Fuck the payout. Yeah. Stay here. This is the place, Marlene. What did Peacock call it?'

'Cheeseville.'

'It's your place.'

I looked at her. I looked at the face of Henderson, that beautiful, strange face; but I could not look into her eyes.

'I'm scared, Bev. I'm scared.'

'Me too.'

'But you can handle it. You can do it.'

'Yeah, I'm the motherfucker.'

'Really. You can do it. You can take the suitcase, if you like. It's you doing all the work anyway, these last few days. I'm too ill. Sell the pieces. Forget Kingsley. Whatever. You can do that.'

'Marlene, I just washed the piss off my legs.'

I took my wallet from my bag, pulled some money from it. 'Here,' I said. 'Take this.'

Henderson wouldn't touch the money. She wouldn't touch what was offered. Instead, I felt her hand on my face, pulling me round, gently now.

'Myself, you, Peacock. This new girl. Sad and crazy fuckers, one and all. Look at me.'

It was painful and scary being so close to her, but I could not help myself now. I had to look there.

'You're not sick, Marlene. You do know that? It's in the space between us, that's all.'

'But why me? Why does it get to me, so much? What's the problem? My family . . .'

Henderson let her fingers touch my lips. There was something hidden there, in her hand. I could feel it.

'Look at your eyes,' she said. 'Two colours. Brown, and blue.'

'Two colours.'

'You're a sweetheart, Marlene. You know that?'

'Am I?'

She placed the capsule in my mouth and I pressed at the coating with my teeth. I pressed hard, breaking it open. The Lucy was on my tongue now.

'I think so,' said Henderson. 'I think that's the answer. You're a good-hearted woman and your daughter got killed. And that's it.' She gave me the water bottle to drink from. 'What do you say?'

'Keep it sweet.'

The phrase, well-practised. But too quietly said, I think. Whispered only.

The moment went by.

'You'd best give me the key,' said Henderson. 'If you're leaving us.'

Without thinking, I bent down to untie my left shoe. This is where I kept the key to the suitcase, inside the sock. A grey woollen sock. The key had slipped down, under my foot. I took off the sock and the key fell out. It was a small silver key, and it was nothing much really because Henderson could easily get the case open without it, I'd always known that.

'That's the one.'

And straightaway Henderson lifted the suitcase to her lap, and she put the key in the lock.

'What are you doing?'

'Here we go.'

152

The lid of the case was open.

'Henderson . . .'

The pieces of glass, the velvet coverings. Six pieces altogether. The story, the mirror. Everything we had found or stolen up to now. Henderson checked to see the mechanic was not looking our way, and then she lifted one of the pieces out from the case.

'You want to see it? Last chance, Marlene.'

Henderson folded back the first layer of velvet.

'This is wrong,' I said. 'It's dangerous.'

'People do it.'

'I know that. I know that people do it.'

'So then, I'm doing it.'

'What are you doing?'

'Just looking,' said Henderson. 'Nothing more.'

'Just looking?'

'I'm not stupid. Just looking.'

I turned away. We were sitting there next to each other on the low wall of the garage forecourt, with my head turned away from Henderson as she lifted the velvet from around the glass.

I could hear a voice.

A soft glow of violet light misted the air, bringing with it the voice of a man. He was singing. And I knew the glass then; the first one we had found together, when Henderson and Peacock joined me, digging in the earth side by side. The one with the voice inside it, the song, the unknown song. And I knew that Henderson was looking into the glass just then, and she was taking a hard breath. I could hear the breath being taken. And then Henderson was crying.

I could hear the crying.

And I waited there, turned away. I waited all the time until the glass was folded back in the covering; the song, folded back, and the light, folded back. I waited until I could hear the lock of the case being closed and I hadn't felt so lonely, not for the last few weeks, not since Angela. And there was little else to do now.

It was time to leave.

I stood up. There was nothing else to say. I started walking away from there but Henderson called me back, and for one moment I really thought she was going to ask me to stay. I really did think that.

'Your shoe,' said Henderson.

I went back for the shoe and the one sock. I didn't put them on, but just carried them with me, the black shoe and the grey sock. And then, with the ground cold and hard against my one bare foot, I was doing it.

I was walking away.

>

I walked out of the petrol station and into the market-place, the crowded area. I had left behind my change of clothes, the various items. More or less everything. The car, even. The mirror, in its pieces. The good things I had left behind, and all the bad things also. Only the shoulder bag was left, and what was in there: some money, a few odds and ends, bits of rubbish; and the book.

This book. The photograph.

The music dragged the smiling crowd of people all around me until I looked up to see the blue sky swirling, and then down, and onwards. It was the same tuneless glee, the same benign smile all over, except for one old man who came to me from an angle, suddenly, wearing a tall red hat, and a red gown, and his voice was wild, burning with passion.

'Repent! Repent unto the Lord, for he dwells deep within the frequencies.'

'What?'

'Repent, I say! The Lord is the strangest attractor; he moves across the boundary of complex knowledge, there to punish thee, and there to embrace. And that

155

which is broken, shall be mended. And that which is mended, broken in turn . . .'

And then he was gone. The old man scowled, and he moved off, pouring out his message to one after another, as he met them.

'And that which is broken, shall be mended. And that which is mended . . .'

I walked on, through the crowd. The people pressed against me tighter now but that was fine; it felt good to be there, drifting away, halfway lost. The same faces would come up again and again, and already I was seeing aspects of myself in them, dissolving; variations, tones of skin, the smile, the one smile repeated.

'Look,' said Tupelo. 'I've bought a magazine.'

The girl pushed her way through to me.

'See? It's about chess.'

'Yes. That's good.'

'I got food for everybody.' She opened a plastic bag. 'Sandwiches. Fruit.'

'That's good.'

'What's with the shoe?'

I looked at the shoe in my hand. I was a little puzzled by it.

'I'll put it on.'

'You do that.'

And I bent down to slip the shoe onto my foot.

'There's someone over there,' said Tupelo, 'looks just like you.'

'Where?' I stood up.

'She's gone now. What about the sock?'

The sock was lying on the ground, by my feet. I looked down at the sock, lying there.

'Marlene? What's wrong with you?'

'Nothing.'

'You want a banana, maybe? An apple?'

Tupelo pulled a bright green apple from the plastic bag, and I took it from her.

'I think you should get back now, Tupelo.'

'I can't. It's not my turn yet.'

'What's that?'

'What colour are you?' she asked.

'Colour?'

'I'm white. What colour are you?'

'I don't know. I saw a man in a red hat. I don't think he liked me.'

'We're on the same side then. Watch out for the knight. He's around here somewhere.'

'I will.'

Just then, a small boy came up to Tupelo. He was dressed in a red pullover, and he smiled the smile, the usual smile, as he touched her on the arm.

'Hey,' she said. 'Leave me alone.'

The boy smiled. 'En passant.'

'Oh come on. I only just started.'

'Even leisure,' said the boy, 'must one day come to an end.'

He spoke the words kindly, in a well-practised manner, and then his smile turned cold, and the crowd closed around Tupelo and she was gone, lost to me. Pulled away. And the people moving slowly now all around, and more slowly the further I wandered. A song had come my way, a tender little melody. I was singing it softly and only to myself. A young man danced with me awhile and then the song was singing all over, and the steps of the dance whirled me away, melting the crowd and the blue sky swirling all overhead and inside me also, the swirling all around until the music ended, my partner drifting from me and then I danced alone a few more steps, until finally, I could dance no more.

Something was wrong. When would the drug take charge of me? When would the crowd fall for me, fall in love with me? When would I feel myself enveloped, fully, and set free from all memories, all hunger, all this stupid desire to keep running away?

And through the crowd I saw a horse approaching. A woman was leading it onwards, slowly, with care. It was an old chestnut-coloured beast of great former beauty, but now far past those days. The horse came up, pushing its huge head close to me, and the skin of the horse was hot and covered in sweat. The animal was giving off a mist, a stench. It was a sick animal. I saw along the horse's neck a series of jagged cuts, some of them scabbed over and some not, but seeping still with blood and with some clearer fluid and there were flies crawling around on the wounds.

I put my hand on the wounds, gently.

I felt the heat there and the power of the horse coming loose from the wounds. My hand was wet, and when I put a finger to my lips, I knew the taste of it.

The sweetness.

The creature swung the vast, slow cradle of its head to one side. The horse looked at me with its huge black eye, which was an eye filled with a pool of ink, and there were silvery stars sunk deep into the ink, many miles deep, and my reflection was in there, all folded up into the eye's black realm.

>

The muscles of the eye tightened and the lid of the eye closed around me, capturing. It was the night folding into the day and my reflection was standing there in the darkness and the both of us looking at each other.

'You can't leave yet,' she said. 'Not yet.'

The reflection took a bite out of a green apple and then the eye opened up once more and I was set down. I was set back down from the eye's confines, standing there in the crowd looking at the horse and then at the woman holding the horse. The woman was telling me to please leave the playing area.

What had happened?

I looked down at the apple. There was a bite taken out from it; a good wet mouthful I could not remember tasting.

I made my way towards the edge of the crowd. The circuit road curved around me, and I walked across this, towards a line of trees. Loudspeaker units hung down from the branches, the leaves moved to the sound of their cold lullabies. Through the trees, a more secluded area could be seen. There were fewer cars parked here, good cars, expensive cars. A family was sitting on the grass beside one of the cars, eating a picnic lunch. There was nobody else around.

One of the cars was a limousine.

I saw it now, clearly. It was a long red limousine parked on its own in a corner, on the far side of the space. I was drawn to the car. I made my way through the trees, and then on past the smiling family, across the park. Even stationary, the limousine gave off a negative energy, a glow, a settled heat. There was no sign of any human occupancy. I moved closer, walking round the car, and seeing all the cuts and bruises, the wounds in the skin of the vehicle, all taken no doubt from previous affairs and battles. My reflection was there. Marlene was there, a black ghost in each dark window; but we have all become skilled, these last months, in the act of not looking directly at any passing shade of ourselves. There were three windows on each side of the limousine. Was there anybody inside? Was there a person inside the car, a sick and downhearted businessman perhaps, or even a faded pop star, staring out at me?

I knocked on the glass of one window.

There was no response.

I pulled the lipstick out of my bag, and wrote some words with it, on the window. I wrote the words, the two words, in such a way that a person inside the vehicle would be able to read them.

NO ESCAPE

I don't know how long I waited. A minute or two. Maybe longer. Again, there was no response. I looked around the area, but nobody was paying me any mind. The trees circled the park. Grey clouds were gathering here and there, and the sun was halfway down the sky; a sudden cold claimed the air. And then, and just as I turned to move away, the driver's door opened up and a man stepped out from the limousine.

'What are you doing?' he asked.

He was a tall, well-built specimen, dressed in a chauffeur's uniform. This was made from a fine material, maroon in colour, but the cloth was stained in places, and torn. The man carried a peaked hat with him, which he now placed on his head and he stood there, looking down at me.

'What do you want?'

'You know what,' I answered.

'Do I?'

'Who's inside here?'

'The passenger.'

'You attacked us.'

The chauffeur stepped closer. 'The passenger has certain requirements. I carry them out.'

'Why?'

'Nobody's hurt.' He gave a brief laugh. 'I mean, if I'd wanted to hurt you . . .'

'And if I wanted to hurt you, what would I do?'

'Well then, there's no rules any more.'

'That's right,' I said. 'No rules.'

And I let my eyes move away slightly. Peacock was standing there, and his fist was already moving at speed even as the chauffeur turned, and the blow caught him clean and square on the chin. The chauffeur's head snapped back and his body fell onto the bonnet of the limousine, and then to the ground.

'Shit, I needed that.' Peacock rubbed at the knuckles of his hand. 'I've been looking for you, Marlene. I've been looking all over.'

'Have you?'

Some people were watching from nearby, from their own vehicles, from the picnic area, but none came forward.

'Beverly said you'd left us.'

I looked beyond Peacock, to where the car was parked, my car, at the other side of the area. The cheap and dirty car, the halfway broken car. It was waiting for me.

'I don't know,' I said.

'Bev's pretty upset. We all are.'

'Right.'

I walked over to the car. Tupelo was sitting in the

back, her face against the plastic window. Henderson was in the front passenger seat. Peacock climbed in beside her. He was driving, once again.

I looked at Henderson. Her face was held firm, unreadable. She was staring at the limousine, and at the chauffeur. He was struggling to his feet. A voice came from the nearest loudspeaker, announcing the start of the next game. And now the sun was clouded over.

I climbed in the back of the car, next to Tupelo.

'It's two forty-nine,' the girl said. 'And fifteen seconds.'

'Let's go,' said Henderson.

'Sixteen seconds, seventeen . . .'

\>

Peacock rolled the car slowly past the limousine, and then back onto the circuit road. I watched the scene as we moved along. I looked out at the people crowded there and the flags hanging down and the children and the red dogs and the white dogs running all over, and I couldn't help thinking that I'd lost all control now; that I was just being carried along, come what may.

The pull, the pulling . . .

We drove past all the various forms of leisure, seen and unseen, and from there towards the exit barrier. A young official was standing at the barrier and he told us to have a lovely time wherever we were headed, and that was that, and we were through the barrier and back onto the motorway.

'That was joyful,' said Peacock.

'It's been a most beautiful day,' said Tupelo.

And we drove on down the motorway; falling down the country, towards the coast.

>

This was the place. All the bars and cafés, amusement arcades, cinemas; all the rundown buildings, made up for the night in cheap and gaudy neon and the colours smeared out by the rain; all the symbols and letters floating free from the signs and bringing a spell to my eyes; these ghosts of desire, this electric parade, and the streets crawling heavy with ragged blasts of old-time rock music coming from doorways and windows; all the people that wandered and no matter the rain that fell, arm in arm, where did they come from, where were they going? Tupelo had said that the place would be deserted. Who were these people? One group suddenly rushed across the road in front of us, cheering, singing a wild song. All this we drove through, and then away from, leaving the brightness behind, bulb by bulb. Peacock turned away from the main drag, down one small street after another, searching, until at last he stopped the car.

'This is it.'

Across the way from where we were parked, a row of buildings could be seen. A few houses, three or four shops, a young couple walking by, the blurred outline of a tree; everything pale and muted, secretive, the rain falling. And the theatre, its bright red sign giving the only true colour.

'Marlene will come with me,' said Henderson.

'What?' said Peacock. 'Marlene? Why Marlene?'

'Can I come?' asked Tupelo.

'Marlene. Just Marlene.'

Henderson got out of the car, expecting me to follow. I didn't know what to do. I looked down at my hands.

'Fuck,' said Peacock.

I couldn't stop looking at my hands. Just these two strange objects lying on my lap, held flat with the palms showing and then the fingers curving round, lined with dirt and with the nails broken in places. There was a small cut at the end of one finger.

These hands. Trembling. They had caused such trouble already, upon this day.

'I'd like to walk on the beach,' said Tupelo.

'It's dark,' said Peacock. 'It's raining. It's cold.'

'I'd like to. I was promised.'

Nothing else was said. We had arrived in town a few hours previously, found a hotel and just sat around there under Henderson's orders. I had worked on my journal a little, and then slept for a while and now, really, I only wanted to go back to the room alone, and to lie down in the dark for a long, long time. But that was not happening. It was not happening.

And so, finally, I climbed out of the car.

It was the kind of rain that made you wet from the first contact and I stood there with my face upturned in the night air and my feet standing in a puddle of water, and I let the rain fall onto my face, without heed.

Peacock called to Henderson from the driver's window. 'Beverly,' he said.

'What now?'

'You want the gun?'

'No.'

'Fine then. Hey listen.'

'What?'

'Take care.'

I couldn't see the look that was given in return, I couldn't even imagine what the look might hold, but then Henderson bent down at the window of the car and she kissed Peacock. I watched the kiss taking place. It did not take that long a time, but there was something good behind it, there must've been.

And then Henderson broke the kiss and she walked across the road towards the theatre.

>

It was a nondescript back-street affair called the Pinhole, well-hidden, squeezed in between two boarded up shops. It seemed to have little to do with the attraction of holidaymakers. An old tramp was slumped down in the doorway, sleeping. But this was the place Kingsley had indicated, and tonight was the night. For the first time in this journey, we had arrived at just the appointed hour, thanks to the girl.

Why was the theatre not open?

Henderson was knocking on the closed doors, without any luck. I stepped back to look at the building. The neon sign was a bright wet blur, above which a camera was fixed to the wall; it was looking down at me, staring at me. There were another two storeys to the building; on the top floor a light burned dimly in a window.

'Here,' said Henderson.

A small door just along from the main entrance swung open at a touch.

'See?' Henderson nodded to a piece of card pinned to the wall, just inside.

'What does it say?' I asked.

'Theatre.'

The doorway led directly to a flight of stairs, where the shadows gathered.

'I'm not sure about this.'

'What's the problem?' said Henderson.

'I don't know. Something's wrong.'

'Come on.'

I followed Henderson up the stairs. At the top, there was a small landing. An old woman was sitting there, in the light given off by a decorative lamp. She was gazing at a chessboard, with the pieces arranged in their starting positions. Only a single pawn had been moved.

'We're here to see the play,' said Henderson.

The woman shrugged.

'What's the show called?'

'Oh well,' the woman answered. 'I don't think it has a name.'

On a shelf behind the desk, a video monitor showed a flickering picture, a stretch of empty pavement. It was the scene outside the theatre, taken through the camera I had been looking at. The scene broadened as the camera opened its eye wider, and then moved up, expanded, to show the street itself and the old pitiful car waiting there. The two figures of Peacock and Tupelo, barely visible. And the rain falling down. It was the film of the town at night, dreaming of itself.

'Is Jamie performing?' asked Henderson.

'You know Jamie, do you?'

'Oh sure. We've come a long way to see him.'

'He's a very special young man,' the woman said. 'Very talented.'

'We know that. We heard that.'

Money was exchanged, and the old woman gave us a ticket each, a bright orange ticket with 'Admit One' written on it; the words pulsated in my hand. I heard a gentle whirring sound. There was another camera here, attached to the wall above the desk. I looked at the camera. The zooming mechanism extended itself, just slightly.

The camera was looking at me.

A second flight of stairs turned off the landing and the woman told us to climb up to the next floor and then just to follow our eyes.

'Enjoy the show,' she said.

We climbed the stairs; they seemed to twist round one time too many, in darkness, and only upon reaching the top could we see any light, coming from the open door of a living room. I looked inside. Two people, a middle-aged couple, were sitting in armchairs, watching a television. A simple wooden chair was set between them. A black dog lay curled on a rug. I couldn't see what was being shown on the television screen, holding the couple entranced. Directly opposite, there was a small window, the one I'd been looking up at a few minutes ago. Next to the window, a painting hung on the wall. This, the only decoration, was the image of a child, a young girl holding a doll in her hands.

And a gentle sound could be heard.

The two people did not seem to notice me, not at all, but the dog looked up as I stood there by the door.

I moved away. Along a corridor, another doorway led into a kitchen, where several plates of sandwiches were laid out on a table. I had the sudden urge to take a bite from one of them. It was a ham sandwich, with cucumber.

One last door stood at the end of the corridor.

'Now listen,' said Henderson. Her voice was quiet, held close. 'Listen. No trouble, Marlene. We've got no business with this guy, except to get the name off him, the supplier. That's all we want.'

I nodded. Sometimes it's like this; Kingsley directs us towards an effect of the mirror, not the thing itself.

Henderson opened the door.

Carefully now, gathering clues.

The door opened onto a small room, softly lit, furnished only with a table, a number of chairs set out around it. A black curtain hung down across the whole length of the room. A young man was sitting alone at the table, staring at the curtain in silence. We took our own places, one to each side. There was a single candle on the table, a cold pool of light.

'When does it start?' asked Henderson.

The young man turned to her but his eyes would not settle, neither on Henderson, nor on myself.

'Soon,' he said. 'Are you here to see Jamie?'

'I hope so. Do you know him?'

'What's your name?'

'Beverly. And this is Marlene.'

'I'm him. That's me. I'm Jamie.'

'Is that right?'

'What do you want?'

He was a nervous young character, in his late teens, I guess, with long straggly hair hanging down over his eyes, and he was staring back at me now. It was as if he had worked his eyes sufficiently to get a hold on me. Immediately, then, I felt a deep sorrow for the boy.

'What do you want? Why have you come here?'

'To see the show,' said Henderson.

Jamie touched at a piece of string he wore round his neck. His fingers were shaking as he pulled the string into view from behind his T-shirt. And I knew then why Kingsley had sent us here. The necklace. This was the property, the found object. Evidence.

'Can I see that?' said Henderson. 'It's nice. Who gave it to you?'

The beads were giving off a faint light, a violet glow, and I felt my skin crawl. It was the feeling.

'Are you going to hurt me?'

'Why would I do that?' said Henderson.

And I wondered about the spell; about what might be given out by the necklace, and what taken away.

'I don't know,' said Jamie. 'I don't know.' He would not look at Henderson. 'Please don't hurt me . . .'

The lights in the room were fading. There was a barely heard sound. The candle lost its flame. All was dark now, inside the tiny theatre. The curtain was slowly being pulled aside by some hidden mechanism; as this was happening, something touched my hand, soft, delicate. It was the young man, Jamie, touching me.

His voice, whispering . . .

The curtain had drawn back completely, revealing a small stage area, the perfect representation of a living room. A middle-aged couple were sitting in armchairs, watching the television. A third chair was set between the two people, an empty wooden chair.

Where was this place?

I felt uncomfortable. The two people did not seem to

notice me, not at all, but there was a dog curled up in front of the television, and the animal looked up at me as I sat there, watching the drama.

'When does it start?'

'I think it already has.'

This was the dialogue, the two characters speaking to each other; they were talking about the television. There was no sound coming from the machine. I couldn't see what was being shown, what the programme was, not from where I was sitting, only the glow of light from the screen.

I stood up. Marlene stood up. This is what happened. I watched myself standing up.

Marlene watched herself standing up.

Marlene stood up at the table. She walked round the table and across the floor, feeling a slight pain as she crossed over into the lighted area. Marlene was on the stage now and the two characters noticed her, at last.

'Oh, it's you. My sweet.'

'Bloody cheek. Where have you been, all this time?'

Marlene looked out from the stage. There was a darkness, a table and chairs, some people sitting there. Marlene wondered who they were, these strange people.

This was the audience.

Marlene turned back to the couple on stage and she said, 'Can I watch your television?'

'It's so lovely, having you back.'

'Just turning up like this, without any thanks or apologies.'

'You come and sit down now.'

Marlene sat down in the middle chair. From there she could easily see the screen.

'Oh why did you leave us, Marlene? Oh why?'

Marlene felt sure that there was some answering line she had to make, but how could it be found? She could not resist the television's charm. It was the first good clear image she had seen in weeks and there she was now. It was herself. It was Marlene on the television.

Marlene watched herself.

The shot was taken from above. It was a small landing at the top of a flight of stairs. Marlene was standing there next to Henderson, in front of a desk where an old woman was sitting. A chessboard could be seen, and the camera moved in slightly, to show the game well under way. The old woman gave a theatre ticket to Marlene. The ticket filled the screen.

Admit One . . .

And then Marlene was standing there with the ticket in her hand and she was looking up at the camera. Marlene saw herself on television. The two Marlenes were looking at each other. Marlene was looking at Marlene.

'Climb up to the next floor,' said the old woman. 'And just follow your eyes. Enjoy the show.'

'Are you coming?' said Henderson.

Marlene dragged herself away from the camera. 'Yes,' she said. 'I'm coming.'

Marlene and Henderson climbed the dark stairs, up to the next floor, and then one more. How many floors were there? Finally, they came out onto a corridor, with an open door leading to a front room.

Bare floorboards, the walls stripped of paper, one dirty window. A pallet bed. A painting. There it was, hung at a crooked angle; the portrait of a young girl, a broken doll in her hands. Marlene felt sure she had seen it before, somewhere.

They moved away, into a kitchen. Here, a selection of sandwiches were laid out on a table. Somebody had taken a bite from one of them.

Along the corridor, there was a third door.

'This must be it,' said Henderson.

The door opened onto a living room. A young man was sitting in a chair, watching television. At his feet, a black dog lay sleeping, curled up within itself. There were two other chairs, and Marlene and Henderson sat down on either side of the young man. They stayed there in silence for a while, all three of them looking at the television screen. The test card was being shown.

'When does it start?' asked the man.

'I think it already has,' said Marlene. The line came to her, as though remembered from some other time.

'What's your name?'

'Marlene. And this is Beverly.'

'Hello. I'm Jamie. That's me. I'm him.'

Marlene looked at the young man. He was touching at a necklace he wore over his shirt collar.

'Can I see that?' she said. 'It's nice. Who gave it to you?'

Marlene reached out. It was just a piece of string on which some wooden beads had been threaded. The beads were warm to the touch. Marlene counted them. There were nine beads altogether, five blue, and four yellow, and the beads were giving off a faint light of their own, a soft glow tinged with violet.

Something was taking place, here, in this room at this moment. Slowly now, a curtain was being drawn aside. People were sitting there, beyond the curtain. They were sitting round a table, in the darkness. Marlene could not see them properly.

This was the audience, she thought.

She did not know how many people were out there, watching her.

'Are you going to hurt me?' said Jamie.

'Why would I do that?'

'I don't know. I don't know.'

The young man let his eyes slip from Marlene. The television was making a noise.

'It's beginning,' he said.

An image appeared on the screen. A lonely street at night, with the rain falling down. A white car was parked across the way, with two women walking from the car, towards the camera. And the camera chose one of the women to follow; it focused on the one woman, who stood now, staring up at the camera.

Staring upwards, downwards . . .

Marlene was sure she had seen the film before but she could not think where, except that she recognized the woman. A number of beads were moving back and forth, yellow and blue, back and forth. The woman on the screen. It was herself. Marlene was looking at herself, looking up at herself.

And the rain was falling.

An old tramp was slumped in the doorway, mumbling to himself. Marlene looked up at the building. The Pinhole Theatre. The neon sign was burning her eyes; the rain sizzled against the letters. A security camera was looking down at her, making a gentle whirring sound.

'Here,' said Henderson. She was standing near a small door, just along from the theatre.

'I'm not sure about this,' said Marlene.

'What's the problem?'

'I don't know. Something's wrong.'

'Come on.'

Marlene followed Henderson up the stairs. The place was empty. A small video monitor showed only grey smoke, tiny sparkles. A chessboard was set out on the ticket desk. Only a few pieces were left on the board.

'What now?' said Henderson.

'I have a ticket already.'

'Where? Let me see that. Where did you get that?'

'I don't know. Admit one, it says.'

'That's you then.'

Alone now, Marlene climbed the second flight of stairs. She felt detached from herself, and cold, as though she could only watch herself from a distance, a great distance. Reaching the top floor, the quietness closed in. Three doors led off a corridor.

In a room at the back of the building, where the theatre should've been, Marlene stepped round a black curtain, half torn from its runner. Some chairs, a television, layers of dust. The television was lying screen downwards on the floor. Fragments of glass were scattered around.

Marlene walked out of the room and back along the corridor. Briefly, she looked into a tiny kitchen. There was a terrible smell of rotting food. Flies were buzzing around a plate of sandwiches.

She moved on to the front room. Somebody had been living here. Just a pallet bed, a one-bar fire, a few items of clothing. A picture was hanging on the wall at a crooked angle; the portrait of a young girl, holding a doll. The girl and the doll, they had the same face exactly. Marlene picked up a paperback book that lay on the bed. It was a copy of Lewis Carroll's *Through the Looking-Glass*. Marlene stood by the window as she turned through the pages.

The rain made a strange effect against the glass, a flickering effect. Her own car was parked across the way and Peacock was standing there, leaning against the car. He was wearing his porkpie hat. In the middle of the road two people were standing close to each other, Henderson and a young man. They were arguing.

Marlene looked directly down.

A woman was standing just outside the theatre, watching the argument. Marlene felt uneasy, seeing this woman. She could not stop herself from shivering, and she pushed her hand against the window. There was a softness to the glass, a misted effect, and her hand did not stop moving.

It was herself. It was myself.

What was happening? It was myself down there on the street, watching the argument. And I moved through the rain, the glass, the pages of the book.

The flickering . . .

I was worried about the young man. He was nothing much more than a boy really; Jamie, that was his name. A teenage boy, shaking with cold, with fear, and soaked through by the rain. A thin cotton T-shirt, transparent, glued to his skin; and Henderson there, grabbing at the boy, shouting at him.

I stepped closer.

'Stay out of it.' Henderson looked at me, and then turned back to the boy. 'Where did you get this?' She had the fingers of one hand wrapped round the necklace.

I had to say something. 'Leave him alone.'

But Henderson would not do that. She wouldn't leave the boy alone; she was twisting the necklace round her fingers tighter now, against his neck, and the boy was struggling and the rain was coming down hard on them, on all of us standing there. I felt the rain on my face. The boy fell to his knees on the wet tarmac and Henderson followed him down.

'Where's it from?' she said. 'Who gave you this?'

The boy was crying.

'What's the name? Who is it?'

I could no longer see what Henderson was doing, not precisely; something bad.

'What's the fucking name?'

They were so close together now, I thought they might be kissing, but they weren't. They were not kissing. The boy was speaking some words and then Henderson pulled up suddenly and the necklace was in her hand. She had broken the string from the boy's neck, and the beads from it were scattered. I felt that something was being pulled loose from myself, just then, some spell cast aside, and I could see the boy clearly now, rolling over; he was crawling along the dirty wet street trying to grab hold of the beads before they were lost. But they were lost.

The beads were lost, I could see that.

The boy was down on his hands and knees, searching through the pools of water and the litter in the road. A black dog ran past him.

Henderson came up to me. 'Where the fuck were you?'

'I . . .'

'You wouldn't come with me.'

I didn't know what to say.

'Oh, fuck this.'

Henderson moved away. She took one step towards the car and then turned back, and came directly to me. 'You see now, Marlene?' she said. 'You see what has to happen? How it has to be, if this thing is to work. You see that now?'

Henderson walked over to the car. And what else was there to do, but follow. What else could I do? Peacock was standing there, with the driver's door held open.

'You got the name?' he asked.

Henderson nodded. 'Cole. Thomas Cole.'

'And?'

'He's a writer.'

'Go on.'

'That's it.'

'Address?'

Henderson shook her head.

'No?'

'The kid doesn't know.'

'He knows,' said Peacock. 'Of course he knows.'

'He won't tell me.'

'Jesus.'

'Peacock, look at him. Look. What else can I do?'

'You want me to . . .'

Henderson opened the passenger door. 'I'll find it,' she said. 'Tonight.'

'Good. You do that.'

Peacock looked around for a moment, passing over me without pause, and then he got in the car. I turned round, taking it all in myself.

The boy, Jamie; the poor boy was still down on the ground, searching desperately. I looked at the theatre. The old tramp was on his feet now, staring back at me from the doorway. The neon sign clouded him with soft waves of colour, the name of the theatre escaping from the glass tubing. I looked down. There was a book in my hands. I must've picked it up that evening. Where was this darkness coming from?

I turned back to the car.

Tupelo was watching me through the plastic on the side window. The rain was falling.

The girl's face was all melted away.

\>

We had some trouble, driving back to the hotel. All
the people were out on the streets. They spilled over
from the pavement, onto the road itself, crowding what
few cars there were, our own, slowing us down.
The rain bathed them. Along this gathering of neon,
brighter now, drenching the scene in a liquid radiance.
The people were slow-dancing to loud manic music,
the beats all broken; and broken also, the rhythms the
dancers found for themselves. And all of them, all
the people, clothed in the light coming free from the
signs in long streams of vapour, of language. Words,
messages, single letters, numbers, brands and
logos. The dancers wearing the words of vapour, the
messages; like dresses they were wearing them, like
cloaks and hats and scarves the people were wearing
the words around themselves, proudly. And the words
writhing across faces, across bare chests and arms. One
face that loomed close; some fiery alien mask made
from a product's name, illegible now, grabbed from the
air and daubed wet and slithering over stark eyes.

\>

Peacock shook his head. 'There's something wrong.'

'Like what?' said Henderson.

'With the car. I don't know. It's sluggish. I'm having trouble steering.'

'It's sick,' said Tupelo.

Henderson looked round. 'Don't start all that.'

'It's got the sickness inside it, in the wires, in the engine, all the parts between.'

'Look now, everything's fine.'

'The car's dying.'

>

Henderson's gone off alone, to find this Thomas Cole, his whereabouts. We know the beads must have come through from a piece of the mirror; it's out there, somewhere in this town, waiting for us. I picture it glittering, a small piece of glass, fragile, sharp-edged, kept safe, hidden away; or else taken up nervously, lovingly, the surface touched at with care. A tiny hole in the world, filled with mist and silver. I see a hand, now pushing through, reaching in . . .

I've written up the theatre visit, as I can. What exactly have I recorded? How can I trust myself, my memories? The words blur on the page; a thin black ink emerging more as smoke than liquid from the pen's nib.

And here I sit, writing, waiting . . .

This little room so squalid, a good way from the sea, and what it all comes down to, finally. So many people here, in town, in the hotel, I don't know why. What's the attraction? Two rooms, the last available; this one, for the girl and me, and another down the corridor some-where, for Peacock and Henderson.

Henderson . . .

Henderson, alone. Why alone? She's taken one of the

syringes with her; a possible payment for information. But why has she gone alone on this job? Why didn't Peacock bother himself to stop her going? Why didn't he go with her? There he sits now, drinking away, laughing with Tupelo, without any much care it seems.

But everyone's worried about me, I know that, I can tell that. About the way I acted earlier, at the theatre. I'm to be looked after. Henderson's words to Peacock, just before she left. *Look after Marlene*. They can't trust me. They can't put their trust in me.

I pull the notebook closer to the bedside lamp, the only light that works. There's no skin on the shade, just the brass frame and the bulb, and the bulb will flicker on and off every so often. Shadows fill the corners of the room. It's crowded in here. Two single beds, a wooden chair, one bedside table with the lamp on top of it. A television. Everything's cheap, second-hand, mismatched. No toilet, no sink. Absurdly, there's an old upright piano standing opposite the beds. Finally, a small drinks cabinet, linked up directly to the workings of the house; Peacock has been at the wires already and now we can drink for free, just not admit to anything when we check out in the morning. If we last that long, that is. If we can get through the night without . . .

Noises from the street below. Breaking glass, wild laughter. A high, yearning cry of despair.

How long will it be, before this is over?

There's a bad smell, coming from all the people who have stayed here over the years, maybe died in here, and there's no escape from it. Bugs are moving around

under the dirty, flowered wallpaper. I can't help thinking about skin disease, and how it looks as if the whole
room is suffering from it. I've tried calling Reception to
complain, but all I get back is an automated message, a
garbled metallic tongue.

This is the place where these things are happening.

This is the room.

On the wall nearest to me, a mirror hangs. It's been
reversed, of course; the glass cannot be seen. But I
can't help looking at it, the blank wooden frame. What
would happen if I dared to turn it back into the light,
revealing the glass and looking in there?

What would happen? What would I see, really?

Whose face would I see?

>

Peacock told a strange story. He told us of the day he killed himself. This all happened, he said, after the war was done and before he met Henderson. It was a bad time for him, without a job or any real desire to find one, and he was staying at his mother's house until something good turned up. But nothing good did turn up. He had a few things left to him, some useful skills. Most of all, he had whatever fire remained over from the fighting days, a residue of poison in the blood, as he called it. He had the gun, stolen from the army. For a time he did security work, and from there he fell into some darker business. It wasn't that much further down than where he was already, but once there, down there, he couldn't make the step back.

'What were you doing?' I asked.

'Putting the love of God in people.'

'Putting the what?'

'Stir yourself,' said Tupelo. 'He was a bruiser.'

Peacock told of how he ended up working for a local firm, run by a man calling himself Billy the Bandit. He was putting the pressure on for Billy, with a dab hand at the more violent aspects, which he grew to love the more with each kick and blow, with each slice of the blade.

'Jesus.'

'I was also playing music. You know, in a few pubs around London.'

'Really? Music?'

'Why was he called the Bandit?' asked Tupelo. 'I'll bet he was like really cruel, am I right? Oh yeah. He was heartless. He was a mean-hearted bastard like who would steal a pet dog's eyes to sell to a blind man.'

'He only had one arm. That was why.'

'He had what?'

'That's it,' said Peacock. 'Just the one.'

'Oh. That is so stupid. One arm.'

'What about it?' I said. 'What about the one arm?'

'Come on,' said Tupelo. 'Get to the part where you kill yourself. That's the part I want.'

'Yes. Tell that.'

A whisper in the ear from some unknown mouth, this is how Peacock got word of a job. There would be no traces, never any traces. A name, an address. A photograph. This last to be burned after the job was done. Peacock had no knowledge beyond that. Sometimes an extra nod would be given, indicating that some further degree of pain was to be included, and the case he now related was of that nature. Some additional pain, to be given out to a man called Jim Spender.

'What had he done wrong?' I asked.

'I didn't know.'

'You didn't know?'

'I never knew. Why should I know? It was a job. I was the message, not the sender.'

'Oh, I love that,' said Tupelo.

'One thing. Studying the photograph, I had a feeling come over me.'

'What was it?'

Peacock was quiet for a moment, his eyes were closed. And then he said, 'I had the feeling that someone was going to get hurt.'

'That sounds right,' said Tupelo.

'And it was myself doing the hurting.'

'That's about right.'

'No,' said Peacock. 'It was bad, that feeling.'

It was a bad feeling to have in a job of this kind. You do the thing without any thought, except for the technical aspects, that was the idea. And he told us that he had never experienced anything other, until this moment.

'And this all came,' I asked, 'just from looking at the photograph?'

'Yes.'

'What did he look like?'

'An ordinary man. A stranger. Nothing much, except he had hair like Elvis.'

'Who?' said Tupelo.

'Elvis Presley,' I told her. 'A popular singer from the last century.'

'I'm joking. Where do you think I got the name?'

We looked at her.

'My mother loved the guy. Jesus, you two are so off the picture. It's where he was born. Elvis Presley. Nineteen thirty-five. Tupelo, Mississippi.'

Peacock shook his head.

'Get on with it,' Tupelo said.

Spender lived in a caravan park, the kind set aside by the local council for use by refugees from the war zone. Peacock got there late one afternoon, a dismal autumn afternoon as he told it, already touched with dark and there was smoke in the air from a small bonfire. Some children were standing around the fire warming their hands and watching a pile of magazines burning. The site had the desolate air of a holding camp. Two young men were sitting on the steps of a caravan and they looked at Peacock with clenched eyes. He recognized the look from the war. A woman was pulling washing off a line. The first drops of a rain shower could be felt. The smoke from the fire must have reached into Peacock's eyes; everything about the place seemed unsettled, allusive. Peacock talked to the children. He asked them where Jim Spender was, showing the photograph. 'He's leaving,' said one boy and he spat, and another boy pointed over towards a pale blue car that stood beside a caravan.

Peacock walked over that way; something strange happened. He still had the photograph in his hand, and now he looked down at it. The face had changed, or was changing. Even as he looked, the image of the face was changing. It was melting. Peacock stopped where he was, right there on the dirt pathway, and he rubbed at his eyes. When he looked again, the face was back to normal. The same face, except that Peacock felt that some slight change had been registered, made permanent. He could not tell, not for sure.

'So?' said Tupelo. 'What's so weird?'

'It was just a moment. That's all, just a moment.'

'Oh, I get it. Your first time.'

Peacock nodded. He looked disturbed now, troubled by the memories.

'I didn't know what it was.'

This was in the very early days of the sickness, he explained, before anybody really knew what was happening. It was in the days before the medicine, before Lucy came along. Peacock had read about the problem in the papers, of course, but that was something that happened to other people, not to him, not here, not now. He was a soldier, a hired man, a tough.

'You were living with your mother,' said Tupelo.

'Nothing could hurt me.'

'Remember your first time, Marlene?'

'What?'

'Your first time? Remember it?'

'Oh, well. I . . .'

'The strangest thing,' said Peacock. 'In that sudden glimpse of another face, I thought he looked familiar. That's what got to me, really. Almost familiar. As though I'd seen him before somewhere, a long time ago.'

'And had you?' asked Tupelo.

Peacock stared at her. 'I was scared.' And then he said again, 'It was just a moment.'

The caravan was smaller than the others in the park and cleaner, a more recent model. A dull light shone through the curtained window. Peacock wondered what Spender was doing in a place like this. He looked around. The two young men were still watching him. Usually, he would have waited a while to find a more suitable time and place for the job, and he had to admit that the episode with the photograph had unnerved him. But now, with the fact that Spender was set on leaving, Peacock felt he had little choice, not if he wanted to be paid and to keep himself in this useful employment. He tapped on the door. Almost immediately it was opened to him and Jim Spender was standing there.

He was smiling. Spender was smiling.

This was the moment when Peacock should have taken control, turned on the heavy manners, the business. But something stopped him. There was a brief confusion. It took Peacock a few seconds to recognize the man standing in the caravan's doorway as the target figure.

'Billy boy sent you, I suppose?'

Peacock nodded. And the moment was lost.

'It's raining. You'd best come in.'

There was an antiseptic smell to the caravan, which made Peacock think of a hospital ward. The seats were still protected by clear plastic coverings and for some reason a picture hanging on the wall was covered with a tea towel. Peacock also noticed a white sheet fixed over a wardrobe door. There was a suitcase on the floor and a sports bag on the small table. Near to the bag there was a hat, a good-looking hat. The bag was open. Peacock could see a passport, and what looked like an airline ticket. Jim Spender sat down on one of the seats and the plastic made a loud creaking noise.

'Drink?'

Peacock shook his head and watched as Spender calmly poured himself a whisky. He was a strange man to look at; intense dark eyes set in a pale face, a thin body set around some hidden weight; energy, kept in reserve. He was controlled, confident, and yet there was also about the man, Peacock thought, a certain sadness. The thick wave of hair from the photograph had been shorn away to the skull, made brutal.

'So then. Billy the Bandit. Now there's a little character.'

'You know why I'm here,' said Peacock.

'Oh well. A nasty business. I have done wrong against the man, and now I take my punishment. Will you be very cruel to me?'

Peacock could not understand why he felt so frozen. He was known commonly for his expertise, his vigour.

'What's your name?'

Peacock told him, and Spender smiled at the name as though there were something unusual about it.

'Is that my photograph? Let me see.'

Spender took the photograph from Peacock's hand. He looked at it. He studied the image, as though a secret was held there, concealed.

'What's with the tea towel?' asked Peacock.

'The what?'

Peacock turned to the covered picture; he lifted the edge of the towel draped over it. He thought it might be a painting under there. It wasn't a painting. Peacock's own face stared back at him from the glimpse of a mirror. And then he looked at the wardrobe, at the white sheet hanging over the door, and he knew what was being hidden but he did not know why. It was the first time Peacock had seen such a thing, the covering of all reflective surfaces.

'Are you fucked up?' he asked.

'Yeah, I'm fucked. Totally. This isn't me.'

'What's that?'

Spender threw the photograph down on the table. 'This isn't me. It's not me.'

'It's you.'

'Look at it.'

But Peacock wouldn't look at the photograph. He had to get control now, he had to do the job and then get out of there.

'It's you,' he said, and he pulled the gun from his belt, and he showed it to Spender. He aimed the gun at the head of Jim Spender.

Here, Peacock stopped off from the story.

Tupelo looked at him. 'Come on then. What happens next?'

But Peacock remained quiet.

'You killed him?' I asked.

'Is that it?' said Tupelo. 'Of course that's it. He shot him. Peacock's a killer. He's a cold-blooded killer and nobody dare trouble us, not now.'

The three of us were sitting on the two beds, the girl and myself on one of them, Peacock on the other. We were eating sandwiches, and making our way through the drinks cabinet, bottle by tiny bottle. Tupelo had started on a souvenir jar of sweets. I couldn't think why Peacock had chosen this moment to open up like this, except that Henderson was away; this was the first time, really, that they had been parted since we had all got together.

'You didn't kill him?' I said. 'Not really?'

'Which is it?' said Tupelo.

'You have to understand something,' said Peacock. 'I killed a man, in the war.'

'Just the one?'

Peacock explained it, as best he could. He told us there wasn't a lot of killing, not by the soldiers. The killing was done from afar and what they did then, the soldiers, is they went in and they cleaned up the mess. That was all. It was a nasty job and you had to be tough about it, but that was what they did. One time a man was hiding inside a hut and he ran out at them and Peacock killed him, he shot him, it was simple. It was simple and at first he had felt something about it and later on he didn't, he lost the feeling. It made the giving out of pain a little easier and when the war was done, Peacock brought the lack of feeling back with him, and he let it get stronger. But since then, he said, the gun was for show only. Since the war, he had not killed anybody.

'Except for yourself?' said Tupelo.

'Except for myself.'

'Get to it.'

Jim Spender looked up at the gun and he said, 'Will you kill me then? Are you the type?'

'You're pissing me off, Spender.'

'You don't know why you're here, do you?'

Peacock didn't answer.

'I thought not. You're a low-level thug without a clue in the world.'

'You're still pissing me off.'

'Well I'm sorry for that, I really am. But all I'm saying is that I know how Billy works. He doesn't want me killed. He wants me damaged, as befits. As befits the crime, that's his saying isn't it? I think I'm correct in this. Do you think I'm correct? Because he's a stickler isn't he, the Bandit.'

'Go fuck.'

'You would go against your orders?'

'Go fuck.'

'Well then.' Spender poured himself another shot of whisky. 'Well then, let me be equally honest. Billy doesn't know. Billy the Bandit does not know the score. The situation is beyond him. Do you understand me?'

'Tell it.'

'It's simple enough. The Bandit does not know the full seriousness of what I've done against him. But soon he will. And when he finds this out, he's going to wish he had placed a more severe order upon me. By then, however, it will be too late for him.'

'What did you do?'

Spender smiled at the question.

'Everything is prepared. I have my new passport here, and my new papers.' Spender arranged each item on the table as he spoke. 'I shall become somebody else. A new identity.'

'What did you do to Billy?'

'I've arranged to have him killed.'

There was a moment of silence.

'Are you sure you won't take a drink?'

Peacock saw himself then as if from the outside. He saw a young man with a gun in his hand and the hand was shaking. Peacock realized that pulling the gun had been a mistake, a bad mistake.

'Are you saddened with your life?' asked Spender.

'What?'

Peacock was losing focus. There was a black feeling inside his head, and his eyes were tightening, growing pained. His target was becoming blurred at the edges.

'I mean, what kind of life is this that you lead?'

Peacock tried his best to keep the gun in line but now he seemed to have more than one target. There seemed to be more than two people in the small space.

'Oh shit,' said Tupelo. 'You were getting the noise, right? The swirling? Yeah, a nasty one.'

Peacock ignored her.

'So then,' said Spender. 'Here's the situation. Now will you kill me?'

'Do you want to die?' asked Peacock.

'What does it matter? I have the sickness.' Spender gestured to the covered mirrors but Peacock could not yet put it all together; he was confused and the talk of disease made him wonder about himself.

'Are you suffering?' said Spender. 'You look like you're suffering.'

Peacock picked up the photograph with his free hand. He looked at it. He kept on looking at it.

'Is something wrong, my friend?'

'The face . . .'

'Nothing can be trusted. That's the worst of it. Nothing can be saved, nothing retrieved. Nothing can be stated, nothing mapped out. Nothing can be fixed. Where then shall we go from here?'

Peacock looked up from the photograph. He looked at Spender, and then he looked at the mirror; the covering had fallen away. There was a rush of noise in his head, and within this noise he heard a voice. 'Now will you kill me?' It was the voice of his target. Peacock looked at his target.

'I tell you now, my fellow, that one of us is not leaving this place.'

The target raised itself from the seat. Something was happening, Peacock felt sure of that. The target was standing there in front of him and Peacock had the absurd thought that he was looking at himself, looking back at himself, and that he too was now a target. Peacock had his gun in his hand, and the target also had a gun.

'What a performance.'

Who was speaking? The two guns were pointing at each other across the blurred surface of a disturbed mirror. A noise was drifting through the glass and one of the guns was fired, or else both of the guns were fired. The target was killed. There was blood. It splashed across the table and also across the plastic seat covers. The gunman felt empty, of a sudden. He felt all emptied of emotion.

What now?

The gunman picked up the passport. He looked at it. There was a picture inside. It was his own face looking back at him. There was a name. John Peacock. That was the name written there. The gunman slipped the passport into his pocket.

'Hang on now,' said Tupelo. 'What's happening?'

The gunman picked up the hat from the table. It was a porkpie style hat, made of brown leather, and he placed the hat on his head. It was a perfect fit. He also took with him the photograph. That too was him. The gunman left the caravan. It was fully dark now. There was half a moon. It was shimmering.

'What the fuck is going on?' said Tupelo.

The two young refugees were standing there, outside the caravan. One of them nodded at the gunman. Some other people were coming out of their homes. They were all staring at the gunman. They were staring at the gunman's right hand.

'Peacock!' said Tupelo.

He had the gun held loosely in his right hand. The gunman walked away from the caravan site and now, in the small, dingy hotel room there was a silence. I didn't know what to say, how to explain it. Tupelo's head bowed down.

Peacock would say no more.

The yellow flowers of the wallpaper, with their silky black centres, the green shoots that twined around each other, the spray of leaves; my fingers, tracing a pathway through the tangles. Where did each stem lead to, from which point, which root, towards which flower? Fingers tracing, or trying to, and only getting themselves lost in the details; possibilities, impossibilities.

'Can we go out?' said Tupelo.

'No.'

'Peacock, come on.'

'No. We wait here.'

I stepped back a little, moving along the wall. I was searching for the pattern's repetition; that point where a certain discrete arrangement of flowers, of stems and petals, would be seen again, and then again. But there were no repeated motifs, none that I could see, not even when and where a new line of paper began.

'I'll go out alone then.'

'You do that,' said Peacock.

'Alone.'

'You do that, and you're not coming back here.'

'What?'

'You won't be coming back.'

And underneath the damp, peeling paper, as I watched, the bugs were crawling. Tiny undulations; the hidden pulse of the room, pursued in darkness. The bugs must live in tiny crevices. They live in brickwork, plaster, feeding on starch, on glue. The room will die of their endeavours. It will crumble, fall. It will fall away. It will fall. I could not tear my eyes away from the wall, the flowers, the leaves and stems, the bugs at work, the colours swirling around, and I felt faint, suddenly.

Painful, adrift.

I stepped back, further, away, and the wallpaper followed me.

>

The room was at the back of the building, on the top floor. I was looking out of the one small window. A thin net curtain hung over the window and through this the moon could be seen with its lonely worn-out face staring, and I stared back at it.

'How long does it take? How long does it take, for the moon to reach us?' I turned to the room. 'The light of it, I mean. How many minutes?'

It was the kind of thing the girl might well know and that was why I'd asked it, but there was no reply, not from anybody. Peacock was too busy getting drunk; Tupelo was pressing her hands one after the other against the television, without heed. And that was that, and I didn't know what else to say.

I glanced at the wall, at the mirror that hung there, reversed.

'Shit now. Where is she? Where's Henderson?'

Nobody answered. Peacock was sitting at the piano, rolling a joint on the closed lid.

'What time is it?'

Peacock gave me a smile in return. He flicked at his

lighter and the joint caught fire and then he drained the last of his whisky.

'It's not good, drinking so much.'

His face turned cold, and the sudden coldness only made me feel more uneasy.

'Tupelo,' I said. 'The time . . .'

The girl ignored me. She was sitting cross-legged on the floor with her face some few inches from the screen, as if she would burn her eyes freely. A blue ghost of light moved over her skin.

Peacock had wired up the set so it worked without payment, but so what if the thing kept switching channels whenever it felt like. I could not watch the thing myself, it was too sickening, but the girl, she didn't seem to mind it. And I wondered again about her age, and the way she had made herself a part of the group; without consideration, this had happened. For all of her passion, I doubted that she would ever know the true concern of what we were doing.

Glances, flashes. High-voltage moments thrown from a game-show, the single repeated word of a news report, jump-cut footage of old rock stars, a gardening programme, all the cracked adverts, the slow flight of a cricket ball, these sudden lurid glimpses of amateur porno, the push-button shopping on cable.

I'd made it a rule that Tupelo had to watch with the sound turned off. We'd had a falling out over this and the bad feeling was still there between us. What could I do to make it come right?

Just then, Peacock lifted the lid of the piano. He was working the keys, finding a song.

'What's that?' I asked.

'Britney Spears. I told you already. I used to play Hits of Yesteryear at the Matador, Bethnal Green. You ever drink there, Marlene? Maybe you remember me? I used to get them singing.'

'No. I don't think so.'

Peacock started to improvise then, badly, but with a certain offhand tenderness. This giant of a man, hunched over a worm-eaten piano with a joint in his mouth, there he was, tapping out some cheap and nasty melody, in a soft and broken way. I just couldn't understand it.

'Peacock, it's just noise.'

'That's right. But it's my noise.'

I moved back to the window, pulling aside the curtain. It was a dismal view, looking out over the back yard of the hotel, onto a main street. Beyond the buildings, the town was stretched beneath the night's fabric, and lit with random flickers all up the slope of a hill until darkness claimed the world completely. A fire was burning halfway up the hill. There was a strange wailing sound that I couldn't recognize, and over the road a neon sign was pulsing on and off, a bright electric green. There were no cars. The rain had stopped a while back, but still I could not make out the wording on the sign. I thought the place might be a nightclub of some kind. I kept staring at the sign, waiting for the moments when it clicked back into life. If I could only concentrate for long enough, keep myself in focus; but no, the letters remained indistinct. A smoke was floating there, between myself and the word.

Again, I felt light-headed, as I had that moment

before, gazing at the wallpaper. I had to find a stable presence, something to fix upon.

Below the sign a group of people could be seen. They were standing around watching a young man. He was caught in the movements of a wild dance, and then he fell to the pavement and he was screaming, I was sure of it. If only Peacock would stop making that noise at the piano, I would know for sure. Another victim, and the sight of the young man made me think of my own welfare.

A sudden doubt. Had I followed the ruling? Had I taken the Lucy that afternoon? I could clearly recall taking the morning dosage and that Peacock and Henderson had taken theirs alongside, but the day since then had been long, too long, and filled with too much incident. It was difficult keeping track. The trouble with the limousine. We'd pulled into a motorway service area. At some point the gun had been fired. When was that? And why? Around the various known points there was only a darkness, as though a soft fold of night had been put in the day, and I wished then that Henderson would come back soon, and that she would bring the good news with her. Or else the bad news. Any news. I wanted this over with.

Something moved. I saw my image in the glass of the window, and I let the curtain fall on it, fall on myself, that other self.

For good or for ill, I wanted this over with.

'Why are you doing that?'

'Doing what?' said Peacock.

'Playing it wrong.'

The piano was louder now, with the notes sounding

icy and pink and brittle, the keys frozen.

'Sounds good to me,' said Peacock. 'Tupelo? What do you reckon?'

The girl looked at Peacock for a moment or two, and then at me, but she didn't say anything; and then she turned back to the screen.

'There you go. The girl loves it.'

'It's not right.'

'Oh what the fuck.' Peacock stopped playing. 'What do you want? What's wrong with you?'

'Nothing. Is it time for Lucy yet?'

'Not yet. You took the afternoon dose?'

'I took it.'

'I didn't see you take it.'

'I took it. I'm sure I did.'

'You're sure?'

'I . . .'

'Marlene, you want me to sing, maybe?'

'No. I want this over with.'

'Right.'

'I want it done with. That's all.'

'It will be. Soon.'

'Henderson will do this, right? She'll find the guy?'

'You know she will.'

'What's his name?'

'Thomas Cole.'

'She'll find him?'

'Now sit down. Marlene. Relax.'

'Yes.'

I sat down on one of the beds, holding my knees, and looking down at my feet. I noticed that only my right foot was covered by a sock. The left foot was bare within the shoe. Why was that? I could not remember taking off the sock. What was going wrong? Why had everything come down to this? A missing sock? I looked around the room; there was something about this place, it was making me feel ill.

I picked up my notebook from where it was lying on the bed, on top of a pile of dirty clothing. This was the story, I thought; this was everything that had happened already, all the things I had seen, and done. This was the secret, the box of clues. All I had to do was look through the pages, read the words; I would start to make sense of myself once again, find the proof of myself, by doing this, by reading.

And yet, the book was filled with some kind of alien language, page after page of indecipherable markings; all the words crawling around the paper, merging together, separating, and all the time losing themselves before my eyes, my cold staring eyes. Even the pages I had been working on just a short while before, they too were cast in this strange manner, and lost. The story, lost. Only here and there amongst the pages would a few lines of text emerge clearly from the black, smoky mess of ink, words I could not recognize as my own. Some other person had taken over the writing of the book. And then I bent my head a little, and brought the book closer, towards my face. There it was, on the edge of silence, a gentle fizzing sound.

The book was making a noise.

Peacock had started up with another piano tune, so I had to press my face tight against the paper. The paper was hot, and tinged with violet, as though it might burst into flame at any moment, and there was the noise; not louder, but more pronounced, brighter. It wasn't coming from the book; the noise was coming from the cover, from the pocket on the inside cover, from some object that was tucked in there, and which I now pulled loose. It was a piece of card, about three inches square, with white edging. It was, I realized, a photograph, a kind of photograph; except that where the image should be, a mist was rising, a mist that would pop and fizz with tiny sparks of red, of blue and yellow stars. And this was the noise being made; the image rising from the surface of the photograph, rising some few inches and then exploding softly in tiny bursts of colour.

What was being shown here?

I looked over at Peacock and the girl. They were both turned away from me, at the piano, and the television. Perhaps only I could see the photograph, the puzzling effect of it. But still, and no matter how hard I gazed at the object, I could not make out the image. It was only after a good while, a dreadful while, and only by dragging the memory from deep within me, shamefully, that I managed to recollect the image, the people, held in the photograph.

Myself, my daughter. The newly mown lawn at the back of the house we lived in, that summer.

That summer . . .

That day, changed now, dissolved into these whispers of smoke that I let my hand move through, my fingers feeling the warmth of it, the sparkle.

I went to replace the photograph. Something fell out of the pocket, a small object. It was a key, a small silver key. It was the key to the suitcase and Henderson had given it back to me. She had given it back in secret. And I remembered then just how it was that I'd lost the sock. It was good to have the moment well gathered and I sat back a little, and tried to relax.

There was a potted meat sandwich on the bed, a few small bites taken out of it. Empty miniature bottles lay around, of vodka and whisky and gin. Hidden amongst them, a lipstick with a shiny blue case. These things. Our few possessions. Tupelo's chess set all folded up, Peacock's hat, and the medical kit and a few books and magazines lying around. A road atlas of Great Britain, lying open; all the towns and cities, known and unknown. A tiny piece of paper used as a bookmark, orange in colour, the words 'Admit One' written on it. Nearby was a copy of Lewis Carroll's *Through the Looking-Glass*. I let my fingers trace over the cover image, a picture of Alice reaching into the mirror. I looked at the medical kit.

These things . . .

Surely I did take the capsule, earlier. I must have done. I must have. Why couldn't I remember?

There was a noise coming from the next room along. It sounded like some kind of weird sexual act, taking place just beyond the wall. I felt confused, dizzy, and I looked at the girl, embarrassed now, but Tupelo appeared not to notice the crude sounds. I was fixed upon the long black hair that the girl kept tied in a knot. Was it coming loose? Somebody spoke then, a word or two whose meaning just floated away from me. I was hot and sweaty, crowded. There were too many people in the room. The girl's hair came free of the tie. The faulty bulb was stuttering, moaning. Bugs were

214

moving over the pages of the atlas; ugly black words crawled out of my notebook. The walls seemed closer than before. Somewhere, a pop song was being sung. I could taste the melody in my mouth, clogging the tongue. A snake of hair came slithering across the bed. A thick brown juice seeped out of the sandwich.

'Marlene? Are you . . .'

A sudden rush of sound. The girl had turned up the volume on the television.

'Please . . .'

The noise came louder still. I climbed off the bed and I was walking over towards the girl, stumbling, and speaking as I went, just words, nothing but words, a cloud of words. Something had slipped away from me; what was it? There was a picture of a tiger lying on the floor. Alice was there, disappearing. I could no longer plainly see Peacock or Tupelo but only various areas of heat and colour. The room was melting. It would not keep still enough, and I thought I heard a name being called from somewhere near, my own name, but all the sounds of it were scattered, and swarming.

Noise. Noise was everywhere.

Static, broken signals. Crackle and hiss.

Only one small thing remained pure, a tiny burst of gold. A flower. It was a yellow flower coming loose from the wallpaper, the only thing I could grasp hold of. It was a flower made of my daughter's voice and her face and my sweet daughter's eyes, moving towards me, wrapping itself around me, with a sharp stab of pain suddenly but still at least now I was safe inside the flower, cradled dark and golden, allowing the petals to fold themselves all the way over.

A man's voice, a face. A touch. 'Marlene? Marlene, you OK?' A man's face in a blur and a voice all drifting and fingers caressing me, now shaking me.

'Come on.'

Dragging me back from the shadows that clung. Come on. Come on. Falling away from somewhere . . .

'Jesus. What a case.'

A woman's voice this time, a girl.

The girl. The man. Information was being gathered up, glance by glance. The room, the flowers on the wall, the full moon glimpsed through a piece of net, an old piano, the television. A pale wash of light. I was lying on a bed, feeling sick in the stomach.

The girl came into view. 'You finished with this?'

'We're done.'

The girl handed something over to the man; a needle's tip gleamed, briefly, and the man worked at the mechanism of the device.

'Oh my Lucy. Oh my sweet.'

'Waste of a good shot.'

I looked down. There was a tear in my trouser leg over the left thigh and the flesh was exposed there. A little blood. The pain I had felt, the quick stab.

The girl sniggered.

The drug. Lucidity. They had forced the needle into my skin.

'She's messing it up.'

'Tupelo . . .'

'Well she is. Going under like that.'

The girl, Tupelo. The man, Peacock. It was coming back to me.

'Oh shit. Did I . . .'

'Stay there.'

'Let me . . .'

'What is it? What's wrong?'

Something was lost. If only I could remember, find it again. What had gone wrong? I looked over towards the television. It was turned off.

'Fuck. The girl . . . Oh fuck.'

'What's she saying?' Tupelo leant over the bed. 'I didn't do anything. I never touched the television, OK? It went loud by itself.'

'No . . .'

I backed away, coming up against the wall. I was trying to get off the bed, falling, falling and slipping back, and the girl was laughing at me.

'Be careful,' said Peacock.

'Look at her.'

'She's not down yet.'

But Tupelo came nearer, putting her face close to mine. 'I never touched it.'

I could feel all the various effects of the girl, the stickiness and all the smell of her. The movement of her breath, the sudden dilation of the pupils. The heart beating in close-up, the blood coursing loud through the channels. The girl came rushing in and all at once, overloaded, too well known, too human, suddenly, far too human and she cried out as I caught at her.

'Shit.'

Peacock grabbed at Tupelo. He was trying to pull her away from me but the girl was fighting back, using her fists, her nails, she was fighting back against both of us, and then there was a clicking sound and Peacock had pulled the gun from his belt.

The gun was pressed against the girl's head.

'Huh . . .'

The breath had lodged in Tupelo's throat and she let herself be drawn away, gently, and all three of us had stopped breathing, until finally:

'Girl. Just leave it.'

And he let Tupelo go. Peacock left her alone where she was, with her back against the far wall.

'You . . .' The girl hit the wall with her fist. 'You people.' And then she slid down the wall. 'Jesus! You fucking people!'

'It wasn't loaded,' said Peacock. And he opened the chamber of the gun. 'It wasn't loaded.'

This was the room.

The loneliness. The exact loneliness of each of us, and the fear and the various pains that had brought us here, this far, and even in Peacock I saw this.

'Oh fuck . . .'

Peacock was scared. He was scared of what he had offered up from himself.

'It wasn't loaded.'

I nodded. I thought there was nothing left to say, not at all, until the girl spoke.

'What's the good of it,' she said, 'if it's not loaded? What's the good of it?'

Tupelo looked at us both.

A man standing there useless with a gun in his hand; a woman lying on the bed, myself, completely inert.

The girl, just starting to laugh.

This was the room. This was the place where these things were happening.

These were the people.

A bad smell. The floor wet, the toilet seat cold, sticky, and the light didn't work when I pulled at the cord. So then, in the near darkness I did the necessary. It was like a long stream of poison coming out of me, that's how I saw it. I'd suffered attacks of noise before of course, but none like this one, none as bad as this, and that was one big shot of Lucy that Peacock had fed into me. The eyes, the ears and tongue, the fingertips, the tiny hairs in my nostrils, all were tingling. A dull pain inside my head, the skull being cleansed. It was good being in the dark, alone, enclosed, while this was happening.

The flush was broken, there was no paper, but I was done and washing my hands at the cracked basin. The light blinked on and off a few times. Sparks were passing along through the night, through the wires of the town, and the bulb caught at them, flickered, and then held on dimly, enough to let me see the state of the place, the damp, the stains, the bugs whispering, the messages scrawled on the walls.

The wooden frame above the sink.

I stared at the frame, at the painted surface, at the

maker's mark, Thomas Monroe and Sons Limited. The paint was a dull rust colour, dragged away in places, as though fingernails had scratched down it. I knew that beneath this one thin layer there would be a film of chemical solution, of silver nitrate. And that below the silver would be a sheet of plate glass.

The mirror.

Kingsley had told me a little of the history. How, by looking into a pool of water, man first became aware of himself. He spoke of the myth of Narcissus, and this strange, bittersweet love affair we have with our own image; how all mirrors are only copies of that first pool of water, gathered up, bound in glass. Framed. 'Do you think they like it?' he said. 'Do you think reflections like being caught, measured out like this? We force them into staring at, returning, the same old faces, day after day. Marlene, they are creatures of the sea, of the lake, the river. They will go back there.'

Here now, this one small collected part of the world, set aside, disregarded, turned to the wall and just left hanging there, lonely there, with its chain hooked round a peg. Waiting there . . .

Do not look upon thyself, suffering.

It got me thinking of Peacock's story and what had happened in the caravan. And I thought as well of the day gone by, the visit to the theatre, the whole day and the last week or so and the weeks gone by and the way that Henderson had been earlier, with the rain falling down. 'You see now, Marlene. How it has to be, if this thing is to work.' With such a cold passion in the words, such anger. And now here I was, in a cheap, stinking hotel toilet, staring at the back of a mirror.

It would take another few minutes or so, I felt sure, before the Lucidity got all the way into my system. Peacock had told me this. Be heedful, he had said. Keep in charge, he said. Keep it sweet. But the thought of my own face, kept hidden for so very long . . .

Yes. Fine. Keep in charge.

I turned the mirror round.

I turned the mirror round where it lay on the wall and I kept my eyes closed as I did so. And then I opened my eyes.

I looked at myself.

Marlene. Marlene Moore. I looked at myself. Thirty-five years old. What was I? A journalist? Well, I used to have the gift for a story, that's what I was told, but these days, what was a story anyway? Who could know? A series of broken gestures lost on the way from here to there, and all the meanings set adrift, dreaming. Adrift and dreaming, and yet. And yet I'd made it this far. I'd put the connections together. I had hooked up with Peacock and Henderson. The girl, Tupelo, the special girl. Together we had done some work and the suitcase was heavier now than when I started out alone.

What was I? Marlene Moore. A flow of shapes in the looking glass. A stranger to myself, I looked at myself. One stranger after another dissolving into each, under the sick-coloured lamp. And for one long moment there, I was reflected back lovely. Fine. Bright of hair, fair of face, a tender smile. Younger. And then younger still. Sunlit. How long did it take before I realized I was looking at my daughter's face, and then the image passing by, diseased, even as my fingers moved over the

222

glass, how long? These fingers still wet from the sink, tracing the shapes, how long?

Angela.

Another face now. A monster. A face of bone, ghastly white, the skin hanging off in shreds. But all was lies, I knew that. The signal was corrupted. In the smallest distance travelled between myself and the image of myself there was breakdown. This was the danger, the noise being caught in a loop. A face was screaming at me, making me hit the glass with the flat of my hand. The glass did not break. I hurt my hand. But what could I do?

What could I do but stand there, watching, watching, as the bad thing melted away, changing. It was my own face this time, Marlene's face, but still not fully formed and Marlene looked at herself, myself. She looked at herself and carried on looking and holding herself to the grief of it until the drug got to work all the way home.

Recognition.

That woman in the glass, she was becoming herself once again, the one true message of herself. One hand tracing the glass, the other checking the evidence. Did they correspond? Which was more real? Tracing the lines worn around her eyes, along her brow, the knots in her hair. I had known it would be bad, but really, where had all this damage come from? Most of all, the terrible look in the woman's eyes, the twin points of darkness. The pain that lay dark within each of the two colours, the brown and the blue.

Marlene. Marlene Moore. What was she? Thirty-five years old. She looked at herself. Journalist. Jobber.

223

Hack. A lost soul. Runaway. Divorcee. Criminal. Petty thief. Mother of a dead child. The child, herself, held within. In many ways, a ghost.

Transmitter, receiver.

The pathway between . . .

>

I walked downstairs to Reception. There was a pay-phone opposite the desk, and the old guy sitting there eyed me suspiciously, before going back to his jigsaw puzzle. I picked up the receiver, put in some money, and dialled Kingsley's number. Waves of hiss came down the line. I don't know what I was expecting really, only that I had to try this. And then, with the sound of something being set on fire, many miles away, a small voice came through. Distorted, spectral, filled with crackle. A voice, a whisper. I pressed my lips against the mouthpiece.

'Hello? Hello. Who is this?'

'Who is this?'

'It's me. Marlene.'

'. . . Marlene?'

'Kingsley? Is that you?'

'. . . is that you?'

'Listen, I'm coming home.'

'. . . home.'

'I've had enough.'

'. . . enough . . . enough.'

'Listen to me.'

'. . . listen to me.'

'Now listen . . .'

'. . . listen . . . listen . . .'

The man at the desk was glancing up from his puzzle now and again, and smiling now, a cruel smile, as if he knew what was happening to me, all my secrets. And the voice continued in my ear, answering with dark echoes; I was being caressed by my own shadow.

'What's your name?'

'. . . your name.'

'Who's there with you?'

'. . . there with you . . .'

>

Peacock and Tupelo were sitting together on one of the beds, playing chess. The bedside lamp cast its soft, unbroken glow over them. The television was still turned off and all was quiet and nobody looked at me as I came into the room, and I stood there for a while, watching them move the pieces around the board.

'Henderson still not back? No sign?'

Peacock shook his head. He was taking a drink from a bottle of advocaat.

'We should have gone with her.'

'Bev didn't want that,' he said.

'We should keep together.'

'We are together.'

'No, I mean—'

'How's the toilet?' said Tupelo.

'What?'

'The toilet? How is it? Because, you know, I've been putting off going.'

'It's bad. Nasty.'

'I knew it.'

'There's a pot,' said Peacock, 'under the bed.'

'Yeah right.'

'I shall avert my eyes.'

The room seemed too well-defined around me; I was not used to such clarity.

'You know what she's like,' said Peacock.

'Who?' said Tupelo.

'Beverly.'

'Beverly? She's mad.'

'These days, every day,' said Peacock. 'Ever since I've known her, the woman's been rolling her own.'

'But you love her, right?'

'What's that, girl?'

'You heard me.'

'Whatever.'

'That's fine,' I said. 'I'd like to . . .'

But I didn't know quite what to say to Peacock, nor to Tupelo. I watched them play for a while longer.

'I'd like to apologize,' I said.

'What is this stuff?' Peacock was trying to read the label on the miniature bottle.

'Peacock—'

'Tastes like shit, it does.'

'Eggs,' said Tupelo.

'What?'

I tried to speak. 'Both of you, listen to me—'

'The drink,' said Tupelo. 'It's made out of eggs.'

'Eggs?'

'Raw eggs, brandy, sugar.'

'Jesus.' Peacock took another mouthful. 'Fuck. That's horrible.'

The way they were with each other, I could imagine the gun had never been placed against Tupelo's head.

228

'Peacock . . .'

'What? Marlene, can't you see I'm busy?'

'I'm sorry. For what happened.'

'You fucked up.'

'Yes.'

'The capsule. You said you'd taken it.'

'I took it. I remember now.'

'You took it? You said you hadn't.'

'Henderson made me take it.'

'She's getting worse,' said Tupelo. 'That's it.'

Peacock looked at me. 'Marlene?'

'I don't know. I just don't know.'

The girl sighed. 'Peacock, it's your move.'

'I'm doing it.'

Peacock was playing the red pieces. He moved one of them now and Tupelo made her own move straight off.

'Check. Didn't you see that?'

Peacock shook his head, sadly. 'Eggs! Now fuck me, but who'd make a drink out of eggs?'

'Raw eggs,' said Tupelo.

'Christ, you think they'd at least boil them, or fry them first or something. Eggs. What was it? Brandy. What was it?'

'Sugar.'

'You sure do know stuff. You hear that, Marlene? Girl knows everything, near about.'

I walked over. 'Tupelo, do you have your watch?'

'The watch? Sure.'

The girl took the watch out of her bag. I looked at the face of it, at the shivering, ghostly hands which now, even as I stared at them, slowly became fixed.

'It's five past eleven,' I said.

'Let me see.' Tupelo looked at the watch. 'There you go. Five past eleven.'

And the day became my own then, creeping in, crawling out from the hidden spaces, bringing knowledge.

'OK,' said Peacock. 'Listen, Marlene. I'm not sure about the needle. I don't know what type it is.'

'That's OK.'

'I don't know how long it will last.'

'Look now. I just want to thank you, both of you. That's it. For helping me. That's it.'

'Fine,' said Peacock. 'Good. Whose move is it?'

'Peacock, you're in check.'

'Right.'

I watched the game for a moment, Peacock making his move, Tupelo replying, and then I walked over to the window. I could clearly read the sign now, the green-lit neon sign over the way. It was a church. I didn't expect this. I thought it would be a club, a nightclub. It was a church. The word itself spelled this. Church, it said. A small yellow cross floated above the word. The group of people could no longer be seen. A police car moved slowly down the street.

'Ah, I'm fucked here, girl,' said Peacock.

'I guess so.'

'I can feel it. Shit. Will you look at that. Look at the board.'

'Mate in three,' said Tupelo.

'Fuck. I feel sick.'

I looked up at the sky. The moon was drifting away behind a cloud. The night was closing its eye.

'One of these days, you know what, girl? I'm gonna kill this game.'

'I'd like to see that.'

I moved away from the window. I placed my hand flat against the wall, the damp wall. I was searching for the flower, the one particular yellow flower I'd fallen into whilst suffering the attack. I'd seen my daughter there, inside the flower. It was only a trick of the noise, I knew that. It was a trick the noise made happen; whatever was most in your thoughts, most treasured, became mixed up with the world.

'Marlene, what are you doing?'

'Nothing.'

'Leave her be. Are you playing?'

'Ah, what's the point?'

My hand moved on across the paper. It was the same wall I'd heard the moaning through before, the strange cries. There was a softness to it now. It was yielding. There was one small area, just there. Soft and wet, pliant, and not at all how it should be, fitting exactly in colour and size the centre of one of the flowers. This must be it. This is the one. I pressed at the flower and it gave slightly under my fingers. A moist substance. The flower accepted me. I felt I could push right through into the heart of it, the root of it.

'Marlene? Marlene, what the fuck are you doing?'

'Um?'

'You've got your finger in the wall. What's wrong with you?'

'It's soft. The flower is soft.'

'What?'

'It's soft.'

Peacock came to my side, reaching out.

'No. Don't do that.'

'Marlene?'

'Leave me alone.'

'Right. Fine then.'

My finger was halfway into the flower and then the whole way and I pulled it back out. I pulled my finger back out and something came with it.

'Oh,' said Tupelo. 'Let me see.'

She took the thing off me. It was black and pulpy and wet. There was decay in it.

'What is it?' said Peacock.

'Old cloth. Scrunched up. Damp.'

'Maybe it's a map.'

'A what? A treasure map?'

'Could be.'

Tupelo unfolded the cloth. It was only a piece of old material torn from a black towelling vest or some such.

'No treasure.'

'Marlene?' said Peacock. 'What is it now?'

I was staring at the wall, staring at the wall where the flower was.

'It's a hole!' said Tupelo. 'I don't believe it. A fucking peephole. Some randy sod peeping through there and watching me getting undressed and everything!'

'Girl, nobody's getting naked.'

'Please . . .' I said. 'Please.'

There was a hole in the wall where the cloth had been. It was the size of a large coin, with the petals of the flower radiating outwards from around the edges, and I felt hypnotized by the effect.

'What is it?' said Peacock. 'What's there?'

'My love . . .'

'What?' said Tupelo.

'Angela. Angela . . .'

'Who's she talking about?'

'Marlene? Come on now.'

I lowered my face closer to the wall.

'Who's there?' said Tupelo.

This was the last I heard. A silence took hold of me, as, carefully now, I placed my eye against the hole.

It was dark. There was no light coming through from the other side, and I thought at first the hole was empty. It wasn't. There was something at the other end that came into view gradually, and it was soft in the darkness. It was alive. I could not make out what it was, and then I could.

It was an eye.

It was a dark but human eye lodged no more than a few inches away from my own. The colour of the eye could not be made out exactly but there was a wetness to it, a black glistening.

I stared deeply.

The lid of the eye blinked. Closing, opening.

It was looking at me.

>

I could not speak. I tried to speak. I pushed myself away
from the wall, from the hole in the wall, and I turned to
Peacock and the girl and I tried to speak but just could
not. I pushed myself away.

'Marlene . . .'

'What did you see?'

'Marlene?'

I looked back at the wall, moving away, reaching the
bed. And I sat down there, with my head lowered into
my arms. All I could see, in the darkness, all I could see
was the eye, staring back at me.

'Marlene,' said Peacock. 'What was it?'

'What . . .'

'What did you see?'

I couldn't answer him. Wetness glinted. I looked up to
see that Peacock was moving to the wall. He gave one
last look at Tupelo and myself, and then he put his eye
to the hole.

Peacock looked into the hole. I heard him draw in his
breath and hold it inside.

'What is it?' said Tupelo. 'Come on.'

Peacock lifted his face from the wall just slightly, and

235

then he lowered it once more. He made the noise once again, and then he turned back to the room.

'Shit.'

'Do you see it?' I asked.

'I see it.'

'What the fuck is it?' said Tupelo. And then she said, 'You're scaring me.'

'It's an eye,' said Peacock.

'What?'

'It's an eye.'

'No it's not,' said Tupelo. 'Don't be stupid.'

'It's an eye.'

Peacock moved away from the wall and he gestured for Tupelo to see for herself.

'I don't want to,' she said.

But she did. Really she did and the girl moved to the wall. She put her face against the wall and she looked into the hole. It was only a glance.

'Ah, no.' Tupelo backed away from the hole. 'No. It's horrible.'

And the three of us were quiet then, not knowing what to say or do. A knock came at the hotel door.

'Jesus,' said Peacock. 'Who's that now?'

'Let me in, come on.'

It was Henderson. It was Henderson back from her travels. Peacock opened the door for her, and she came into the room, saying, 'I found him. I found out where Cole lives.' And then she stopped, looking at the three of us there, all three of us looking at the wall.

'What's going on? What the fuck's going on?'

'It's a peeper,' said Peacock.

'A what?'

'A peeping tom,' said Tupelo. 'There. In the hole.'

'Let me see that.'

Henderson moved to the wall. She moved to the wall without any trouble and she put her eye to the hole.

Henderson looked into the hole.

She kept herself there for a long time. It was a longer time than either Peacock or Tupelo had taken, and then she lifted her face from the wall.

'You stupid fucks,' she said.

'What?' said Peacock.

'You really are a bunch of stupid fucks.'

'Beverly . . .'

'It's a mirror. It's a mirror on the other side of the wall, in the next room. And the mirror is turned to the wall and the glass is placed against the hole.'

'Shit. Oh shit.'

Henderson was laughing. 'You stupid, stupid fucks. Oh, what a party.'

Peacock turned away from her, shaking his head.

'Marlene,' he said. 'Are you OK?'

I couldn't answer. My eyes were wet, filled with longing. And the soldier, Peacock, the killer, he came forward then to sit down on the bed next to me.

Peacock. He put his arms round me.

>

Tupelo sleeps on the other bed, breathing gently, and sometimes sighing. I have covered the lamp with an old shirt from my bag; now the light barely touches the girl, but falls steadily on the notebook, as I write. I have taken advantage of the needle's sweetness, to hold the day in words; and the pages I have just written, and the pages already written, they seem to make a kind of sense now. I have knowledge of the story once more, my own story, my place in the story.

I am tired, on the edge of sleep . . .

But I have not looked at the photograph. I am scared to. Scared, not so much that it might still be damaged in some way despite the drug, but scared that it might not be damaged. That I might see it again, clearly. My daughter and myself again, clearly.

Just now, I could not stand that.

\>

It was a black room. It was a small black room in a house somewhere and Marlene was in the room. The walls were covered in paint, still wet to the touch, and swollen with pustules that would break open with a dull popping sound here and there, and a thick yellow juice would seep out. There was no light but there was a light. It was a soft low light without any source. The walls of the room curved round to meet themselves making a circle and there was no door. There was no door to the room but Marlene was in the room. A church font stood alone at the centre of the floor. There was a pool of water in the font, a black water that carried no reflection. Marlene made no image in the water and she leaned over further because she needed to see herself there but she could not. Some beads were floating in the water. Marlene counted them. There were nine beads altogether and five of them were blue and four were yellow. Marlene put her hand into the water to pick up one of the beads, but when she pulled her hand back out and she opened it, the bead was not there. She thought it must have slipped back, it must have fallen, but no, there were only eight beads in the water now, and five of them were blue and three of them were yellow. Marlene tried to pick up another bead but when she opened her hand the bead was gone, and there were only seven beads in the water, four of them blue and three yellow. Marlene was afraid. She felt that she would never be able to lift the beads from the water. Rolling up the sleeve of her blouse, Marlene let her hand go deeper than before and the water was warm, it pressed at the skin. She moved her hand through the water but she could not find the two missing beads. Her fingers touched the bottom of the pool. It was soft. There was an object soft and giving at the bottom of the pool and Marlene had touched it. She had pushed into it. Marlene felt sick and she pulled her arm out of the water. The beads were still there floating in the pool and Marlene counted them. What had happened? Only six beads were left, and four of them were blue and two were yellow. Marlene bent over the font and she lowered first her arm, and then her face into the pool of black water. Marlene let the water cover her face and the water was warm to the skin. There was no light but there was a light. It was a black light at first but then a soft glow came into it and Marlene could see the thing that lay at the bottom of the pool. It was an eye. It was a large human eye exactly the size of the pool and it was looking at Marlene. The pupil of the eye was black and it opened up wide to receive Marlene's image more fully. It was a damaged eye. Marlene saw that now. She had pushed her hand into the white of the eye, making a wound, and a thin trail of yellow pus was streaming out from the wound towards her face, her open mouth. Marlene tried to keep from choking. She had seen that the black pupil of the eye had no covering to it. The pupil was open and the water flowed upwards from it, into the font, and Marlene saw the three missing beads down there, inside the eye. They floated there, two yellow beads, and one blue. Marlene put her hand inside the eye. The thick pus was in her throat now but Marlene kept on, she pushed her hand further down, inside, and the pupil contracted round her wrist as though in pain but Marlene kept on. She had caught hold of something within the eye. It was something precious, some wet pulpy substance that Marlene pulled loose. She had not meant to pull it loose but she did so, and a cry of pain came from within the eye. The eye went blind. The soft light went out and the eye was blind now, and no longer looking at Marlene. It was a blackness. It was the feeling of not being looked at, not now, not by anybody, and not for any time to come and Marlene felt a panic, a sadness, and she tried to pull herself out from the eye but she could not, the pupil was tight round her wrist. The pupil clutched.

The bedside lamp had been pulled away from me, along the table. The girl was sitting there in the pale, shaded light, with the chessboard opened flat on the bed in front of her.

'Can't you sleep?' I asked.

'Don't want to.'

'I was sleeping.'

'I know that,' she said. 'You were making a noise.'

'I was dreaming.'

'Dreaming?'

'Yes.'

I sat up on the bed, put my feet on the floor. Once again, I'd fallen asleep fully clothed. I'd taken my shoes off, that was all, and now, as it rested on the carpet, one foot was colder than the other. I was still wearing only the one sock.

'Yes, dreaming . . .'

I got up and went to my bag to find a pair of socks, my last good pair.

'What was the dream about?'

'I don't know. I can't remember.'

I had not dreamt, not properly, not since the trouble

began. The clouds of noise got right into the skull. The noise got in the sleeping skull and it was like watching a television with one million channels or more, and all of them being viewed at the same time. It was painful, and dangerous, and the nightly dose of Lucy kept this at bay, diluted it, so that only glimmerings came through. Gleamings. Some unseen object might give off a sudden heat. Perhaps a dull, brief light would flicker, or a small cry be heard, and be remembered on waking. The fingers might touch at fur, or at thorns. But nothing more. And people did not dream, not properly, but tonight, tonight I had been dreaming.

'Are you OK?'

'I don't know.'

'You look a bit . . .'

'What?'

'Sit down, Marlene.'

I sat down. I sat down on the edge of the bed to put the new socks on. Everything had fallen to the floor: the books, the clothes, all the rubbish, the bits and pieces of the journey. Everything. What was it for, where was it going? I rubbed at my face with my hands. The dream was hidden somewhere behind the face that I touched. The dream was there. The black room, a pool of water, and . . .

I reached for my notebook, but the dream would not come back to me, not sufficiently.

'Do you dream?' I asked.

'Of course I dream. Every night.'

'Every night?'

'There's nothing wrong with me, Marlene.'

'What time is it?'

Tupelo looked at her watch. 'Just gone two.'

'OK.'

My hand knocked against some object, hidden amongst the sheets. A tube of lipstick. Memories.

'I got lost today. At the service station.'

'I know that.'

'I got lost. I was confused.'

'Beverly was upset.'

'Was she? Really?'

'She was upset.'

'Were you?' I asked.

'What?'

'Tupelo, were you upset?'

'I don't know,' she answered. And then, 'Perhaps you should have carried on. When you ran away. You should have carried right on, maybe.'

'Maybe.'

I was looking at the wall. There was a strange shape there. It was a patch of clean wallpaper, the shape of a mirror. Henderson had taken the mirror off that wall, and the ghost of the mirror was still there.

'I didn't run off. I got lost.'

I turned to the opposite wall. There was the mirror now. Henderson had fixed it there, with the glass facing inwards, over the hole I'd discovered. I thought about the two mirrors facing each other on each side of the wall, in this room and the other room. I thought about the mirrors looking at each other through the hole. I imagined the eyes still being there on either side of the hole and looking at each other, and the image of each eye being repeated for ever into the distance that the two mirrors contained between them. I had the picture clear in my mind. And then, as I was looking at the mirror, quite simply, some moments from the dream came back to me. I moved nearer to the light, to write the dream into the notebook.

'You want to play?' said Tupelo.

'I'm working.'

'All that Lucy inside you, I don't know, maybe you can play. Normally, I mean. Maybe you'll win.'

'Let me do this, please.'

'Well then. Whatever.'

'Yes. Whatever.'

'Who's Angela?'

'Uh . . .'

'Angela. You were saying her name, in the dream.'

'What was I saying?'

'Just that. Just the name.'

'Angela . . .'

'She's your daughter? Peacock told me you had a daughter.'

'Let me work.'

It was good to be writing. It was the job, the one thing that I was good at, or that I used to be good at, and now I was doing it again.

'I'm the only person I know,' said Tupelo, 'that I can't win against. Have you any idea how that feels?'

'No.'

'It's sad. That's what it is. It's just sad, you know? It's sad.'

I looked up from the work. The girl had picked up the copy of *Through the Looking-Glass*, the stolen copy. She was flicking through the pages.

'Perhaps you'll meet somebody.'

'What?' Tupelo glanced at me.

'I don't know, a boy, maybe. A normal boy.'

'A normal boy?'

'You know . . .'

'Oh, please.'

I watched her. She was looking from the book to the chessboard and back again.

'Tupelo, you know this morning?'

'When?'

'At breakfast.'

'What of it?'

'When you told me what I looked like?'

'Oh that.'

'Yes. That. Did you mean it?'

'Henderson told me to.'

'Oh what's wrong, girl? Why don't you like me?'

'What do you mean?'

'Tupelo, I helped you.'

'You helped me?'

'We gave you the lift.'

'There would be others, other cars coming along.'

'But none like ours.'

'No,' she said. 'None like yours.'

And then she lifted up the book. 'I've been reading this. Chapter thirteen.'

'Let me see. There's only twelve chapters.'

'It's here. Someone's been writing in it.'

I took the book off her, glanced at where she was pointing, the new words . . .

'What does it mean?'

I looked back at the mirror where it lay reversed on

the wall, thinking once more of the two eyes staring at each other.

'Marlene? Tell me.'

Again, I looked at the new chapter. *Alice often awoke at night, from some dream or other.* And through all the lost moments, all the broken signals of days gone by, I thought of Kingsley telling me more or less the same story. I had taken it, then, as purest fantasy, a way of persuading me to accept his proposition. Now I saw it more as a simple explanation, at least for the workings of his own mind.

'Marlene . . . what is it?'

I looked over at Tupelo; the girl was staring back at me, her eyes never leaving mine. Truly now, with the drug's respite, and even from some few feet away, I felt myself being held within the eyes' black depths. The dream came back to me, complete in all its details. And I had been keeping myself locked in place for so long now, for so very long, that I could not help from spilling over. I told the girl everything that I knew, or thought I knew, regarding Kingsley, and the true nature of the mirror. I had not spoken so easily, so intimately, with anyone, not for a long time.

Tupelo smiled. Nothing more; no words, no answer was made. The girl smiled at me.

It was done.

I picked up the lipstick, twisting the case open. The slash of colour was the brightest thing in the room.

'Here. Use this.' Tupelo was holding out her little mirror, unfolded, the glass exposed.

I took it from her. And then, moving still nearer the lamp, I applied the lipstick to my mouth. The face stared back at me. I had the sudden feeling that this might well be the last glimpse given of my real self, and I would not leave the mirror's grasp. I would not leave it.

'They have mirrors on the moon,' said Tupelo. 'Did you know that? It's true. The astronauts took mirrors with them.'

'What?'

'To the moon. They took mirrors with them.'

Finally, I pulled away from the glass. 'Why?'

'To look at themselves.'

'Really?'

'And when they blasted off from the moon, they left the mirrors behind.'

I thought about this. I saw the mirrors lying there amongst the dust of the moon, with the dust gathering on the glass. Over the years, the centuries, nothing good was reflected there. I thought of the mirrors as being lonely, upon the cold moon.

'And what they do now,' said Tupelo, 'is to shine a laser beam from the earth to the moon. And the beam hits the mirror and is sent back, and the time it takes for the light to get back from the moon is measured. That's what you wanted, right?'

'Sorry?'

'You asked how long it takes for light to reach us, from the moon. You asked, earlier.'

'Yes. How many minutes?'

'One and a quarter seconds. More or less.'

'Is that all?'

'Why did you want to know?'

'Oh, I was thinking, yes, I was thinking about how

248

could I trust what I was seeing. I was looking at the moon. I was thinking about how tired the moon looked tonight, and whether it really looked like that.'

Tupelo was placing some of the chess pieces on the board.

'You can't trust anything, Marlene. Not any more.'

'No. No . . .'

'So then?'

'Listen, I'm sorry for all this. For dragging you into this.'

'Do you think I mind? Do you think I care?'

'I guess not.'

And I looked once more into the mirror.

'You look fine, Marlene. Just fine. Beautiful eyes.'

'But you don't know me, not really. You can't know what I'm really like.'

'I'm trying to.'

'Angela died.'

'Right. I guessed that.'

'She died.'

'Was it the sickness?'

'She was nine years old. Only nine.'

'What happened?'

'I remember now, I came into her room one evening. She was sitting at her desk, looking into a mirror. A small hand mirror. She was staring at herself, her face. Her body was shaking just slightly. I asked her what was wrong, and at first she did not answer me. I asked again, stepping closer. Her computer was switched on, a video game playing. There was a dog, now I see it; a robotic dog, moving round and round in circles. And a strange humming noise. It was coming not from the screen, but from her lips, from Angela's lips. A tune of some kind, I don't know. And then she spoke. She asked me if she would ever be beautiful. Can you imagine that?'

'What did you answer?' asked Tupelo.

'I told her . . . I said to her . . .'

'What?'

'I told her to stop being so stupid.'

'Oh.'

'You see now? You see what I'm like?'

'People say these things.'

'I know. I know that. But then she looked at me for the first time. Angela. She told me that a demon lived in the mirror. This is what she said. A demon. It was eating her, she said. It was eating the way that she looked, her appearance.'

'Didn't you know what it was?'

'I should've done. That's the problem. I'd already heard a few stories from America, about the sickness. I should've realized. Instead, I thought she was only becoming grown-up, becoming concerned about herself, about the way she looked. This is what I thought. Oh god, if I had only realized.'

'Marlene . . .'

'I could've saved her.'

'That wouldn't be possible.'

'Wouldn't it? If I had taken her then, right then and there, to the doctor? How can I know? It might have been possible. She might've been saved.'

'Come on . . .'

'The truth is, we were not getting on that well. Not for a while, not since my husband left us. It was hard. I don't know. Just one argument after another. What could I do? How to make the love come back? I didn't know what to do.'

'I know what it's like.'

'Do you? Really?'

'I'm just . . .'

'Angela died in a tank. A tank of water. Isolated. They say her own heartbeat killed her, the rhythms of it. A terrible music. She drowned. She drowned in herself. So cold, so alone. This is how she died.'

My eyes found themselves in the mirror. My face, with its unforgiving stare. Accusing, hateful. My lips were moving inside the glass, speaking these words.

'Angela already was beautiful. She already was. This should've been my answer. You already are, and will be in years to come, even more so than now. Even more so . . .'

And all the lost years never to arrive, I saw them as moments passing by, passing away.

'I'm sorry. Really, I am.'

I looked over at Tupelo. Her words seemed to reach out to me. It was a feeling barely remembered.

'Come and play.'

And so I closed the mirror, and I went to sit on her bed. I would let this happen. The chessboard lay between us and, using the book as a guide, Tupelo set out a small number of playing pieces, on various squares. The two kings, the two queens. A red knight, a white knight. A white rook. The pattern was immediately familiar. Only the single white pawn was missing.

'All the moves are listed,' said Tupelo.

I looked at the board.

'This is what you want? To go through with this, all the way? Marlene? This is what you want?'

'I don't know.'

I could only think of Kingsley, sitting alone in his darkened chamber, playing this game against himself. He was trying to find the solution. This one same game, night after night, over and over . . .

'It's white to play. To play and win, in eleven moves.'

'Yes.'

'You can be Alice.'

The white pawn was lying there, in the palm of Tupelo's hand. I reached over to pick it up, this tiny carved figure which I studied for a moment, and then placed down on the board. I placed it down where it belonged, four squares along from the left-hand side, two squares in.

This was the starting point.

'OK,' said Tupelo. 'That counts as your first move. You meet the red queen.'

I looked at the red queen, standing there on the square to the right of Alice. The two characters would be speaking to each other.

'Where do you come from?' said Tupelo. 'And where are you going?' She was reading from the book. 'Look up. Speak nicely. And don't twiddle your fingers.'

'What does Alice say?'

'I've lost my way.'

'I've lost my way?'

'That's it. Now then, I'll play all the other pieces, white and red. You just move Alice. OK?'

I nodded.

Tupelo moved the red queen away, along the diagonal.

I slid the white pawn two squares forward, and that was it, we were playing the game. We were playing the game together. We played it there in the pool of light given out by the lamp, in this cheap hotel room, and following the patterns laid down.

>

Alice, becoming a queen, and then losing her crown. I've been reading the Carroll book, just lying here on the bed, reading. Dusty, worm-eaten, yellowed pages, the cover torn. Angela loved all this, I remember; all this mad invention, and then the final poem. That last line, the question.

Life, what is it but a dream?

And then, turning over, there are a few blank pages before the book ends. Here, in this one particular copy, in a fine, precise handwriting, somebody has written some words of their own. Did Jamie, the theatre kid, write this? I don't know.

In effect, it's an imagined final chapter to the Looking-Glass story, chapter thirteen.

Alice often awoke at night . . .

>

Alice often awoke at night from some dream or other, but how pale and ill-fed they seemed, these visions, compared with those inside the looking-glass. With the house still cold, in darkness, the young girl would creep downstairs to the drawing room. She would test her hand against the mirror's surface. A spider was building his web over the glass, as though to catch any moths or bluebottles that came through from the other side. But no matter how she tried, Alice could not make her hand pass through the glass, not a second time. Her reflected face gazed back at her, with a mocking expression. Until, one night, when her dreams were so ordinary they seemed not to be dreams at all, Alice found herself standing in front of the mirror without any recollection of how she had got there. And now, her hand did go through the misted glass, quite easily.

A few minutes later, Alice's father roused himself from sleep, his heart beating, drops of sweat covering his brow. A noise had woken him. He looked in on his daughter, only to find her bed empty, the sheets ruffled. He went downstairs to find her. Strange whispering shadows moved along the walls, the ceiling. He was about to call for help, when he saw a hand, a small delicate hand, emerging from the mirror. A child's hand. It was Alice. Her face appeared next, all sticky and veiled by a spider's web, and then the rest of her body, until she was caught exactly halfway between the two worlds.

Her father could hardly believe what he was seeing, and he grabbed at his daughter's hand, to pull her free from the cold grip of the looking-glass. Once this was done, he picked up a heavy stone paperweight from his desk. Alice tried to stop him, but it was no good. Beside himself with anger, and fearful now, he threw the stone at the mirror.

There was a dreadful sound, a cry of agony that came from the mirror as it cracked and splintered. Some few shards of glass were still lodged in the frame, many others had fallen to the floor. Alice ran to these pieces where they lay scattered. She tried to pick them up, she had to put them back into the frame, if she could. She had to. Tears ran down her face, the glass cut into her fingers. Her father dragged her screaming from the room, and only then did she feel the pain. Only then.

Alice's hands were covered in blood.

>

We could not finish the game. Something kept going wrong, we could not finish it. Something went wrong, despite all the Lucy inside me, and the white pawn could not make it to the eighth square. A cloud would come into my eyes and the board would melt away and bend into new shapes, the straight rows and columns would twist and turn around themselves and the white pawn would always end up a few squares back from where she was meant to be. And not even Tupelo, when she played the white pieces, could bring the game to an end. And Alice could not make it to the final square, she could not become a queen.

>

Sleep would not stay with me. Something travelled through my restless body. I was not dreaming, as far as I could tell, but something woke me up and I lay there in the dark, listening to Tupelo's soft breathing.

A dull green light was coming through the window, from the neon sign over the way. I got up from the bed and walked over to the window, looking out. And then I turned to the mirror. I reached forward. I was touching the back of the mirror with my hands, with both hands.

I lifted the mirror from its hook.

A beam of light came streaming from the hole, from the hole revealed there.

I placed the mirror on the floor. I stood there by the wall, watching this beam of light come freely into our room. And I put my face to the hole. I set my eye against the hole. I placed my right eye against the hole, making dark the room I was standing in, and I looked through into the next room. The mirror had been taken down from the wall in this next room along, and now I could see through, clearly.

The room was brightly lit, a small space, the same shape and layout as our own, except that only one bed could be seen, a double bed. There was a man lying on the bed. He was naked, lying sideways on to me, on top of the covers, quite still. The mirror was propped up near to him, as though he had been looking into it. The frame was empty. Pieces of glass were strewn around the body, some of them touching the man's flesh; at the feet, the legs, the groin, at the stomach, the chest, the arms, the neck.

I don't know how long he'd been there, lying there like that. Lines of blood ran down the body. His hands especially, the one hand I could see, it was dark red in colour, a broken mess of skin. And all over, fragments of light were catching on the glass, bringing a haze, a sparkle, and the body was shimmering.

The man's head had lolled to one side, turned towards me. He could almost be looking at me. I had to imagine those final moments, as he took up the longest piece of glass . . .

\>

And I let my eyes come open. My head was resting against the side window. My hands, I found, were holding the steering wheel. A shadow fell across me, and I looked up to see Peacock's face at the window. He was tapping on the glass with his knuckles, and then he opened the door. Henderson and Tupelo were standing a little way off, both of them looking at me. Peacock said something, I don't know what. I can't remember how I got there, round the back of the hotel, into the car. The driving seat. What was I doing behind the wheel, sleeping, or dreaming, or setting myself on some plan of escape? But where would I go? All my chosen destinations were behind me. And then Peacock took hold of my hand, and he led me from the vehicle.

>

We drove down through the main part of town. It was that strange time, that period of the day when most people have already made their way to work, and the streets seem lonely, without purpose. A cloud of steam rose up from a grating. We passed through it and I saw a grey figure, a wraith of vaguely human shape floating there, its body of mist dispersing around us as we moved along, and then vanishing.

Presently, we found an empty place in an underground car park not too far from the beach, an all-day ticket. We walked in silence along the seafront. A screech of gulls drifted above the road. According to Henderson's source, Thomas Cole lived in one of the flats that looked out over the water. It was an old building, tall, of strange shape, and salt-eaten, squeezed in between buildings of a similar nature.

We stepped up to the entrance. There were seven flats listed; Cole was supposedly living on the top floor, apartment G, but the little card slotted in next to the letter was blank. The door was locked. Henderson pressed her finger against the button. She spoke into the grille, raising her voice. There was no answer.

I felt a sudden darkness inside. Darkness, and then splashes of colour, becoming shapes; the hole in the wall expanding. And then the picture forming, perfectly. The night before . . .

'Marlene? What's wrong?'

It was Peacock. I shook his hand away. There was nothing I could say. What could I say? I had seen too much, and now the vision scalded me. There were too many people, all bunched in the doorway. Stepping back from the group, I found myself held tight against the door, with the glass panelling cold against my cheek, stinging. A movement caught my eye, through the glass.

A young security guard was sitting behind a desk, his head moving slowly from side to side. His features showed no expression, no regard. No feelings. He had fallen away in there, inside himself, leaving only this blank mask in place.

If I could fall so sweetly . . .

>

Halfway along the pier there was a small games arcade with a café in one corner. The four of us were taking breakfast there. Instant coffee in paper cups, sticky buns, cigarettes and powder. Not much was being said. The machines had just been started up, making a quiet music; electronic sorrow. Peacock was going through the medical kit to dole out the morning's supply.

'Tell me now, where are we keeping it?'

'Oh sure,' said Henderson. 'You know.'

I felt my eyes close. It was all I could manage, just to let the melodies play over me.

'Marlene's sweet enough, I think,' said Tupelo.

'Sweet? She looks terrible.'

'Come on, Bev,' said Peacock. 'Take the stuff.'

'I will.'

'Do it then.'

'Just give me a moment, won't you? Let me consider. What does it mean?'

'What?' said Tupelo.

'Marlene's sweet enough. What is that?'

'Well now,' said Peacock.

266

'What? What have I done?' said Tupelo. 'I thought you'd have told her.'

'No he did not tell me. Fuck. Where is it?'

I opened my eyes. Henderson was holding the medical bag upside down, letting all the capsules fall out onto the table.

'Where is it? Where's the needle? Marlene?'

'I took it.'

'Right.'

'We had to,' said Peacock.

'She got the swirling,' said Tupelo. 'Real bad. We had to give it to her. We had to jab her. We had to.'

'What is it?' said Henderson. 'I go away for a few hours, you all go crazy on me.'

'That's it,' said Peacock.

'Shit. I already sold one last night, for the info, and this is what I come back to.'

'We had to do it,' said Tupelo.

Henderson placed a Lucy in her mouth. She took a long drink of coffee. For a moment then she sat there, looking at each of us in turn.

'We're throwing it away.'

'It was my fault.'

Henderson looked at me. 'It's not your fault.'

'Right,' said Peacock. 'Blame me.'

'Why not? I left you in charge.'

'Nobody's in charge, Bev.'

'Nobody's what?'

'The whole world's going crazy,' said Tupelo. 'And she wants somebody in charge.'

'What are you saying?'

'Nobody's in charge,' said Peacock. 'It's simple.'

Henderson got up from the table.

'Where are you going?' said Tupelo.

'Do you care?'

Henderson walked away. She walked along the corridor between the machines, towards the door. A young kid was standing there, a boy. Henderson said something to him, and then she pushed him aside, against the door. The kid was sent sprawling.

We watched this happening, the three of us. We didn't do anything, we just sat there, watching Henderson walk out through the door, onto the pier.

'OK,' said Peacock. 'That's fine.'

He took a Lucy of his own, his eyes on Tupelo now.

'Good job, girl.'

Peacock took his first measure of the day, but he did not say the motto. He could not keep it sweet, not this time.

'There was a man, in the next room.'

'Yeah?'

'A dead man. I think he . . . I don't know, but I think he killed himself.'

'Is that so?' Peacock would not look at me. He was placing all the capsules back in the bag.

I grabbed his hand. 'He stabbed himself . . .'

'There you go then.'

'Why won't you—'

'Marlene, it's his choice.'

'He stabbed himself, with a piece of glass. In the eye. The eye. Oh god, I wish I hadn't looked at him. He pushed the glass into his eye.'

Again, I saw the picture of last night, forming in front of me. No matter where I took my thoughts, the picture followed.

Peacock shook his head. 'Does the girl know? Did she see it?'

'No. She was asleep.'

'Good. That's good.'

He looked over to where Tupelo was playing at one of the video machines.

'Peacock, this man—'

'There's a lot of it happening.'

'I didn't know what to do.'

'People killing themselves. Shit.' He held out one of the capsules. 'You taking this?'

'No. Not yet. What could I do?'

'You did right. Do nothing.'

'I saw it, through the hole. The man, he was—'

'Marlene, I don't want to know.'

'What could I do?'

'That's the way, these days. Do nothing. Run away. Climb in the car, like you did. Go back to sleep.'

'You believe that? Really?'

'Sure. Or else kill yourself in turn.' Peacock shook his head. 'Sure. That's the way.'

'Peacock . . .'

'What?'

'Let's go back now. Let's not bother about today. We don't need today, we have enough already. Six pieces. Let's go back.'

'No.'

'We could go back, no trouble.'

'Beverly told me. She said the theatre was the best yet, the worst yet. The most powerful. Is that true?'

I nodded.

'OK then, this Thomas Cole guy, the writer, he's got some magic around him. Some good slice of the mirror, some beauty. We need that.'

'Beauty?'

'Some goddamn fucking beautiful thing. For once, you hear? For once in my life, I need that.'

I let my head drop.

'For fuck's sake, Marlene. What can I say? I'm trying to hold this together, I really am.'

'I know.'

'Go on then. Take the case. What can I say? Take it. And me and Bev, we'll just carry on, whatever . . .'

I thought about it. I thought about myself, in the car alone, going back. Home. The cold house waiting for me. And all this sounded both good and bad, but really, there was only one answer.

'No.'

'No? You sure?'

'There's too much . . .'

'What?'

'Too much between us.'

Peacock nodded. He was quiet for a moment, and then he said, 'I won't tell you my real name.'

He rolled himself a cigarette, taking his time over it. A bunch of kids had set themselves up at one of the machines nearest to us. Peacock gave them a look. He put the cigarette in his mouth, set it alight.

'When I left that caravan, everything changed for me. Everything. I had killed off my old self. There was no choice. I became this new person. John Peacock. There I was, waiting for me. Spender laid it all out. I had everything I needed. A name for myself, an image, the proper documentation. A mission.'

He took a drag of smoke.

'There was little difference from my usual work. I had a new target, that is all.'

'Billy the Bandit?'

'I walked away from the caravan site. I wasn't sure what had happened, not really. But the next time I met

Billy, I found myself calculating ways of getting him alone, of getting a mark on him. The thing is, Billy had found out by now that Spender had put an agent on him. So he was pleased, the Bandit was, he was pleased with me for removing Spender. What Billy didn't know was that I was the agent. I was the agent sent to kill him. I wasn't even sure myself, until I fired the shot.'

Peacock stopped. His face was hardening.

'What happened? Did you kill him?'

He looked around the arcade. Tupelo had moved to stand close to where two boys were working one of the machines. She was watching them play the game.

'I didn't have the skill for it.' Peacock laughed, just briefly. 'I've been on the run ever since.'

'Where does it end?'

'It doesn't. When I left that caravan, I didn't just become somebody else. I became myself. Do you understand that, Marlene? Do you?'

'You became yourself.'

Peacock looked at me through the smoke he was making. 'That's it,' he said. 'That's the outcome.'

I wandered over to where Tupelo was cheering on the young players. They were lodged within the machine, these two boys, firing laser beams at figures in the globe of the game. All around, the lights were stuttering, and the music breaking apart with every note; the noise had made its way deep inside the mechanism. But still, the boys worked the controls with a manic expertise, and when they swung themselves around on the balanced chairs, I could see a concentrated, faraway look in their eyes.

'What's happening?' I asked. 'Too much Lucy?'

'No Lucy,' said Tupelo.

'What then? They're immune?'

'No. Not that. They're playing it, Marlene. They're playing the sickness.'

The boys were not yet teenagers, perhaps nine or ten years old. Children. Tiny cameras fixed to the machine were following their every movement. I looked further into the game, into the shining globe. There was a world contained there, imperfectly realized, but alive with strangeness. The machine had captured the boys' own images, and given these images to the figures in the game, hundreds of them, multiples. Animated versions of the two boys were crawling out of gutters, from doorways, they were swinging down from billboards and from fire escapes. The representations were cruel, mutated, filled with the noise; flickering, fading, tumbling. The boys didn't mind it, they did not mind the noise, not at all. They were firing at each other, within the game. The boys were killing each other.

'Watch where they're aiming,' said Tupelo.

These two young boys, with their faces, their eyes, all daubed with a viscous glow. Colours sparked on broken circuits, and I watched the boys as they aimed not at the figures, but slightly to the side of them, or above or below the figures, and sometimes they seemed to aim far off the target on purpose. The lasers crossed over each other at speed, leaving their golden trails like dust in the air. Flames burst within my eyes. Soft explosions, disembodied screams. And one by one the boys were killing each other.

'They've cracked it, Marlene. Don't you see? The code. They've broken through.'

'Code?'

'The noise. A way of living with it, a method. Shit, I don't know. A technique. Watch them! Watch!'

'Yes.'

I glanced over. Tupelo was smiling, the happiest I had seen her. She pointed me back towards the machine. One boy now had the game to himself. The last image of his opponent had been blown apart and the mechanism was flashing up a winner takes all message, a ruined message, but the boy would not stop playing. He could

274

not stop from playing the game and he was firing the gun at those few images that were still alive within the globe. And all the time allowing himself compensation, degrees of latitude. Adjustments. Using the sickness against the sickness. In this way, he was killing the damaged shapes of himself, and I wished then that I could gain access to his skill, his secret pathways.

One by one, the boy was killing himself and he was laughing.

>

These were the final days of the season. The morning air was cold, and yet a good number of people were already gathering as I walked out onto the pier. The tarpaulin covers were being pulled from the fairground rides, the wooden doors of the ghost train creaking open. The first ride of the day had just set off, along the twisting rails of the roller coaster. I watched this, until, at its furthest pitch, the tiny car was suspended directly over the waves, dragging screams from the occupants. And all around now, people were queuing to join the other rides. I could not understand. Did they have no fear of their senses being filled with confusion?

For myself, I felt as though I was suffering from some cruel hangover, the kind which makes the world seem too real, too fierce. The cries of the gulls pierced through me. My pores were damp with the smells of diesel oil, salt, the saturated fats floating around the hotdog stand. Even the planks I walked on, the grain of the wood, the patterns were too well-defined. And yet, strangely, whenever I turned away from these details, everything became fragile, brittle. I felt I was moving inside a kind of theatre set, that I might step through completely, and fall.

The sea would take charge of me.

I kept returning to that image, the body in the next room. Now that I had finally told somebody about it, the whole episode was taking on the quality of a dream. Is that all it was? I could no longer be sure.

Oh let me use this well, this period of the needle's bloom. If I could only find my purpose.

I saw Peacock and Henderson. They were separate from each other, standing a few feet apart. Henderson was looking out towards the sea, with Peacock facing the other way. The suitcase rested on the boards, between them. Peacock was looking in my direction. He should've seen me there, watching him, and yet he showed me no recognition. Neither of them gave any sign. And what else could I do, but leave them to their problems.

Once again, I walked around the pleasure rides. Below my feet, through the cracks, I could see the waves pounding against the iron struts of the pier.

Only one attraction was closed to the public. This was the Hall of Crazy Mirrors. A government health warning was pasted to the door, and beneath it, a sign reading 'Under Repair'. And I imagined the mirror repairman, this mysterious character who was travelling around the country with his bag of tricks, with his brushes and his paint, his book of techniques, his magic spells, his chemical solutions, his protective mask and his gloves. His little jar labelled *Silvering: use with care*. Could such a man exist? Could such a process be possible?

And then I thought of Kingsley. Because, wasn't he performing just such an operation? The same magic? And what did that make me? I had stepped freely into this role, his dark-spangled assistant, his seeker of charms, his collector. Another part of his collection?

Was that my worth, these days?

I felt something touch my sleeve. It was a girl's hand, a little girl who stood beside me, holding a tiny dog at the end of a lead. She smiled at the closed door of the Hall of Mirrors. 'People go funny in there,' she said. 'Their eyes blow up!'

And then she ran off along the pier, following the dog through the crowd.

>

'How long would it take? Do you think?'

'For what?'

'I was expecting sand, Marlene. Golden sands. And now I'm wondering, just how long will it take for all these pebbles to be ground down?'

Tupelo and I were standing on the promenade together. We were leaning on the balustrade, looking down at the beach. Henderson was down at the water's edge, going through her t'ai chi movements. There was no sign of Peacock. A line of grey mist clouded the far horizon.

'Is that how it works? They become ground down?'

'Yeah. How long for the sea to crumble them all into dust? How many years?'

'I don't know. Thousands of years?'

Tupelo turned to look at me. 'Millions of years. I think so. Whatever. A long wait.'

I watched Henderson for a while and then turned to look further along the shoreline, towards the pier. It was only the middle of the day, but already the pier was lit up with sparkles, with dancing colours. I could not look that way, not for too long. Instead, I let my eyes be drawn by the clouded horizon. This was the place where nothing was happening. There was no purchase out there, nothing to cling to, and I felt myself being lulled by the moment. Stillness. For too many days now I had been travelling, or fighting, or else succumbing, or running, hiding, or just simply hanging on, as I could, or else not. And sometimes . . .

'Do you think it's right?' said Tupelo. 'Is it right what you're doing? Stealing things. Stealing the mirror, the pieces of it?'

'What?'

'Is it right?'

'I don't know.'

'You don't know?'

'Kingsley . . .'

'Ah, Kingsley.'

'He's only reclaiming the pieces. This is what he says. Mending the glass.'

'And you believe that?'

'I don't know.'

'Well there's the trouble, you see. Nobody knows much of anything any more. There's no big picture. We're all just doing stuff, going places, falling out of cars. Running away. Fucked up, strung out, broken. Mended with bits of glue, string, masking tape. Stealing things.'

'Anything else?'

'Plenty.'

'Tonight's the last.'

'The last?'

'The last piece. I've had enough.'

'What then?'

280

'I'm going back, to Kingsley. Finishing this.'

'What about me?'

'I don't know.'

'I can come with you, right? I mean, that's what you want, Marlene? Isn't it?'

'I think you should go home.'

'Home? Jesus, no. Not that. I can't do that. How can I do that?'

'Why not?'

'I just can't.'

'Tupelo, you're a very special person.'

'So? So what?'

'You can help people.'

'Oh, please. Those horrible vampires, all over me.'

'Whatever happens . . .'

'Yeah?'

'Whatever happens, you need your own life.'

The girl looked away, mumbling.

'Tupelo . . . what is it? What did you say?'

'Nothing.'

'You said something.'

'It doesn't matter.'

'Please. Don't hate me.'

The girl shook her head in response, nothing more.

Down on the beach, Henderson was no longer doing her exercises. Peacock had come up to her, they were talking together. It was too far away to tell for sure, but it looked as if they were arguing with each other. I heard a small sound, a tinny bleeping noise. Tupelo had taken out a small handheld device. She was leaning on the railing, with the device held in front of her.

'What's that?'

'It's a spellchecker. The boys in the arcade gave it to me. See?'

'Does it work?'

'It's trying to.'

People were strolling by along the pathway below me, along the paved walk that marked the limits of the beach. One young man was dressed in a sandwich board, with the single word 'TURN' written on the front. The word was fluorescent green in colour, and the paint had dribbled down from the letters. The man walked on, and I saw the words 'TO JESUS' on his back.

Everything and everybody, all seemed calm compared to last night. I had the sense of the town waiting for darkness, perhaps, for the release that darkness would bring. And we ourselves would be a part of that madness, there seemed no escaping it.

A number of archways were set into the structure of the promenade, taken over by souvenir shops, coffee bars, fortune tellers, drinking holes. Directly below was a club called the Snake Pit. It was closed at the moment, with its steel shutters drawn, but we would go there tonight, hoping to find Thomas Cole. This was the one other clue that we had; that Cole would sometimes visit the Snake Pit.

'Look at this.'

The girl handed the spellchecker over to me. It was an old model, rectangular, with a miniature keypad and a viewing screen. The screen was filled with letters, with tiny green letters that moved at speed, across from right to left. And no matter for how long I looked, I could not see any sense being made there, no word or phrase of any real meaning.

'What's it doing?'

'It's trying to find the correct spelling.'

'Of what?'

'One of the boys pressed a random sequence of letters into the machine, that's all. But now look. It's trying to find a word that doesn't exist. The machine can't stop searching. It's going through every possible combination of letters. See? You can't switch it off.'

I pressed at the cancel button, but nothing would stop the mechanism.

'Machines with diseases. All the kids have these things, nowadays. They just like to watch the letters coming up, the madness of it. They like to watch out for tiny fragments of sense. They have competitions. Who can find the best sentence, or part of a sentence.'

'What's the best yet?'

'Your pyramids shall.'

'Your pyramids shall what?'

'The boy told me. That's the best, up to now.'

'Crumble, maybe?'

'What?'

'Your pyramids shall crumble. Maybe that's it.'

'Marlene, I don't think you can guess it. I don't think that's the point.'

Perhaps I had pressed a button by mistake, because the letters seemed to be moving at a faster speed now, becoming desperate in their search.

'You know why so many people are here?'

'No.'

'I thought the place would be deserted. But I asked them, the boys. I asked them. And what they're doing, with their families, is they're travelling around the coast. You see that? All these people, travelling around where the noise is most concentrated. Getting jobs where they can. This and that. But living with it, Marlene. You do see that? Living with it.'

I looked down at the pathway below, and then out, along the beach. The gathering: children, teenagers, adults, even a few older men and women. I saw people kissing, running, playing, standing alone, in groups, in a crowd. Suddenly now, so many of them. I heard their voices. Shouts, whispers. The call of the hotdog vendor, the melting of a pop song. The churning music of the roundabout. I saw the glittering horses, trapped in the loop the music dragged around them. The sun had broken through, and now the colours were streaming away from the ride. The children were crying out as the colours tore themselves free from their clothes, their faces, from the horses they were mounted upon. I watched the colours as they floated over the beach in long thin tatters, amongst the crowd, and catching momentarily on people's arms and legs and then drifting away into the air, fluttering, disappearing over the guesthouses and hotels that lined the seafront.

'Are you OK?'

'What? Oh . . .'

'You see now, what I'm thinking, is that maybe you and I, Marlene, we could travel around the coast, just for a while maybe? What do you reckon?'

I looked at the girl.

She was waiting for me to answer, even though her face was turned away. I could tell that. But what could I say, truly?

'Ah, look at that now.' Tupelo was pointing over the crowd, down to the sea. 'Look.'

There they were, Peacock and Henderson, the two of them. They were doing a slow waltz, out there on the shoreline with the water lapping about their feet. They were dancing.

'That's either really sad,' said Tupolo. 'Or else it's beautiful.'

'Yes.'

'Something like that.'

And then, as we watched, Henderson pushed away from Peacock.

'Of course, he's wasted on her.'

'Listen, Tupelo . . .'

'Yeah?'

'Listen. It can't happen.'

'What?'

'It can't. Me and you . . .'

'Right.'

'It can't. You have to understand.'

She spun round to face me. 'Oh sure. I understand. Fuck, I understand.'

'Please . . .'

'Oh, that's it then.'

The girl was walking away. She was walking away from me, along the promenade. What had I done?

'Tupelo, wait . . .'

I followed behind, a few steps behind.

'Tupelo . . .'

The crowd moved in around us both, closing in between myself and the girl, and I let them close in, between us. I let them slow me down, hold me in place.

I had to let her go. I had to.

The little machine beeped in my hands.

I turned back to the balustrade. There was no sign of Peacock or Henderson, only some children playing down at the water's edge. They were covered in a fine spray of mist, a sparkle of colour, caught from the sun and the sea. It gave them a delicate appearance, as though they might drift away at any moment. The mist was creeping in, enclosing the people, the round-about, the distant pier, the whole scene before me; all things grew soft within my eyes. The young man with the sandwich board was coming back along the path-way. Only the word he carried with him, only this seemed clear and bright. It was coming back to me, the noise, and, strangely now, I felt that I should welcome it.

This desire to be ill, where was it coming from? I thought again about Tupelo, about whether I had been right to force her away. The machine beeped a second time, making a little tune for itself, and I looked down at it, at the panel of the spellchecker. The letters were a simple blur of text, moving faster than before. I had the idea that some word had just passed before my eyes. Some liquid green word, or words, or a sentence even, that had passed along and now vanished. I felt that some message was trying to be sent to me, to me alone, and I pressed at the buttons of the machine without thinking, and pressed too hard. The machine slipped from my grasp. It slipped from out of my hands and fell to the walkway below.

I looked down, feeling dizzy. The sandwich-board man was standing there, looking up at me. He was smiling, the word shining out from the sign he was wearing.

TURN

And I realized the word was coloured the exact same shade of green as those letters on the spellchecking machine. I pushed away from the railing. The world was spinning round, too quickly circling round and lost, lost as a flare of light broke in my skull, and a sound and a smell, the hot crackle and stench of two wires fusing together, as though I had looked directly at the sun. And then, in the bloom of darkness that followed, some letters were printed on the back of my eye; once again, this same bright electric green, illuminated.

. . . *sbcyxekaroundvkolizpr* . . .

And I saw the word hidden there. I put the two words together, from the sign and the machine. These were my instructions. I turned round.

What could I see?

The white hotels, the cafés and seaview apartments. A clown on a bicycle. A child's hand, a yellow balloon, the piece of string that joined the two. A poster advertising a firework display. A bus stop. People walking past without care, and the road that stretched away on either side of me. And there, a bruised red limousine was passing by, slowly, only a few feet away.

Its windows were cold black mirrors, reflecting the sky.

A dark and smoky coffee bar, somewhere just off the main shopping square. The meeting place, as agreed. I got there first, then Peacock, and then Henderson, a while later. They were still not talking to each other, not properly. Peacock asked me where Tupelo was and I could only shrug. He made a face, and Henderson shook her head. She had a well-practised expression. I couldn't tell what she was feeling. Whereas Peacock was jumpy, ill at ease. He kept screwing his eyes tightly shut, and then bringing them open, with a sudden release.

And I sat opposite these two, watching them. I felt so distant from them, they seemed like two figures in a landscape. I can explain it no other way. Their voices drifted by.

Some people at a table next to ours were taking the Lucy. They had one capsule between them, between the four of them, and they were passing it around, wet from their tongues, direct to the next person's mouth. It was a kiss that went round the circle three or four times, with the capsule melting in stages from their shared heat, the powder seeping through. It was a highly sensual act, some fascinating process that I felt was taking place behind a gauze screen. Peacock was talking, I could see his mouth opening and closing, and I brought all my attention to bear upon it. He was asking the others if that's all they had, the one capsule, and did they want to take some of ours, and they said, no, this is fine, one is fine, and they shared it between them.

Something was moving across the tabletop. A tiny black object, vibrant, and shiny. I placed my hand in its path, and the thing climbed onto my palm.

It was a fly.

Over in the corner, somebody was playing an acoustic guitar. Music. I had not noticed it before, this long stream of random notes that almost became a tune, and then becoming lost once more. The music folded itself around me, composed from shadows. Other strands joined in, more than could be played by one person alone.

Again, I heard a voice. I could only imagine that a door had been opened, within the music, and I looked through. Henderson was telling us how she had called round at Cole's flat, at various times during the day, but there was never any answer.

'Perhaps he's gone away,' said Peacock.

'He's there. He's waiting.'

'What?'

'I can feel him, waiting.'

'Jesus.'

On the table in front of me there was a menu card, a large ashtray, and a wine bottle with a lighted candle placed in the neck. I could see the word 'golden' written on the ashtray. Just that. The word struck me, for some reason. And then, moving my head slightly, I saw the word 'claret' written on the bottle. The wax had dripped down from the candle, leaving only three letters of the word visible. A sentence was being made.

Golden are . . .

The menu card was hidden behind the wine bottle. All I could see clearly was a single word, the first word from the name of the place, The Black Bag.

My eyes fell upon the word.

Golden are the . . .

What was being said? All I had to do was find the next word, that was all. I looked about the table, and then the wall to my side, which was covered with posters, fliers, personal ads, images, all laid over each other at skewed angles. The fly was crawling across them. So many words, hundreds of words.

Golden are the people, golden are the days, the doors, the dogs, and golden are the skies, the cars, the feelings, and golden are the eyes, the stars, the books, and golden are the dancers, the children . . .

Which to choose? I could not keep my attention from jumping around, word to word. And everywhere I looked, messages leapt out at me, all in secret, all in . . .

'Marlene?'

'Uh?'

'Are you listening?' Henderson tapped me on the arm. 'Marlene, we're making plans, for tonight. Down the club. Are you with us?'

'Yeah. Yeah, I'm here.'

'What if we don't find him?' said Peacock.

'Then it's done,' said Henderson.

Peacock looked at her.

'We're done,' she said.

And so, we made our decisions. I held myself in place, as we drank our coffees, and we took our medicine. Peacock told us he was going to keep it sweet from now on. Sweeter than sweet, he said, most definitely so, and Henderson the same and then it was my turn. And I said the words as though I meant them, and maybe I did, and maybe we all did, I cannot tell.

But the capsule, the Lucy, I only placed it gently against my lips, hidden by my hand, and when my hand came away the capsule was still there, still hidden.

This one decision, being made.

>

I have been doing things. I have been measuring, I have been counting. The streetlights, for example; how many along the promenade, how many back again, checking to make sure it is the same number each way. I have been studying the colour of people's hair, grading them by shade and hue, and to see if more light than dark pass me, in any one span of time. This is called 'waiting for a message'. I have put myself in charge of reckoning the exact amount of litter dropped in a certain square metre of ground. I have been taking note of every person who wears an item of red clothing, be it a shirt, a scarf, a pair of shoes. This is called 'searching for clues'. I have matched people to the parked cars they were walking by, according to whether they wore items of clothing the same colour as the car. This is called 'receiving a message'. I have crossed my hands twice behind my back for every time I have seen a poster I could not read. Every time I see a balloon, I have to whisper the word 'blackbird' to myself. This is called 'acknowledging the message'. And I have been looking for girls who remind me of other girls, for dogs on leads if the leads are blue, for the shadows of men when the shadows exactly reach the edge of the pavement. This is called 'deciphering the code'. I have been searching for a face, one certain face hidden amongst the crowd, a woman's face, with eyes both brown and blue. I have been consulting the signs. I have been counting the seconds it takes me to count the number of streetlights. I have been measuring, recording. I have been doing things.

These few objects, found along the beach: a silver coin, with the King's head nearly washed away; the one blade of a pair of scissors; a small battery; a compact disc of Ornette Coleman's *Tomorrow Is the Question*, broken, one shard missing; a piece of string; a single page torn from a book; a bottle top. These are the seven elements, the various components of the machine. This is how it works. First, choose a location approximately one metre from the water's edge, with the tide incoming; here, the blade of the scissors is buried halfway in the pebbles, with the sharpened point showing; the compact disc is placed horizontally on the blade, with the point of the blade pushed securely through the hole provided; please note that the labelled side of the disc must be facing downwards, and that the disc should be tilted at a slight angle, towards the operator; a knot can now be tied in one end of the piece of string; the other end is tied round the battery. The battery is placed on the pebbles close by the compact disc, with the page of the book held in place beneath the battery; care is needed, to ensure that the printed text on the page is not obscured by the battery; finally, the knotted end of the string is placed within the broken part of the compact disc, in such a way that the string is held there. When the parts are joined in this way, the machine is ready for use. The operator should place themselves in such a position that they can both read the text and see their own face reflected in the mirrored surface of the compact disc. The eyes glance back and forth between the text and the mirror, as the text is read aloud.

Up, and put on my coloured silk suit very fine, and my new periwigg, bought a good while since, but durst not wear, because the plague was in Westminster when I bought it; and it is a wonder what will be the fashion after the plague is done, as to periwiggs, for nobody will dare to buy any haire, for fear of the infection, that it had been cut off the heads of people dead . . .

During this procedure the bottle top should be held in one hand, the coin in the other, with the King's face uppermost. All outside influences should be ignored: the laughter of children, the scorn of adults, the cruel blow to your shoulder, the water at your feet. All that matters is the text and the mirror, the joining of the two, and that the text be read aloud to the final word whilst the eyes stare back at themselves, examining. Only then will the process be deemed complete. The fact that nobody has yet managed this task, not completely, should not discourage us; the machine often falls apart in usage, or else is cast aside and broken by the operator. This is a normal part of the procedure. There will be many attempts, many failures, before the words are spoken into life.

And the mirror holds the face, gently.

>

The locked doorway. The letter G, the little blank card
next to it. Through the glass, the uniformed guard
pacing the foyer. My finger on the button, mouth
against the grille. 'Cole? Cole . . .' Only a dark static to
answer me. And then, listening close, I thought I heard
a whisper, a breathing, a distant moaning; a crying out,
a crude grunt of pain. The sound of paper tearing. And
then silence. Silence. As I turned round, the guard's
face was pressed against the other side of the glass. I
demanded to be let inside. The man wore the same
blank expression as this morning, and would give me
no response. This close up, however, separated only
by this thin barrier, I could see that his eyes were constantly on the move; not dead, but fired with anguish,
seeking connection. He was coming loose inside, trying
to climb out from behind his mask.

I saw somebody. I saw a person that I recognized, or thought I recognized. In the crowd. A sideways glance of somebody known briefly, or well known, a long time ago or recently. A woman. In the crowd that moved along the beach path, she walked there, below the promenade. A woman, somebody. A certain way she had, a certain look about her, half-turned towards me and then away. I followed her. I pushed through the crowd, trying to keep the woman in sight. Sometimes she would seem very near to me, and then further away, and sometimes she would vanish altogether, drift away and then reappear some distance off, and always moving.

Where did she go to?

All the many people around me, the colours they were clouded within; the noises they made, the tumult of their lives, their voices. I could hear them speaking all at once, and their thoughts even, in various tongues.

Where did she go? Where did she go to?

I had to stop. I had to stop then and gather myself. The whole day flooded me. I leant against the wall of a kiosk. Just over the way, people were waiting to take

297

their turn in a fortune teller's booth. A large painted hand was looking at me. The diagram of a hand, with its magical lines inscribed and an eye drawn in the palm of it, looking at me. The eye closed, and then opened again, and I saw the woman a few yards away, turning away from the crowd. A subway went under the promenade here, under the road. I followed the woman, into the barely lit tunnel. A young boy was sitting against the wall, with a dog, and a bowl with a few coins in it. He was playing a wooden flute, sending out high, lonesome notes which scattered into echoes around me, all bright and cold echoes which now, remembering this, I step through once again. The woman walks ahead of me. I recognize her style of dress, the cut of her hair, the way that she moves along. The way that she holds herself, with her hands held clenched against her hips, when she stops at the sound of my voice.

I have called her name.

My name. My own name. We have the same name. And the woman stands there quite still, with her back towards me, as I approach.

'Marlene? Is that you?'

Somebody speaks. The woman turns round. I imagine a mirror turning on a central pivot, shifting through degrees, through slow degrees. Her face is dark and soft, retained by shadows. She will not come forward. Tiny sparkles of colour play around her neck, two colours. Yellow and blue. Two wooden beads, yellow and blue, held on a chain round her neck. I have to move closer myself, one step, one more, to let the face reveal itself. And with these eyes, those lips, this mouth, that

298

strand of hair falling, these bones, that skin so pale,
these hands that reach forward . . .

'Marlene?'

Somebody speaks. Somebody . . .

'What do you want?'

It's not her. No, it's not the person I thought it might
be. It's somebody else, a stranger.

The dog howls behind me. The music plays. The
woman takes hold of my hand. Her fingers fold themselves round mine, courteous, gently pulling, and I
move towards her, closer now. And the light grows
darker around me, around both of us.

>

Black marks, wetness, scratches. In the darkness, a pen moving across skin, across a young girl's skin. Words being put there, on the skin, with Marlene's own hand doing the writing. Words, these words, being written on the skin and Marlene thinking to herself that only by covering the body with words, entirely, will the young girl be saved. And then feeling the sharp, polished nib of the pen cutting into the skin, pushing the ink through into the body of the girl, pushing the words deep into the veins; Marlene realizing that the words, these very words, they will either enliven the girl, or kill her. Only by putting the correct words down, in the correct order, will the girl be roused again. The soft wetness, shreds of skin, scratches, the black ink. Tiny cries of pain, the darkness. Marlene knew that she was failing, she was failing in the task. The writing was a poison. But still, she could not lift the pen away from the flesh. Marlene could not stop writing. And then from nowhere came the idea that all she had to do, to stop herself from writing, was to wake up. She had to wake herself up from this dream, that was all. Marlene had to open her eyes, let her eyes come

300

open, that was all, but she could not do it. She had to wake up. What was the problem? Marlene's body was a slow machine, with only the brain and the hand at work, the writing hand. Marlene's eyes would not come open. She had to seek out the hidden instructions that would activate the machine, set it going. Marlene had to find in the dark of the skull the countless tiny levers that made the eye work. She had to pull at the levers, gently now, allowing the operation to take place. To lift the pen from the body of the young girl, to let the eyes come open finally, blinking at the light that burned into them.

>

Where was I? Painful, curled up on the back seat of the car, coming to, awakening. Alone. Shit. I raised myself up, looking around. Brick walls, a dull yellow light. The underground car park. I couldn't remember how I'd arrived here. This drift of voices inside my head, all speaking at once, all demanding. What time was it? Was it day, or night? There was no way of knowing.

The notebook lay on the floor by my feet, open, the pen lying across it. I must've been writing in the book, and then fallen asleep. A pool of ink had leaked from the nib, onto the page. The young girl, the words, the bare flesh. Perhaps I had been awake, all along. Writing. Imagining . . .

Why hadn't I taken the capsule?

I looked in my bag. Down at the bottom, amongst the bits of tissue, the loose money, the wallet, the boiled sweets, the scraps of paper with meaningless numbers on them, the keys to doors that may never again be opened, the penknife, the pens, the book of stamps, down there, amongst the little sachets of coffee granules stolen from some lousy hotel or other, amongst the matches, the petrol coupons, the government leaflets, all this slow drifting down of life, the dust and the grains of sugar, the flower seeds, the little bits of myself, the flakes of skin, the molecules, down there, a few extra Lucies were hiding.

I took one into my hand; the tiny yellow eye was looking at me, looking back at me.

I remembered the people in the café, sharing just one capsule between the four of them. Perhaps we had been taking too many all along; perhaps the official rulings were wrong. I lifted the road atlas onto my lap, and then pulled the two halves of the capsule apart. The powder fell onto the map, where I smeared it with my fingers and then raised my hand to my lips. This one taste, enough to make me feel sick. I had to force myself, rubbing as much as I could onto my tongue. I found a bottle of water on the seat, and I drank some of this.

The voices grew louder, not calmer. Where was I going to? Where was I going?

I picked up the notebook. I read through the last few entries, the scrawled lines, the mess of words that told my story. The walk on the beach, the strange machine, the random signs. The woman I followed. The darkness. And even as I read, the text melted away in my eyes. Whatever meaning I had seen before . . .

What was the use of it? What was the use of writing? The book was the noise. I couldn't fight it any more. All that was done, fighting was done now, and I tore the page from the book. And then another, at random, another page, the next page, letting them fall. Somehow or other and without realizing I must have cut myself on something, cut my hand; there was blood on the paper, dripping down the words as I tore through them.

I took the photograph from its pocket. There it was, the senseless image. The colours, the various objects depicted, somebody and somebody, something, something else. The strange shapes. For too long now I had carried this thing around.

I took the photograph in both hands, one at each top corner. My hands started the necessary movement. Tiny cries filled the air. Jesus. What was I doing? Tears came into my eyes. I had to stop myself, right there. I had to let the half-torn photograph fall to the floor, alongside the few pages I had ripped from the book. I had to. And then, picking up my bag, I stepped from the car.

This car, this lousy beaten-up old thing, this rusted box, this shell, this sick and dying machine; this car was my home, my one good place in the world.

What was I doing? Where was I going?

The stairs led directly onto a small side street. It was night. Flashes of light came from an office block. I started to walk, without a plan, breathing in the rich, salty air. The voices still lingered inside my head. People were making their way down towards the front and I let myself get lost amongst them. They dragged me along, they took me with them down one street, round a corner, down to the coast road. The vehicles moved slowly by, their headlights coming out in long streams of white amidst the tiny scarlet sparkles of the brake lights, shining out, burning to the rhythms of the music I could hear coming on loud now as we crossed the road, finding the spaces between the cars and moving there, moving on, across the promenade to the railing, standing there looking out at the sea and the sky all opened up before me, this vast swathe of purple where the stars were caught and the moon held motionless above the water, the water, the moon's reflection dusting the tide, the black water which glistened wherever it touched at the world, the long curve of the beach, the people assembled there from one side where the flames of a bonfire could be seen, the figures dancing around it, and then looking across, below, where the crowds gathered outside the clubs, lost in the brilliance, the music, the voices, the smell of cheap food, alcohol, the neon signs casting their soft spells, along, past the old roundabout with its circle of horses, along, a scattering of gulls, further along, out to where the pier stretched far into the ocean ablaze with lights, with words and numbers floating upwards like smoke, the glittering rides turning and swinging, sending out their colours, cascading, rising, the spectres rising into the night sky and all this I took deep into my eyes, allowing it play, allowing it, letting it mix in with the voices that swirled within my skull, where was I going, where was I going to, the voices, and I raised up my arms then, not caring, not caring of the people all around me, opening up my arms wide to the sky, not caring, and I let them scream, the voices, I let them scream out, I let them out.

Peacock was sitting outside a little bar, just along from
the Snake Pit club. There were some other people at the
table with him, strangers; Peacock was ignoring them.
I stood there a few feet away, watching him. The silver
case rested between his feet. He had a glass of beer in
one hand, and now his other hand went up to his lips,
away, back again, and only then did he drink from the
beer. And I wondered how many capsules he had taken
already that day, that evening, the last few days or
weeks, in secret, away from Henderson.

I walked up to him. Peacock looked at me, his eyes
lost in a film of neon.

'Have you seen the girl?' I asked.

'The girl . . .'

'Tupelo?'

'Why?'

'Have you seen her?'

Peacock shook his head. I asked him where
Henderson was and he shrugged, and then nodded
towards the Snake Pit. It wasn't much to look at; a
door in the promenade wall, a painted banner showing
two snakes twined around each other, that was all.

The whole set-up looked quite temporary. Certainly, it wasn't as popular as the other places, further along the front.

'There's nothing doing, Marlene,' said Peacock. 'No sign of Cole. I think Henderson fucked up.'

'Right.'

'Hey listen . . .'

'What?'

'Keep your head closed down.'

'Sure. I will. Thank you.'

I went over to the club's entrance. A man at the door asked me if I was coming in, or staying there all night? This was the choice. I could walk away now; I could walk away from everything. And then, hearing a cry of alarm from behind me, I turned round. A woman had fallen to the ground, shaking with the sickness. A circle cleared around the victim. A teenage boy had hold of the woman's body, trying to keep her still. He was shouting for help. I turned back to the doorman, paying him some money. In return, he stamped the back of my hand with the crude, violet image of a snake.

Passing through the doorway, I felt a shiver run down me. The cold touch of a security device flickered over my clothing, my skin. From there, a corridor led to the main room of the club, a small, low-ceilinged space with a bar at one side, a central area with tables and chairs, a small dance floor, and, cramped into one corner, a raised stage.

The walls were decorated with painted letters of many different colours and sizes, a jumble of words. I could feel the Lucy, the tiny amount I had managed to take, I could feel it starting to work. On the wall closest to me,

I recognized lines from Allen Ginsberg's *Howl*, from *Moby Dick*, from the poetry of Gerard Manley Hopkins. Such astonishing words, all taken from books I had read many years before, and seemingly forgotten, now brought back to me, alive. These stabs of memory, of detail. And I felt that I was being drawn into the words, just by being in this place.

On the stage, a saxophonist and a double-bass player explored a slow, fiery blues; split notes, broken rhythms, squeaks and howls, animal cries. A young couple were dancing to the music, held loosely, now tightly, turning round each other, their hands stroking at bare flesh. Other people were sitting at the tables, leaning in close to talk to each other. I saw Henderson. Her lips were pressed against the face of a young man, whispering, laughing. The music grew quieter, with long dark notes from the bass, murmurs from the horn.

I got myself a drink from the bar, and then walked over, to sit down next to Henderson.

'Hey.' It seemed to take a while for her to recognize me. 'Oh. It's you. Shit. Where have you been?'

Henderson's voice was slurred. Her eyes closed up, briefly, as though she were bringing something to mind.

'You know Jamie, right?'

'What?'

'You remember Jamie, of course you do.'

The young man smiled at me. The last time I'd seen this guy, he'd been down on his hands and knees in the rain, in the dirt of the street, crying over a few coloured beads. When was that, yesterday sometime? Now, he sat opposite me, smiling, all neat and tidy in clean clothes, his hair combed.

'What's he doing . . .'

'Jamie's helping us.'

The young man looked at me. His smile flickered, and then caught again; his fingers pulled at the piece of string he wore round his neck. There were no beads there, none that I could see.

'We've made up.' Henderson moved her hand through Jamie's hair. 'Haven't we now?'

On the wall next to me, painted words were shifting, changing; along the floor they crept, along the ceiling. I tried to keep hold of one line of sight, a fixed point. *In the darkness.* I watched this phrase crawling across the wall beside Jamie's head.

'Where's Cole?'

'Cole?' Henderson looked at me with pale, washed-out eyes. 'Oh, you know . . .'

'Where is he? You said he'd be here.'

'It's not like that.'

'What is it like?'

'He never leaves the flat.'

'Oh, Bev . . .'

'Fine, I got it wrong.'

'Shit.'

'It's OK, Jamie will get us in. Later on.'

'When?'

'Later. How it works, is that every Friday night—'

'Friday?'

'Every Friday, Cole sends out his reader. OK? And then, up on the stage, the work gets read out, the latest stuff. So what we do, when the reader goes back—'

'It's Friday? Today is Friday? How do you know?'

'What?'

'How do you know it's Friday? When's the last time you knew what day it was? When?'

'Marlene—'

'What date is it, today? What month is it? What year? Tell me.'

Henderson smiled. 'It's fine, Marlene. Sit down. Everything's working out.'

'No.'

I couldn't stay there. I had to stand up, move away. Something was wrong. Suddenly, the room seemed to be far too long, too thin, filled with heat. More people were dancing now, crowding the tiny space. I walked down the tunnel, towards the music. From the scrape of the bow against a string, from the golden soft channels of the saxophone, the music, the black noise of it broken already at source and passed on broken through waves of air, becoming louder, along the sparks that glimmer, broken, amplified, through the mathematics, louder now, louder, more ragged, crying out, broken, cracked and tattered from fingers and lips and the people loving all the remnants, making a dance out of them.

I stood to one side, listening, watching the light catch on the polished brass of the saxophone, hearing the deep fever of the bass inside my bones. It was hot down there, beneath the road. Hot, humid. I was covered in a sweat, sticky, shivering, watching the dancers as they moved against each other's bodies slowly, with a passion that reached out to touch at my skin. This moment.

I had to step back.

This was a flowering. I saw that now. A late, night-bidden flowering, here on the coast. Amidst all the sick mirrors, the lurid signals, amidst the static, the fog, the noise, these people had found a way of releasing themselves, and I had to step back from it, against a pillar. This sudden desire. To make love to somebody, one of the people here, a man, a woman, anybody. What was happening to me? I could not remember the last time I had felt so aroused.

My back was leaning against the pillar, with my head almost touching the stone. Something moved in the corner of my eye, some words. *Surrounded by phantoms*. Just that phrase. I looked more closely. The pillar was covered with writing, with letters and words of differing sizes, and each letter had inside it more letters, more words, and words within these words. My head started to ache, just from looking. The single word, *trembling*, the one sentence, *Where shall we go from here?* Coming into focus, and then being lost, lost, every word ever spoken gathered here inside this room, and then lost, slipping away along the walls, the floor, the ceiling. *Wetness, scratches*. These two words moving across the stonework. *In the darkness*. The single word, *skin*. Nearby, *a young girl*. I was being drawn along. *They will poison*. These words, appearing, disappearing. And there, to the very edge of my vision, I saw my own name. I saw my own name on the wall. The word glistened before me.

Marlene . . .

I let my hand reach forward. The wall had a softness to it, a warmth. Skin. Human flesh. My hand pressed at the skin, at the writing that covered it. The letters of the name were sticky, wet, and my fingers came away coloured by them. And when I looked again at the wall, the word was smeared there, unreadable; fading now, lost to my eyes. I felt myself grow faint in turn, as though I was vanishing along with my name, my sign, and my story no longer my own.

Where do you come from? And where are you going?

In a daze I made my way back to the table. I had to push somebody aside to get there, some stranger. Voices, voices. The music still playing, the words, a chair knocked over. I don't know what happened, some people were looking over, staff, other customers, Henderson holding me back from whatever it was I had done, and the young kid, Jamie, down on the floor, staring up at me. He was talking to himself, mumbling.

If only I could . . .

'Marlene? What are you doing?'

'I . . . I'm not sure.'

'What's wrong with you?'

A member of staff arrived, asking what the trouble was. Henderson turned to speak to him. I knelt down next to Jamie. That look of fear had come back to his face; this was the same frightened boy I had last seen outside the theatre. I touched his hand.

'It isn't me,' he said. 'It's not me.'

That was all. Enough. I now had a strong feeling about what was happening here, and the cause of all my problems that evening. I stood up.

'They want you to leave,' said Henderson.

'I'm doing it.'

I thought Henderson might protest. Instead, she said, 'Marlene, you're not running away, are you?'

And suddenly it came to me. No. Not running. I wasn't running. I was no longer running away.

'You're not leaving us?'

No. Not that.

\>

The moon was a promise the clouds could not conceal. A cold breeze stirred, and there were fewer people around outside. No sign of Peacock. The sea moved in darkness, and yet, climbing the stairs up to the promenade, I felt a calmness come over me. This night would not end unless I myself ended it. There was no other direction.

I walked down along the road until I stood opposite the building that housed Cole's apartment. I could see the window of the top flat, a balcony, and beyond that a figure moving against the pale, violet light. This person stepped out onto the balcony. I saw the figure only as a silhouette. The light flickered.

It was late; people were walking home, or going back to their hotel rooms, lonely or otherwise.

I crossed over the road. Through the glass panelling of the doorway I could see the guard at his desk. The panel beside the letter G was illuminated, and the name COLE was written there, in red. I placed a finger against the button.

'Yes?'

A distant voice. A woman.

'Is Cole there? Thomas Cole?'

'Who is it?'

'Marlene Moore. It's about—'

'One moment.'

That was all it took. There was a low buzzing sound, the door latch being released.

The guard rose from his desk as I walked through into the foyer. He seemed different from before, a different person; the mask had fallen away. His face was alive now with feeling, his voice a mumble of words. I asked if he was all right, and he backed into a corner, his hands moving slowly through strange patterns. There could be no translation.

Beyond the foyer, a short corridor led to a single lift, a black chamber. I stepped inside. The walls of the lift were made from mirrored glass, the ceiling also, all of them now painted over. Fingernails had scratched down the paint in jagged lines. A knife of some kind had made other, more detailed, patterns. Letters, words, numbers, obscenities; diagrams of the female body sliced open. And there, amidst all the madness, one item that cuts through me. One word. A name. A girl's name.

I pressed the button for the top floor.

>

Upwards, through blades of grass, through sunlight.
The lift ascending. Through the waves of daylight,
the fields, the plumes of pollen disturbed. Through the
crystal notes of a melody, upwards; through the warm
breath of air a bird's wing once sent to me, as a child,
standing on the brow of a hill. Sunlight, daylight.
Upwards, the lift ascending. The one small bulb that
flickers on and off, the tiny glimpses of myself seen
through the scratches in the paint. Memories. The
distance of stars caught beneath the surface of a frozen
pond. I remember now, placing my hand against the
ice. The burning. Upwards. This fragile apparatus that
holds me, carries me. The twinkle of the bulb. Through
starlight, moonlight, the moon-yellow beams of a car's
headlights. All these thoughts coming to me, unbidden,
precisely detailed. My father being taken away, that
night, that cold winter's night. The way his words
clouded from his lips, remembered. The exact shape of
the cloud. Where did he go to, oh where did he go?
Upwards, the lift transporting me, through the voices,
the shaded contents of the mouth, the tongue that could
only ever speak by dipping itself in ink. I see myself,

filling my schoolbooks with endless lines of writing, all the things that would happen to me, day by day. The lift ascending. Through the whispers of the story, this one story that holds me now, that carries me along into the pictures, upwards, into the garden. Finally, the garden. The young girl with her eyes that shine both brown and blue, turning away towards the camera. Angela. I remember now, we had been playing a game. A word game. That moment when the lens opened up to capture her, the smile that she gave. That one brief moment. The game. I had forgotten. Upwards. The lift ascending. Through sunlight, starlight, moonlight, headlights, the lights of the skull, the lamps of the eyes, gleaming. Wordlight. The tiny sparkle of the lens, and then my daughter turning back towards me. Her voice, the word that she had found . . .

The door of the lift breathed aside. I stepped out onto a small landing, to see that apartment G was directly opposite, the door slightly ajar. I pushed it further open, entering a hallway. Some coats were hanging against the wall opposite, and from within their folds, low down, two eyes were staring out at me. It was a boy; a young boy of five or six years. He came towards me, out of the garments.

'Did you see me? I was hiding.'

'No.'

A loving smile came to his face. 'My name is Alex. What's yours?'

'Marlene.'

He held out his hand for me. I saw traces of writing on his palm, the faded shadow of words. The boy led me down a corridor, into the kitchen. The place was a mess, with plates stacked high in the sink, food left to rot on the counter, something disgusting on the floor that flies buzzed around. A woman was sitting at the kitchen table, smoking a cigarette. The boy sat down at the table, next to the woman. He opened a book and started to read. The woman was simply staring into space. She had not yet looked at me, but I knew her to be the same person I had seen on the beach earlier, the one I followed into the tunnel beneath the road. There was a passing resemblance between us. Beyond that, I could not say what it was I had been following.

The woman poured herself a drink; only then did she look up at me, raising her weary, haggard face. One of her eyes, I saw now, was stained purple. A bruise. She still wore round her neck the chain with the two beads upon it. Whatever I was now caught within, it had started then and there, in the tunnel, with the woman reaching out towards me. When we touched.

'I'm here to see—'

'I know what you want.' Some of the wine spilled down her chin. A frown creased her brow, and then she nodded over to another doorway. 'He's waiting.'

'Does Cole know—'

'In there.'

I moved to the door. The light came shimmering from within, violet and pale, draping itself softly over objects and furniture, and bringing with it a perfume, a chemical sweetness. I had not felt such a concentration before. I felt faint, my head reeling; a crackle moved around my skin, as I stood in the doorway, barely able to move. There was a large, full-length window opposite me, half open, which led out onto the balcony, and the view over the dark ocean. The moon still kept me in its vigil, following me everywhere. Rain had started to spot the window, through which I could see the hunched figure of a man. Another small boy was sitting at a coffee table, studying a chessboard. Neither person gave any sign of knowing I was there.

I stepped further into the room. There was a fine leather couch, framed oil paintings on the walls, a plush chequered carpet, a long line of bookshelves. But as my eyes grew accustomed to the light, I saw that the couch was scuffed, the cushions torn open. The carpet was freshly stained with wine; a pile of salt was sucking up the colour. The painted landscapes were smeared with some brown substance. Behind me, a noise of breath being drawn in. The woman was standing at the kitchen door, a cigarette gleaming in her mouth. I walked over to the nearest bookshelf. Nearly every title was by the same author, a writer of detective novels famous some years ago. I pulled one book from the shelf; *The Severed Helix*. The pages fell loose as I opened them, releasing a scent of mildew. Words crumbled into dust.

I turned back to the room, and the space seemed to shift around me awkwardly. There was a brief darkness. Dull blobs of colour danced before me; they pulsed and slid apart, forming themselves back into the shapes of the room. Things had changed.

The door I had come in by was no longer opposite the window, but adjacent to it. The woman was standing on the balcony; there was no sign of the bent, male figure I had seen there previously. The paintings had moved around, occupying different walls. A beaded curtain hanging over a second doorway trembled, the beads clacking together as though somebody had just stepped through them.

My eyes would not keep still.

The boy at the chessboard had been behind me, now he was sitting close to my side. It was the same child that had led me into the kitchen. Had he somehow slipped by me, unseen?

I brought my hands up to my face. How could I control these messages, this sickness? I felt a sudden need to have Tupelo standing by me, to give direction.

Another person walked in from the kitchen. It was the boy, the same boy. Another boy.

'Hello,' he said. 'Did you see me? I was hiding.'

'No.'

'My name is Alex. What's yours?'

'Marlene.'

The boy went to sit with his twin, at the chessboard. They both had long blond hair, cut in the same style, and they wore identical outfits: green trousers, and bright red pullovers with the letter A printed on them. I could no longer tell which boy was which.

One corner of the room was occupied by a large desk. Thin strands of violet swirled in the beam of a reading lamp, beneath which an old typewriter glinted. The sight of a pile of manuscript paper, set to one side of the machine, drew me forwards. I had to find out what was written there.

The woman came in from the balcony. One of the boys got up from the coffee table. The woman walked over to sit on the couch; the boy headed for the kitchen. The three of us moved around the room, slowly, at strange angles to each other. The desk kept drifting away from my sight. Two boys were sitting at the chessboard; a third boy, identical in every respect to the other two, stood next to the bookshelves.

'Did you see me? I was hiding.'

'No.'

His face came alight with a smile. 'My name is Alex. What's yours?'

'Marlene.'

I reached the desk. Everything was set out neatly; the pens, the ruled notepad, the scissors, the liquid eraser. A small clock, with its blurred numbers.

The typewriter, I saw now, was broken. The spindly arms with their tiny embossed letters were bent over or else snapped in two; the ribbon was pulled loose and tangled around the keyboard.

A silver frame held a photograph. I picked this up, tilting it this way and that in my hands, until, through the sparks of noise, I could see the image of a young boy. He was of similar looks to the ones who moved around the room in front of me, but of rougher cast, dirtier, more real, more human.

I read the title page of the manuscript. *Maxwell's Demon. A novel by Thomas Cole.* Letting the pages fall open one by one I saw that the entire thing had been written out by hand, a rough and imprecise hand. The ink had a strange quality to it, a wetness, no matter which page I turned to. I could imagine it would never dry. Words swam before my eyes for a second or two and then came into focus.

Death can have no knowledge of itself. Let us imagine a creature then, a woman say, who has died and does not know it; and therefore she lives on. A ghost. Ignorant of her true status, in thrall to a loneliness that cannot be understood, the woman can only drift through this world. All that she may think she touches, she touches not. And all that she loves . . .

Drops of water fell onto the paper, and the words

blossomed, pale and blue, into wet flowers. There was a brief darkness. My eyes burned with colour.

The room floated before me.

Only one boy was sitting at the chessboard. The other two were sprawled on the couch, and speaking out loud, each in turn, the letters of the alphabet. The woman had vanished. Shivers of heat moved through the room. A light flared amongst the beads that hung over the second doorway. Something moved at the window. There was a face pressed against the glass, looking in at me. This fourth boy mouthed some words in my direction. He smiled. The pages of the manuscript slipped away from my fingers.

'Do you like it?' the woman asked.

'What?'

She was standing by my side, appearing from nowhere. 'I'm supposed to be reading this stuff, tonight. Out loud, you know? At the club. What do you think? Is it good?'

'I . . . I'm not sure.'

'No. Well, it's fancy, isn't it?' I could smell her wine-heavy breath. 'Oh yes, fanciful.' She glanced at the beaded curtain. 'He's like that, these days.'

These days? I looked over to the bookshelves. All the best-selling novels lined up there, their pages filled with murder, with clues, alibis, solutions.

'Is Cole his real name?'

The woman laughed at my question. 'I know what you're after.' She leaned in close, her lips hot against my skin, whispering. I thought she would mention the beads, or the mirror. Instead, it was but two simple, dreadful words.

'A child . . .'

My heart leapt. I tried to move away, but the woman had too tight a hold, and she pulled me close a second time, with the same two words, louder now . . .

'A child.'

'Where is she?' I cried. 'Angela . . .'

'Oh well.'

'Please, where is she?'

There was a noise from the kitchen, a bell sounding. The woman turned away from me.

'Who the fuck is that?'

'No. Wait . . .'

Her body slipped aside. I felt we were standing close together, and yet I now saw the woman across the room, a great distance away, walking through into the kitchen. Coldness ran along my skin, and I tried my best to follow her, shaking now, the room drifting in sleep around me, the walls growing hazy, the floor rising slightly and falling, melting, falling, and no matter where I stepped, I could never reach . . .

The fourth boy came in from the balcony, brushing the rain from his hair.

'Did you see me? I was hiding.'

No words would come to me.

'My name is Alex. What's yours?'

The boy waited. I could not answer him; I could not remember my own name. Where had it gone to? The smile wavered on the boy's face, on his lovely, ink-speckled face, and then he shrugged, and he walked past me to join his companions. All these children in the room, where had they come from? They were moving around, stepping from square to square along the carpet's design. One boy was down on all fours, licking at a pile of salt, the wine-flavoured salt. The room held me in its spell. The playing pieces were knocked over on the board; the pages of the manuscript lay scattered about. My legs were giving way beneath me.

What was I doing here? I had no hope of finding my daughter. She was dead. Drowned by her own heart.

I fell to the floor.

Angela, Angela . . .

And I fell to the floor, cursing myself, my weakness, and a love that comes too late and too slow, and closed down within itself. It will not blossom.

'Look at you.'

It was the woman. She had come back into the room, and now she stood over me. 'That was Peacock, at the door. He wanted to know if you were here.'

What could I say?

'I told him you weren't, of course.'

Right, good. This was good. To not be here, to be nowhere. To be free of all this struggle. To be nameless. The fading shape of a word that, the further it travelled away from me, the more at peace I felt. With no sign to guide me, without direction. Without conclusion. And I knew then that I was falling into darkness.

The woman picked me up. She grabbed at my collar and she pulled me up, to hold my face close to hers.

'Look at you. Jesus. What is it? What is wrong? What the fuck is wrong with you!'

She hit me. The woman held me in place with one hand, and the other hand swung round to slap my face, again, a third time. I let them happen, one by one. A fourth time, and again. Another. Allowing the pain. Until, finally, the woman let go of me. I slipped back to the floor, to my knees. The window. I could see through.

The moon, this one pure signal. The one and a quarter seconds it took for the light to reach me. I let my eyes close, and the moon was still there, a strange warmth inside me. Acceptance. A giving away.

I opened my eyes again. Now I stood before the second doorway, with its beaded curtain. The beads were coloured either yellow or blue, many hundreds of them, arranged in no clear pattern. They moved gently, of their own accord. A glimmer of light could be seen beyond; a soft light that flickered, died, and then stuttered back into life. Was it a flame, a candle flame perhaps?

With one hand I held aside the curtain. The beads made their music around me as I passed through.

>

My presence in the room, the tiniest gesture of my
body, my breath, even the pulse of my heart seemed
enough to set the flames in motion. They danced more
brightly, bent sideways, almost lost their purchase,
and then righted themselves hesitantly. I counted six
candles altogether, and then realized that each performed the same action twice, simultaneously. Three
candles, at different points of the room, each placed
before a mirror, each with its own small halo of violet
light.

All else was darkness.

I could no longer see the beaded curtain. It must
have closed, or closed up. There was no door. All was
darkness, from which I heard now a low moaning
sound. I took a step forward, and something brushed
across my face, soft and wet; something soft and wet,
tingling, fibrous, clammy, gently holding at my skin
where it was bare, the hands, the face, the back of my
neck, turning my blood ice cold. Memory. The image of
myself, pacing through the fields at night, a child; I
was running home late, beneath trees, fearful, and
the floating ghost of a spider's web attached itself to

my face. This was the same feeling exactly, the same revulsion. Another step forward. There was the slightest resistance and then the strands broke apart.

I could make out the shape of a bed, a double bed, emerging from the gloom. Was there a figure resting beneath the covers? I could not tell. The moaning came again, followed by a tiny scratching sound, recognized; a pen moving across paper. The noise came from a corner of the room where no candle burned, and where the shadows enfolded some darker object.

I was standing a few steps away from the bed, with the filaments of web pulling away from me. The mirrors gleamed from the walls, all set just below eye level. I had to take care to avoid their gaze, oh but there they were; the fragments of a dream. Three of them this time. I had not seen so many in one place, not since Kingsley's house. And I knew that the beads would be found within one, and perhaps the strands of web came from a second. What kind of miracle would the last contain?

'Marlene . . .'

A voice spoke from the darkness. Hardly that, hardly a voice at first; the moaning, the harsh breath, a tongue that seemed to drag words from deep within the throat.

'Marlene? Is that your name?'

'Yes.'

Something moved in the corner; the shadows crawled, the candles flickered. I could feel the sticky threads being drawn tighter, a secret mechanism at work. A small light was reflected from each mirror; it gathered itself, this concentration, each beam meeting to dispel and melt away the shadows. And there, yielded up from the dark, a man's face appeared.

'Cole?'

'No. No closer. Please.'

It was an old man's face, shivering within the pale glow of light. Long straggles of white hair fell over the brow. The skin had a dull complexion, like thinly poured wax, almost transparent except where it was speckled with darker spots. The eyes were closed to begin with, and then came open; one held wide, staring, and the other a dreadful hole in the face, a blackness. The dry mouth drew in what air it could, moaning the while, as the words came to the lips.

'What do you want?'

I could not bring myself to speak.

'You want to steal from me.'

'No.'

'Kingsley sent you, am I right?'

'You know Kingsley?'

'I know of him.' The mouth smiled, and then turned cruel. 'I know of the people in search. Most of them. Their various agents, the pathetic travels they venture upon. All of that. The money involved, the suffering. Also, I know how it will end. Closeted. Alone in the dark with their glittering objects, crying.'

The old man coughed, as though the speech had pained him. He struggled to calm himself. Phlegm dribbled down his lips, and a trembling hand came up to wipe at his mouth. And the three mirrors, each with the same face angled within them, Cole's face, they trembled also, in sympathy.

329

'Marlene . . .'

He was dying. I saw that now.

He was dying slowly in this room, in the near dark. Only the mirror's embrace to keep the breath going, the heart; the hand, even now scratching at paper; the mouth, the tongue.

'You are not the first to come here, begging of me. Begging. No, not the first.'

The light around his face gleamed brighter. The webs pulled off me and then settled, as the old man brought something up from his lap. The light dimmed momentarily, caught again, dazzling. The man's eyes; one rich and full, the other darkly cast, hollow, both of them held wide as he brought the object closer to his face.

It was a further piece of the mirror, sending its rays across the walls. And now I could not see the man's face at all, only his hand, his shaking hand, as it approached the mirror and kept on, and kept on, the hand pressing against the mirror, and further on, inside, into the glass, the silvered glass.

I could hardly draw a breath, watching this.

'Please . . .'

That word, that one word, the way it came out of him, slowly, filled with anguish. His hand seemed to be caught within the mirror; something had a hold of it, something that brought only pain. Only pain. The flame of each candle, each in turn, burned higher; the webs tightened around me. Until, finally, a stillness came. Cole sighed, and he pulled his hand clear of the glass. In wonder, I saw the blackened fingers emerging, wet, glistening, dark as night. This hand, touching now at the man's brow, the line of the cheek, leaving its mark, along the mouth, the lips.

I thought of the manuscript I had seen, those few lines I had read, and the ink, still moist. The mirror held this ink inside it. This was the treasure.

The old man's face, as the light came back to it, was parched, almost drained of life. His one good eye was starting to close; the other seemed to bleed a little, some dark substance dribbled from the sightless orb. His mouth worked feebly, producing a whisper.

'What have you lost?'

As these words were spoken, the room took on a warmer aspect. The webs, I now saw, looked more like hair, long wisps of hair, human or otherwise. They pulled at me. My attention was drawn towards the bed. Something was lying there beneath the thin sheet, giving off a soft and violet light. It was the colour, the one strange colour I had been following these last few weeks, at first on Kingsley's behalf, and lately just to keep myself on the move. And I felt then that I had been travelling towards this moment.

I stepped forward, feeling the hair break around me, clutch again, break again. My hand touched at one corner of the sheet, gently now, gently; and the covering slid off the body, like water poured over a rock, over marble.

Revealed, the sleeper.

Revealed, the pale violet body of the sleeper. The featureless body; quite small, childlike. The legs laid out straight, the arms resting at each side. There were no fingers, no toes; the hands and the feet still to be made. The skin was translucent all over, and a darker liquid pulsed beneath, along the veins. The belly was smooth, with only the slightest indentation at the navel. The pudendum, not yet formed, hairless. The meagre breast lifted and fell under my hand, lifted and fell with the tiniest movement. It breathed. No heat could be felt, but still, the body breathed, as my hands caressed further, up to the neck, the head. The perfect oval of the skull, and the lovely face. Revealed, the face of the sleeper. The barest signs of the nose, the eyes, the ears, the mouth. All closed up, as yet. A child. A girl child. Unadorned. Sleeping, or more than sleeping.

I felt my heart stir with pain. The more I gazed at the child's face, and the more my hands explored her ghostly body, the more I felt sure I could discern my daughter's features hidden there.

Waiting, only waiting . . .

I looked up at Cole. The mirrors' light had faded slightly, and now I could not tell if his eyes were open or closed; I could not tell whether he looked upon me kindly, or cruelly, or at all.

'Is she real?' I asked.

In response, a long, drawn-out cry rose from his lips. The sound was caught by each candle in turn; the light flared up, the shadows recoiled, wavered, caught, returning, the light coming to rest once more, and the cry fading to a murmur, to a breath, a whisper.

'Go on. Go on . . .'

And he nodded. With this direction, I turned to the small nightstand that stood beside the girl's bed. An object lay there, a fountain pen. The nib was sharp and wet against my finger. I thought of the boys in the other room. Had Cole lost a son? Was this the reason he had brought these pale reflections into life? With this pen, this ink; the mirror's spell. And now, in its pool of dusky light, the body of the girl lay before me.

'What shall I do?'

Cole nodded again. He gave no other answer.

'Please. What should I write?'

Again, silence. It seemed that I would have no guide in this task, none but my own. My own talent, my small talent at words. I was a journalist, a reporter. Paid by the line, not by the heart. What was the use of it now? On what could I report, what possible expression could be found? What was I supposed to do?

All those stories I had made my living from. Lost dogs, flower shows, music and book reviews. The vagaries of fashion, royal weddings, drug dealers, murderers. The state of the nation, the varied states of the heart, interviews with strangers, the sickness beginning, the noise. And then this journal, these broken words.

What was the subject matter that would bring the girl more fully to life? Should I write of dogs and flowers, would that do it? Of melodies and words, poetry, of bright scarlet dresses, disguises, kings and queens, brides, of needles and bloodshed, my country and my part in it, of desire, of the strange, of strangeness? Of the sickness? The roads I had travelled, day by day? Of what should I write?

'Please. Please help me.'

There was no reply. Cole's face had merged once again with the shadows. I had been given this chance, this one chance; to love again. To love. To love again.

Alone now. Closing my eyes . . .

To press the pen against the body. Against the cold

belly, the pen. The darkness that flows from it. From the pen, the darkness. The wet darkness flowing from the pen. The ink. The pen, the body, and all that flows from one to the other.

The dog, the flower, the song . . .

>

The dog, the flower, the song, and all that flows between them. The dog we found that time amongst the flowers, with the birds singing all around, remember? The petals all fallen on the creature and the fur so cold we thought it dead but no, not dead, not lost, sleeping, the petals bright upon, fallen upon, bright upon, sleeping, waking, and the music the birds were making for themselves and of themselves, remember? And how we went home then, taking the dog with us, the scarlet flowers, the birdsong, and the poem we made from all of that, all that happened, together, and then home, and the book we chose, writing the poem down in the book, dark upon, dark upon the page, no, bright upon, falling, no, dying, no, but sleeping, awaking, the words awaking, awaking you, remember? How we fashioned it, the book, how we dressed it, caressed it, the book, how we disguised it, made a king and queen of it, together, how we married it, the book, made a bride of it, remember now, all to keep you from sleeping, the drugs we gave you, the powders, the golden dust that fell upon you, arousing, so bright upon your body, remember, the needles that pushed into you, to poison

you, no, but to save you, save you, with these few black
marks, the wetness, scratches, no, the pen, the body,
and all that flows between, not to murder you but to
bring desire to you, Angela, and if this could only be
the country of, the nation of, this will be the nation of
your skin, your body and blood, fallen, befallen, no,
arousing, dying, no, arousing this state of love, my part
in it, a pen moving across skin, across my daughter's
skin, the pen, the body, and all that flows between,
bright upon, dark upon the skin, poisoning, no, bright
upon, and that which is broken shall now be mended,
with these words, these words to set the heart beating,
across the breast, the face now, the face that slowly
takes on a shape, these words, fallen upon, failing, no,
the face becoming strange, malformed, no, the soft
wetness, shreds of skin, scratches, the black ink. Tiny
cries of pain, darkness. The writing become a poison,
and the face, a stranger's face. And the pen, now
finding only sickness, should lift from the body, from
the skin, but no, how can I stop from writing, how can
I, no, the dog, the flower, the song, no, to wake myself,
arouse myself, to let my eyes come open, the countless
tiny levers, to lift the pen from the body of the girl, to
let the eyes come open finally, blinking at the light that
burns into them, no, no . . .

Where was I? Painful, curled up. Shivering. Lying on a concrete floor, somebody standing over me, talking to me. A drift of words. A fog of colour in my eyes, a sparkle of sounds, pops and fizzes, and a face amongst them, a girl's face lowering, amongst the colours and the noise, a face coming down to greet me.

'Marlene?'

All cloudy in its form, in its beauty, wavering.

Angela . . .

'Marlene, come on.'

And then the face melting into view, properly now, with her arms round me so tightly, down on the floor with me and holding me close, and I tried to speak but could not.

'Marlene, for fuck's sake.'

I could not speak, my tongue all powdery, dry with words that had broken down, become dust; and then, with my spit, become a paste.

It was not her. No. Tupelo dragged me up with her, to a sitting position. I saw where I was then, the brick walls, the yellow light overhead. The car parked where it had always been, all day, waiting.

'Here, drink this.'

I took the bottle from Tupelo and drank from it, a long and shocking draft of liquid making its cold way down my throat, all the way to the stomach.

'Come on now, stand up.'

All around me lay strange objects: sachets of coffee, bits of tissue, keys, boiled sweets, leaflets, a book of stamps, coins, banknotes, a penknife, petrol coupons. The contents of my bag strewn about the floor where I was kneeling. A pen. The capsules of the drug, broken open.

'I got them inside you, as best I could.'

'How many?'

'Both of them.'

'Two?'

'That's all I could find. Jesus. Stand up.'

I did so. Tupelo held her hand out to me and I took it, and she pulled me to my feet. I was feeling a little better, the colours had settled within me, the noises also. The Lucy doing its job.

'Christ. What happened? What time is it?'

'I don't know.' Tupelo smiled. 'I threw it away, the watch. It's gone.'

'Oh . . .'

'It's late.'

'Right.'

Something was nagging at me, a flicker of doubt. I could not remember anything of the night's events. Where had the time gone to?

'Tupelo . . .'

'Yeah?'

'What day is it? Is it Friday?'

The girl nodded. She told me the day, the date, the month. She told the year. And I tried to place myself within the scale of it, within the knowledge. How did I know it was Friday? How did I know that?

'Shit.'

'What's wrong?'

'I . . . I don't know. What happened tonight?'

'Well I came back, didn't I, thinking it might be time to leave.'

'To what?'

'To leave, you know? Anyway, there you were in the car, rocking back and forth all crazy like, and when I got up close . . .'

'What? What was I doing?'

'Writing.'

How cold I felt then, at the mention of the word and the memories it brought back.

'Just writing, just sitting there going crazy with the pen and the book and your head rocking, like I said, and you were talking to yourself all the while, stuff I couldn't make out, moaning like. I didn't know what to do. The door was locked, I had to rip the plastic from the window. I had to . . .'

'OK.'

'I didn't know what to do.'

'You did fine.'

Still, the coldness all over me as I went to the car. The notebook lay on the back seat. I had been scratching at the book, attacking it even; pages had been ripped out, splashes of ink, and words, words were everywhere, scattered around. The walk to the beach, the visit to the club, and then apartment G, and everything that happened there. The night revealed in these few glances. And so sweet it was, to picture once more the girl lying there in the bed, waiting for the hand that would arouse her. So sweet and so real.

Oh god. What had really taken place?

The photograph. There was a small tear in it. Tiny, cramped lines of writing covered the image, unreadable now, unreadable, and it all came back to me then. The failing. I couldn't do it. I could not do it. I could not find the words that would bring the child alive, the sleeping child, I could not do it.

'Couldn't do what? Marlene, what is it? I can't hear you. You couldn't do what?'

A terrible despair welled up inside me. I felt adrift from myself, as though it were somebody else's hands that gripped at the door frame so tightly. Somebody else's blood poured through my body, enough to make the heart work, but no more, no more than that.

'Marlene, what is this?'

Tupelo was touching at the hands, working them loose. How pitiful they looked. How could these two instruments have ever considered putting pen to paper.

'Where did you get this?'

The words brought me back down a little, and then completely. There, printed on the back of my hand, my left hand, a violet snake lay curled.

>

We walked down to the beach together. The rain had just started to fall, and all the lights strung along the front glistened amid a surrounding halo, like blossoms. The neon signs of the pier were going out one by one, each with its attendant cloud of sparks; the colours hung suspended around the dead bulbs, unwilling to leave the sky. I was aware of the beauty of the world, and the underlying darkness from which the beauty arose. At one point I glanced in the direction of the writer's apartment, but could not really make it out from this distance, a building amongst others. Every so often a child's face would float upwards into my mind, a blank mask, devoid of signs.

It must have been well past midnight. The bars had closed. Only the clubs were still open, a few people gathered around the doorways. Darker figures could be seen on the beach itself, down by the sea. The flames of the bonfire burned low.

We found Henderson outside the Snake Pit. She looked worried, distraught even.

'What's wrong?'

'It's Peacock. I can't find him.'

She had been drinking heavily. I had never seen her this bad before; her face was drained white, ghostly, and her eyes would not stop moving.

'I can't find him. We had an argument.'

'It's OK now,' I said. 'We'll look for him.'

'Yeah, we'll split up.'

'No,' said Tupelo. 'We stay together.'

And so we set off along the beach. Henderson had the suitcase in her hand, I had only just noticed. Peacock must have given it to her, or else she had taken it off him. The rain was coming down heavier. Tupelo produced a woollen hat from her bag; she offered it to me, and then to Henderson, and we both refused. The girl pulled the hat down over her hair. She took hold of my hand. I did not question the strangeness of the gesture.

'What happened to Jamie?'

Henderson did not answer. She was looking all around, her face still troubled.

'Bev, listen. I was in the club tonight, wasn't I? The Snake Pit?'

Finally, she turned to me. 'You were there.'

'And the kid, Jamie?'

'Jamie, yeah. There was some trouble. You went a bit crazy, and you ran off. That was it.'

'Right.'

'Where did you go? You went to see Cole?'

'No. No, I just went walking.'

We came to a darker, lonelier, part of the beach, a line of closed-up souvenir shops. The giant painted hand over the fortune teller's booth looked down at me, with the mystical eye held in its palm. The lines of love, life and destiny were marked. One area of the hand was called, for some reason, the Realm of Venus.

'There he is.'

Tupelo pointed down along the walkway. Peacock was standing there with another man, just beyond the yellow glow of a lamp. They looked to be deep in conversation.

'Who's he talking to?' asked Henderson.

'I don't know.'

The two men embraced. They looked, with their arms locked around each other tightly, like very good friends who now must sadly part. And they broke away from the closeness. Peacock remained standing where he was, but the other man stepped forward into the light.

'It's the driver,' said Tupelo.

'Who?'

'Fuck,' said Henderson. 'What's he doing here?'

It was the chauffeur of the limousine. The man nodded to us briefly, smiling, and then climbed a set of steps leading up to the promenade.

Peacock came towards us. Into the light, and then through the light, with his big coat wrapped round him, and his lovely porkpie hat on his head, just so, at the exact correct angle, with the rain dripping off the brim. And he came right up to Henderson.

He said, 'Bev, there ain't nobody like you.'

Henderson would not give in, not that easily. 'What were you doing there?'

'Talking.'

'What about?'

'About the passenger. Sorting it out.'

'And is it?'

343

'It's done.'

'This isn't to do with Billy, is it?' said Tupelo. 'Billy the Bandit?'

'I'm telling you, they won't trouble us any more.'

'Good,' said Henderson. 'That's good.'

'Is it time to go?' asked the girl.

'It sure is.' Peacock's voice turned quiet. 'Christ. I've had enough of this world.'

'This what?'

'This place. Come on.'

We climbed the steps ourselves, then, back to the promenade. There was no sign of the chauffeur, no sign of the red limousine. The city was preparing for sleep, or was in sleep already. Only the moon still seemed fully awake, watchful, behind its thin curtain of cloud. And where do we go from here, that was my one question to myself. Where do we go . . .

'Jesus, it's cold,' said Peacock.

We had just found the little street that led to the car park, but Peacock was reluctant to go on.

'What's wrong?' said Henderson.

'I can't . . .'

'Come on. What's wrong with you?'

'Nothing. I just need to . . .'

One of his hands was slipped inside his jacket, and he groaned, and fell back against the wall. We were standing outside a little shop that in the daytime sold second-hand books; now the place was closed up, all dark, and Peacock was leaning against the wall just next to the doorway with his two hands clutched to his stomach.

'Peacock?'

'Cold . . . so cold.'

I had seen this before. The brick wall, the exact markings on it, and Peacock's face held tight with some pain he could no longer keep hidden. There was blood coming through his fingers. And he stayed there quite still for a moment, before sliding to the ground.

'Oh fuck!'

Henderson ran to him. She went down on her knees, pulling open the two leaves of his coat. The wound was there, the terrible stain. Tupelo made a noise, some little noise. How can this be? Why was this happening? Why? Why the fuck was this happening?

'He's not breathing.'

'What?'

'Help me. Oh please.'

Henderson was bent down with the side of her head pressed against Peacock's chest, listening.

'There's nothing there. I can't hear anything.'

'Shit . . .'

'He's not . . .' Tupelo came to my side. 'He's not dead, is he?' Her voice was quiet, so quiet.

'Go and get the car.'

Henderson was just kneeling down next to Peacock's body, touching it, nothing more than that, and speaking, whispering. She used his first name, his one proper name.

'John? Johnny . . .'

'How do you tell?' I asked. 'How do you tell?'

'Here, let me . . .'

'Tupelo, the car.'

'Try this.'

The girl had pulled the mirror from her bag.

345

>

The little mirror, the stupid mirror, the folding vanity mirror. The green plastic casing with its sad and weary corporate symbol. The casing which, when unfolded, lays bare the glass, the pitted surface all covered in marks and hardly large enough to contain a face. The sickened glass, which, held gently now against a man's mouth for a moment or two, a long enough moment or two, can then be examined; and a mist will be found there, the ghost of breath, which is the one true sign and evidence of life itself.

5

>

Travelling, we were travelling. Rolling slowly through the darkness with the rain clinging to the windows, and the wind holding itself hard against our progress. I no longer knew where we were; a long stretch of motorway without any lights, the road becoming any and all roads, all of them empty, all inconsolable. Myself, falling into and out of sleep.

Coming awake, sleeping again, curling myself on the back seat, awakening; little spots of rain finding their way through the plastic sheeting. And always the same image coming to me, lingering between. The face of the child covered in words, in flows of ink, stirring, half-formed, beneath my pen.

Occasionally we would pass a household of some kind, a light far off in the distance that held out its promise, but we could have been lost in another realm entirely for all the kinship I could feel. Once we saw a building on fire, a spirit that danced in the hills.

Tupelo turned on the radio. Music was playing, some highly patterned affair, Bach, I think, with the notes all broken and rearranged into new melodies. They didn't quite work; sudden changes of mood and tonality would startle the ear. Every so often, a man's voice would stray into the music, speaking of love.

Tupelo's doing well. She's driving as best she can, given the vehicle's condition. Occasionally, I will feel the car veer to one side, or else slow right down without reason, faltering, before regaining power.

'It's on its last legs,' she said. 'I mean wheels. It's on its last wheels.'

We did not talk much, the girl and I, during the drive. We were heading towards Oxford, Kingsley's house. This was Henderson's idea, her last insistence. Let it be finished. I have given her a piece of the mirror. Just the one, it was all she would accept. For the sake of Peacock, she said. I don't know which one she has chosen.

Hours, hours of driving.

Traffic signs, glimpsed in the rain beneath their hooded lamps. Words, names, diagrams, circles and arrows, all would flash by, all a blur.

At one point I felt a tingling on my hand, and when I looked, the printed image of a snake was moving there, writhing on the skin. Perhaps we were no longer in England. I let myself picture the car passing through some strange gateway, into a land of constant wandering; no towns, no cities, and no names on any signpost.

There was blood on the seat, from when we drove Peacock to the hospital. I can't help feeling that it was all my fault; not so much that I dragged him into this, because it was always his own choosing; rather, that I never mentioned the photograph to him, the one that I burned in the old woman's house. Or not that even;

no, but that I should have let Henderson know about it, about the foreseen wound.

The deep red stain on the shirt, the stain turning to look like a flower, and then becoming a flower.

I think Peacock knew. His gun is lying on the floor of the car, at my feet. He did not use it. I think he had seen the moment himself, coming upon him. The embrace. And maybe this is why he could cheat it, he could embrace it. He could embrace the knife.

He did not use the gun.

But still, to keep in mind the roads we had taken together; the roads taken, the roads forsaken.

'Look at that,' said Tupelo. 'We're being watched.'

It was not the moon, but the moon's sister. There she was, painted onto a bank of cloud, projected from some building or other; the vast golden eye of the company, looking down upon the world.

>

Awakening. Still dark, but the sky was soft along one edge, the first tinges of the sun. The rain had drifted away. We were no longer on the motorway, but travelling down a smaller road, lined with hedges, the occasional house or farm building.

'I'm looking for somewhere to stop.'

'Are we there yet?'

'What? No. But I'm tired. And we need petrol.'

'OK.'

I felt strange. There was a voice, a whisper, coming from somewhere nearby; from my own head, I thought, but no, the voice was separate from me. It was coming from inside the car.

'Tupelo, is the radio on?'

'No.'

The road atlas lay open on the seat beside me. Pages had been torn out from it, by my own hand presumably, although I could not remember doing such a thing. On the floor, Peacock's gun, and my bag, and the shoes I had taken off many miles before. The suitcase. And my notebook, again with loose pages scattered about it. I picked this up now. I had not looked at the book since,

352

since when? Since the underground car park, that would be the last time. It wasn't too bad; most of the pages were still intact. I flicked through them, I looked inside the pocket. No. It was not there.

The photograph. Angela's photograph.

I found it underneath the front passenger seat. My fingers moved across the rip I had made in the top edge. How could I have been so cruel, to have damaged it so?

This one point of connection.

A purple smoke, lit from within, floated upwards from the image. That's all I could see, with flecks of words suspended in the mist. I remembered the journey in the elevator, and the memories it brought. Playing the word game, when the photo was taken. Angela turning back to me, after the camera had flashed, with the word on her lips.

What was it now? I could not retrieve the word.

And yet, and yet here was the voice. It was coming from the photograph; from the image revealed, its dark swirl of colours, its consummate beauty. And the voice.

The voice, almost heard.

>

We found a place. I don't know what it was, exactly. It called itself a Traveller's Inn. Small, family run, half a cheap motel, half a transport café. There was a petrol pump, a garage, where we filled the tank. This would be the last measure; the mechanic shook his head at the sorry state of the car, and smiled. We went inside to order breakfast. I said to Tupelo that I could book a room for the day, the night to come, if she wanted to sleep. She said to leave it for now, see how it goes. The food was nothing but slop and grease, and the finest meal I had eaten in days. It was still very early, and the place was quiet. A couple of lorry drivers occupied one table; some young people were sitting at another, over in the corner. We had seen a painted van outside, which must have been theirs. I don't know why, but I had the idea they might be a band of musicians. They were playing chess. There was one other diner, a middle-aged man who sat alone, staring into space.

When our coffees arrived, Tupelo searched through my bag for the capsules. We had taken some from Henderson, at the hospital. The girl made me swallow the drug, looking after me. Time was passing, but I didn't know how, or why. The snake lay on my hand, not moving now, just a printed image, nothing more. I felt that I would never be free of this story, not whilst the creature had claim to me. I got some saliva onto my fingertips and rubbed at the skin.

'Marlene, leave that now.'

'It won't come off.'

'Leave it.'

The waitress came to our table, with the cake that Tupelo had ordered. The girl looked at the pastry, and then at me, shaking her head. Her mouth came open as though to speak.

'What is it?'

'How can I say this, but I think you're right.'

'Am I?'

'You know what I'm thinking about? I'm thinking about the tube.'

'The what?'

'The tube, Marlene. The juice. You know, they stick this tube in your neck, suck it out.'

'Jesus.'

'Yeah, it was going to the hospital, with Peacock. All those machines they have, I mean, how's the noise affecting them? Badly, right? Sure, they have their special devices, all that. But I just got to thinking, this isn't right. It's not fair.'

She looked through the window. Another lorry was just arriving; once it had parked, our car could no longer be seen.

'I'm going to let them take it out of me.'

'That's good.'

'It's not good. But I'm doing it. I was always scared,

you know, that they'd take too much out. And then, well, I'd get the sickness.'

'I don't think it works like that.'

'But you'll come with me, right? We'll find a place, a hospital, on our journey?'

'Journey . . .'

'Yeah, our journey. We'll find a place.'

I closed my eyes, nodded.

'Marlene? What's wrong?'

'Nothing. I . . .'

'Tell me.'

I let my eyes come open. The girl was looking at me, her face held soft, and loving almost. There were so many questions, so many desires.

'Tupelo, why did you come back?'

'What?'

'In the car park, you came back. You found me.'

The girl shrugged.

'Why?'

'You know why.'

'Do I?'

'Don't make me say it, Marlene, not out loud. What's wrong with you? We're here now, we're together. Isn't that good? Isn't that, you know . . . enough?'

'Enough?'

'The two of us. Enough.'

'Oh, Tupelo . . .'

'What? What now?'

'Look at me.'

'I'm looking.'

'I already have a daughter.'

'Yes, but . . . but she's . . .'

'No. She's still with me.'

There. It was said. It was painful, saying it, and seeing Tupelo's eyes turn away from me, and the way her lips were set.

'I know that,' she whispered. 'I do know that.'

'Good.'

'But we can stay together, for a while. I mean, I'd like us to. I'd like it.'

'We're not going to Oxford, are we?'

The girl shook her head, just the once.

'Where are we going?'

'I don't know. Anywhere.'

What could I say? And how bad would it be, at that? Just to travel around the country with this girl. We could sell the pieces of the mirror, make some money that way, some good money. We could do anything.

I looked around the café. The man who sat alone, he was staring at me.

Tupelo took hold of my hand. 'You don't mind?'

'No, I don't mind. Anywhere.'

The girl smiled. She nodded towards the young people, the chess table. 'I might have a game?'

'Sure. Whatever.'

'Good. Listen, something I was thinking about.'

'What's that?'

'Peacock won't die.'

'No. I don't think so.'

'I know he won't. Because he's already died once. He killed himself, didn't he? And you can't die twice. I'm right on that?'

'You can't die twice.'

Tupelo stood up. 'There you are. There you are.'

'We're forgetting something.'

'Are we?'

'Keep it sweet. Go on.'

'Me? I don't have to say it.'

'Go on.'

'Yeah. OK then. Keeping it sweet.'

She walked away from me.

Alone now, I let my thoughts gather, allowing the drug to find its course through me. I pictured the veins with their cargo, the plenitude, the flavour. I saw the nerves, the brainstem, receiving the message, open up! The five senses following suit, as they could, to let in this damaged world; the noxious smells from the kitchen, the aftertaste of the food, the chequered shirt of the lorry driver walking over towards the counter, the stickiness of the table top under my fingers, the flawed rhythm of the pop records playing on the juke-box. All this, all this being calibrated by the drug, balanced and counterbalanced, adjusted for, as it could.

Such is the way we now live; only by these constant readjustments can any overall picture form itself, real or otherwise. And yet, could we not instead attend to the details, directly; to the grain of the wood that the table is made from, rather than the table itself? This table here, this grain, this splash of ketchup, the exact and hidden shape and colour and texture of the world, the unknown song.

Surrounded by phantoms in the noonday, trembling under a breeze when the leaves were still . . .

I noticed that Tupelo had left her shoulder bag behind. Good. I lifted the suitcase onto the seat. I had the key in my pocket, there being no need to hide it any

358

more. I looked over at the chess players. Tupelo was playing a game, sitting with her back to me. There was laughter, some joke being told. Under cover of the table, I opened the suitcase. Only the tiniest way, to let my hand reach in and pull out one of the pieces, a velvet-covered fragment of glass. Whichever magic it held, it was small enough to slide into Tupelo's bag, without trouble. Then I looked in my wallet; I took out half of the money, and put that into Tupelo's bag, on top of the mirror. I thought about leaving a note, an apology of some kind, but decided against it. Finally, I picked up the car keys from the table. The cake was still there, left uneaten.

It was done. A sadness unfolded. But I had to leave the girl to her life, her own life. There was no other choice. I walked out of the café.

Tupelo. I never did know her second name.

It wasn't that long a time since I'd last driven the car, a week, perhaps two, but it felt like some months had gone by, and I had changed since then, grown worse in the sickness, and the car the same. We were bound together, held one within the other.

A cold morning coming up, the mist rising from the fields. I was keeping to the back roads, taking whichever turn I fancied, as they came along. I didn't have a clue as to where I was, or where I was heading. I made my way down yet another side road, and then craned round in the seat to look behind me.

The other car was still there.

I had first noticed it a few miles before, a green car tailing me, taking every turn I did, and matching my speed exactly. I couldn't understand it. I had no other desire, just at that moment, than to be on my own, to be rid of all human company. To find a place for myself where I could rest up, sort myself out, maybe work on the journal a little. I would put my thoughts in order, and then decide on the next move. This was all I had in mind, and yet here was this shadow following me. What was it doing? Why wouldn't it leave me alone?

I stopped the car.

The second car stopped as well, a few yards behind, and the two of us waited there, for one or the other to make a move.

Nothing happened.

I reached round to pull the gun from the back seat. I placed this in my bag and then climbed out of the car. The other driver stepped out as well. I walked over to him. His vehicle was a family estate model, with nothing to distinguish it. I could hear music being played, from the car's interior. The man was leaning against the door frame, and he waited until I was but a few steps away before he spoke.

'Where are you going?'

It was the middle-aged man I had seen in the café, the lone diner.

'What?'

'Are you running away?'

'What do you want?'

'I'm just asking. I'm being friendly.'

'I really can't—'

'Are you running away?'

'No.'

'I think you are.'

'What is this?'

'You're running away. You're leaving that girl in there, in the café, alone in there. You're running off from her. I saw you.'

He gave a smile at this judgement. It was a filthy smile, a dirty smile. It fitted well with his face, his slack cheeks and neck, his baggy eyes, his fraying hair. The smell of his body lingered beneath cheap cologne.

'Listen now,' he said. 'Do you like this music?'

'It's OK.'

'It's a piano. You like jazz piano?'

'I don't—'

'Listen to it. Listen!'

His voice turned suddenly angry. I had to work this situation, without showing my fear, and so we stood there for a while, the two of us, listening to the ballad being played. In truth I could find little wrong with it. This was the clearest, brightest sound I had heard in months. There seemed to be no sickness in it. I wasn't used to such expression.

'It sounds good.'

'Oh yeah. Beautiful. What's your name? Come on now, don't be shy. I'm Henry. Henry Jackson.' He held his hand out to me. 'Pleased to meet you.'

'OK. Henry. I'm just going to walk away now. Back to my car.'

'Are you?' His hand dropped away, untouched. 'Who is she? The girl? A relative?'

'No.'

'Your lover?'

'Just a friend.'

'And you run away, from a friend?'

'Leave me alone.'

'What's in the case?'

'The what?'

'The silver case. What's inside it?'

'Nothing.'

Jackson smiled. He pushed away from the door.

'Can I see it?'

'It's nothing. Papers.'

362

'Papers?'

'Documents. Look, I really do have to—'

'I know what's in there. I know it. It's always the same. Something special. Something beautiful, deadly. I can see. I can see your eyes. I know. I do know.'

I looked around. There was nobody else in sight, not a soul, and only fields of wheat on either side.

Jackson held his arms out wide. 'Ah now. What a view that is. You come out here, there's no shit. Everything means just what it means, and nothing more.'

He moved closer still.

'Keep away from me. I have a gun.'

'Oh, that's nice.'

'What do you want? Why are you following me? Tell me what you want.'

The man looked at me. A look of despair crossed his face. 'Where are you going? Really now? Really?'

'I don't know.'

'Oh . . .'

A weariness, a sadness.

'Oh. That is a shame.'

'What do you want?'

'Help me. Please. I need help.'

He brought his hands up to his face, rubbing at the loose skin around his cheeks, his neck. There were tears in his eyes, just then. And he pulled the hands away, staring at them.

'Do you like my hands? Look at my hands. Have you ever seen hands like these?'

He held them out to me, palm upwards, and then turned them over, and back again. They were smooth and clean and free of all blemish, a young man's hands.

363

'You like them? Do you?'

'Yes . . .'

'Of course you fucking do. Jesus.'

'What is it?'

He backed away from me a little. His body seemed to fold up within itself.

'I don't know what to do. Where to go. Help me.'

'Is it the sickness?'

'Help me . . .'

'You want some Lucy?'

'No. Not that.'

He looked at me, nervous now. His hands moved around of their own accord.

'I'm thinking of getting my face done next. What do you think? It might be dangerous. I don't know. What do you think? Do you like my face?'

'I . . .'

'Do you like it?'

'Henry, there's nothing wrong with you, with your face. Nothing wrong.'

'Just like it is?'

'Just like it is.'

'You know, when all this trouble started, all this noise, I was thinking to myself, well that's good isn't it? Nobody will know what I look like any more. But it's not like that, is it? It's not like that.'

His eyes had a cold look in them.

'I am getting tired. I have to tell you. All this disrespect that people are showing me.'

'I'm not—'

'Shut the fuck up. What is it? I talk to you. I show you my kindness, can't you be friendly?'

364

'I don't—'

'Please, there's something I have to show you.'

'Now look, you're not going to—'

'To what?'

Finally, the smile came back to him, softer now, as though the anger had burned itself away. He moved round, towards the rear of the car.

'It's in here.'

He put a hand on the boot. I was thinking about how far this would go. Whether I could shoot him or not. Or else just run away, take my chances.

'I really do have a gun.'

'Let me see.'

I took the gun out of my bag. Jackson looked at it, and then at me.

'Is it loaded? Is the safety off?'

'I don't know.'

'Of course you don't.'

'Do you know?'

Jackson sighed. 'I'm not going to hurt you. In fact, the exact opposite.'

'What is it?'

'You've seen my hands. Look at them. See? How clean they are, how young. And the music? How good it sounds, the purity of it.'

'So?'

'The purity. Listen to me. I have a road atlas. Oh, would you like to see that? The whole country, mapped out precisely. I know where I am, where I'm going. And look here, you see? The time.'

He waved his hand in front of me, too quickly for me to see his wristwatch properly.

'All these things. All cured.'

'What are you saying?'

'In here, in the boot. Travelling around with me. There are others, I think. A woman in Glasgow. Only rumours. Some strange thing in her cellar. These little places where the noise doesn't work.'

I remembered Peacock speaking about the Lucidity Engine. Could this be such a thing?

'Let me see.'

'Why, have you got something? Have you something you want making clean? Have you?'

I thought about the notebook, the photograph. How could I not think about them? Both or either one of them coming clean, being cleansed, made anew. I thought about what that would mean, how good that would be.

'Henry, let me see it.'

'Oh, but can I trust you? Because I've almost been killed, a number of times. People desire this. They want it so much. I don't know what to do. Why can't people be kind to me? Why can't they?'

'I don't know.'

'You don't know . . .'

His eyes clouded over. And I saw then that Jackson was just one more lonely person, on the run. On the run from shadows.

I let the gun drop to my side.

And, seeing this, Jackson nodded. He turned his key in the lock, and the boot sprang open.

'There was something about you,' he said. 'I thought you might be of the same kind. A carrier. Something. In the café I saw that in you. The look, the suitcase. I just knew that you would be kind. I really do value that, in a person.'

He reached into the boot, shifting something aside.

'Take a look. Come on.'

He was speaking in a whisper now, as though scared of what was contained within. And I moved round to stand beside him. I looked inside the boot.

'Well then?' he asked.

'Where is it?'

'What?'

'I can't—'

'What's wrong with you? There it is.'

He pulled aside some more clothing, bits of rag, old newspapers, plastic bags, odds and ends, a petrol can. Some of these things fell out onto the ground. Jackson seemed not to care any more. He was clearing a space in one corner of the boot, working frantically now, and talking the whole time.

'The light, can't you see it? A green light. There! Just there. The sphere of light, flickering. Careful now. It's fragile. Tender. See it now? And the sound it makes. Listen. Can't you hear it? A purring sound. So quiet. You have to listen very carefully. Go on. Put your hands near to it, up against it. The warmth. Can't you feel it?'

'I . . . I'm not sure.'

'You're not looking properly. Here.'

Jackson stepped aside, to allow me access. And I followed his desires; I tried my best to see the thing, I really did.

There was nothing there. The boot was empty.

'Can't you see it? Surely you can see it?'

'Yes.'

'You do? Oh, I knew that you would. I just knew that you'd have the eye for it. Not everybody does, you know? Oh no, but only the special ones. Yourself . . .'

'It's beautiful.'

And what else could I say, really?

Jackson smiled. 'There it is. Yourself. Myself. We shall join ourselves together, in this gift.'

'Together?'

'Surely now, to lay ourselves open, and be cleansed.'

'No . . .'

'But please, if you would only stay with me. I can't stop myself from using it, returning. Alone. Returning. I can't stop. It pains me.'

He let out a breath.

'Will you join me?'

I shook my head.

'You don't want to?'

'I can't. I can't help you.'

'Please . . .'

'I'm sorry.'

I turned round. The long walk back to my own car, the long walk. Jackson's voice, calling. Only when I was safely behind the wheel, with the engine started, did I look back.

The man had fallen to the ground. I saw his hands come up, his lovely hands rising upwards, as though still to be offered.

\>

I moved on. Open country, slowly giving way to trees, and the pale sun climbing. I would pass the occasional other vehicle, or a man walking the roadside, or people working the farmlands. And then the forest closed in and I saw nothing but the trees themselves, still in leaf.

Driving, only driving; only drifting.

The car started to move across the road from side to side, without my command, the wheel slipping in my hands. I should have stopped then; I thought of stopping but then the car would right itself, giving control back to me. The journey was not quite done.

From the radio, only sighs of breath.

The trees extended their branches over the road from both sides, meeting, then mingling, and the sun was not yet bright or high enough to find its way between. The leaves took on a darkened splendour only seen in a dream. Trails of vapour moved through the trees. A bird flew across the road in front of me, so drowsily I could note every flap of its wings. The car slowed down of its own accord, or else made sleepy, embraced by light and air. The instrument panels on the dashboard, the speedometer, the mileometer, the clock, the petrol gauge, the radio dial, all of them were shrouded over by colours, tiny glimmers, sparks of noise. The car's interior hummed with heat, drops of sweat rolled down into my eyes. There was one last road sign, a plain white rectangle from which, as I drove towards it, a large golden flower blossomed, its petals unfurling like smoke, and then becoming smoke, and disappearing into the branches overhead.

Again, I thought of stopping the car, but my foot pressing on the brake pedal had no real effect. All the various lines between message sent, and received, had now been severed.

I took my hands off the wheel.

The car carried on for a short while. It could only have been a few metres, no more, and yet it seemed beyond measuring. Time was a slow liquid through which we moved, now swerving towards the trees. A bank of earth slowed us even more, and we crested the rise at an easy pace and then slid to a halt against an old, blackened tree trunk. The seat belt embraced me round the heart, so gently. I felt that we had caressed the tree, rather than hitting it. A scuffle of birds flew away through the branches, and then all was still.

>

Everything seemed to be fine, until I opened the door and tried to climb out of the car. A dizziness came over me, and I fell to the ground, the air singing around me. And I lay there in the grass for a time, a good time, I don't know how long a time, just lying there. A web of branches intertwined above me, with the sky glimpsed through them in patterns, and the spell of heat moving across my face in copy of the patterns, of wood, of sunlight, all these things in combination holding me in thrall.

The car groaned beside me, a final settling. My hand started to itch, and when I brought it up to my face I saw there the snake curling and uncurling. It was enough to rouse me, and I stood up. The road lay empty and quiet to both sides; a thin plume of smoke lingered over the car. The birds had returned to the trees, with their sparkle of notes.

I went to the car and got from it all that I needed, or thought that I needed. My bag. The notebook, and all the torn-out pages that I could find. The photograph of Angela. I had some other clothes in the boot; I didn't take much, just a few extra items to keep me going.

There was no plan to this, no expectations, beyond seeing where this road would lead.

I had to decide what to do with the gun, Peacock's gun. I couldn't imagine any use I might have for such an object, not now, but in the end I decided it best to bring it along, rather than leaving it for somebody to find. I placed the gun in my bag.

Finally, the suitcase. The key.

All was done. I took one last look around me, and then I walked away from the car.

I chose the same direction I had been driving in, following the road beneath its canopy of trees. At one point a van passed me, going back the way I came; it slowed down and then drove on, and I gave no sign of wanting anything more, only to carry on walking.

I was still a little unnerved by the encounter with Jackson. He had accused me of running away, of running off from Tupelo. And this was true, of course. There seemed no other option, but why was this? To always be leaving people, and places. And would a time ever come when I could dare to surrender myself?

As I walked slowly on, my thoughts began to drift at random, in rhythm with my progress; a series of stray images, pulled from the darkness. Pictures, memories. And once again I was looking out through my bedroom window, that night, that long ago winter's night with my father standing near the car, talking with the driver. Once again I saw the breath issuing from his mouth as he spoke. Across the years, these clouds of white breath, their exact flowing patterns. If there were only some method by which these shapes could

372

be decoded, I would know the words he spoke that night.

I would know.

A voice of mist that fades on the air.

And now, with these thoughts in mind, step by step, I came to realize that some other presence walked along with me. Something moved within the forest, something of silver that crackled the leaves and snapped at branches, and I stopped and waited as, a moment later, it came forward out of the trees.

It was a horse, a most handsome creature, with its ivory coat, its long head; its gleaming eye of the deepest blue, with which it regarded me. A moment passing, as we looked at each other. And then the creature turned the muscled length of its body round the trunk of a tree, and set off deeper into the forest. And I followed the horse, moving through the cool shadows.

The sunlight was finding its way in places between the trees, and where it did, the flowers were opening. They were spreading wide their blaze of petals, and releasing their delicate scents. Butterflies, wasps and other flying insects were responding to these signals without problem, without any problem, and I pictured the grains of pollen transported from stamen to pistil, male to female.

There was evidence of humanity still, in the various small objects that littered the undergrowth: a shoe, some playing cards, a matchbox, pages torn from a pornographic magazine, and so on. At one point I heard a noise, a regular ticking sound that I recognized even before I came across the clock, the old grandfather clock that stood amidst the trees with its face obscured by a tangle of vines. I felt no surprise at this, not even at the fact that it was still going, the slow pendulum still travelling its repeated arc. Fading now, as I moved away, the soft ticking of the mechanism was the very last sign of human life. I took Peacock's gun from my bag, and cast it aside, far into the trees.

The horse walked ahead of me, weaving a pathway. The further we went, the more I seemed to lose all sense of myself, and my surroundings. Now, in recollection, I can use these various words: horse, tree, gun, flower, clock, Marlene. But just then I no longer knew the name of the creature that roamed ahead; I no longer knew the name of the strange objects that grew all around me. I no longer knew what it was I should call myself, not even this; neither my being, my species, nor my given name.

Presently, seen first only as flashes of light, of reflection, the forest gave way to a body of water. The horse led me down to the weed-covered banks of this lake, and then stood watching me for a moment, before moving away, slowly back into the forest.

I was alone.

There was a small cleared area, where I thought I would rest a while. Nearby, tall yellow flowers drooped their crowned heads over the water. The sun's light was lying aslant on the lake, a mild shimmering effect that calmed the eyes. And then, on the bank opposite I saw another person, sitting as I was, partially hidden behind the flowers and the weeds. The figure could not be made out clearly.

Finally, the idea came to me.

I moved right down to the water's edge. I took the key from my pocket, using it to unlock the suitcase. The lid clicked open.

There they were, the pieces of the mirror. Six to start with, and two given away, one to Henderson and Peacock, one to Tupelo. Four pieces remaining, all contained in velvet. I lifted out the first one, pulling open the folds of material. The glass sparkled. I did not look into it. I did not know which particular fragment it might be. Briefly, I thought of Kingsley, and what he would do if he could see me now, his anger. Enough of that. Holding the mirror by one sharp corner, I lowered it gently into the water.

A darkness shifted inside me.

With the next two pieces I did the same, allowing them both to slide beneath the surface. Looking up, I felt that the person opposite was doing the same as I was; some few objects of her own possession were entering the lake's care.

Glass to glass, liquid to liquid.

Reflections caress. And the water, which had been brown and muddy to begin with, this close to the bank, was now taking on a silvery hue.

There was one piece of mirror left, and this I unwrapped from its covering. There seemed little else left to do. And just then I heard a man's quiet voice, a singing voice. It was coming from the glass, from the violet shine of the glass. It was the same piece that Henderson had looked into, at the motorway service station. Something came over me.

I laid the mirror flat on the ground, reflective side

uppermost. I touched the surface with my hand. It was warm, and quite solid to begin with, but then, as I pressed further, the glass seemed to dissolve around my fingers. It became liquid, and then pressing further on, it became a mist, a silvery mist, and now my hand was through, into the mirror's world.

Immediately, I felt the sadness of this world, and the pain, and the song came louder now, with its melody filled with such yearning. It was a song I knew, from my childhood. I had not remembered it until this moment. And then, as my hand ventured deeper within, I found that I was stroking at skin, at the face of the singer, the damp lips, the tongue, the tongue from which the song came, and the tears sprang into my eyes, unbidden.

I pulled my hand back out from the glass. The fingers were wet with spittle. What could I do? What possible balm could there be, to lessen the pain? And so I picked up this last piece of the mirror. I gave back to the water that which belonged to the water, and the song was lulled away, turned to silence.

I leaned over.

Seeing myself. The face that was held beneath the surface, a drowned woman, staring back at me.

I thought, this is my ending. This is the ending shown to me, in the photographer's studio. That one glimpse I had of myself sinking into the pool of silver. Floating, trying to move myself forward and then falling, not sinking, but slowly falling. Submerging. It was a calling within the blood, that I should walk naked into the lake, allowing the water to take hold of me. And I knew that if I did this now, the figure on the opposite bank would do the same, would strip herself naked following me, and likewise lower herself into the water. We would meet beneath the surface and all of this, all of the troubles endured since Angela's passing, they would melt away in the cold depths, and be laid finally to rest. And I remembered Kingsley's words, his dream of what the mirror would bring, once healed. A door of bright and liquid silver, he called it, a way through . . .

This was it. I could not turn away from the drowned woman, this one temptation, and, reaching forward, I let my fingers play amongst the contours of the face. I felt I had dipped my hand in mercury. The image rippled, becoming lost, and then slowly re-forming itself. And I found in there, in place of my own features, the now clearly seen lines of my daughter's face; as though the one contained the other.

Which it did, which it did.

Angela. Her tender, wavering expression.

My hand slipped deeper into the water, without my choosing. The face closed round my wrist. Something stirred within me. A beating heart. It was not of any great notice, all told; a small releasing and nothing more. A simple refusal.

No. It would not end here, and not in this way.

Nothing more. But such a moment; so pure, and so forgiving. The water glistened. The snake uncurled itself. The violet snake shifted on my skin, and was then washed clean, its thin transparent body drifting away through the shallows.

And I rose up. The woman on the opposite bank rose with me, in accord. We had both given something to the lake, and taken something back in return. Here was love. And we turned and walked away, both of us, each to our own direction.

Hushed and slow now, through the trees, through the early morning mist, the clock was sounding the hour.

Around each chime, the forest breathed.

>

I have been working this last week on the book, the story. With scissors, with paste; with pen and pencil, eraser, ink; alcohol and powder. Composing from shadows, from glances, and the voices I can still sometimes hear, belonging to my good companions on the road, lost now, all lost. They have journeys of their own.

These words. Some of which are missing completely, and here, well, I have let desire take over; remembering as I can, even as the noise creeps further into the pages. The sickness grows worse within me, in tandem. I'm taking the Lucy four or five times daily, perhaps more. I do not know where it will end.

Reading, rereading.

This drab little room I have rented, in a village I do not know the name of. The money is almost gone. I have reduced myself. This patch of sunlight on the desk, the blue-striped tiger, the book. The soft colours of the pressed flower, still visible. My hand, this pen, these lines of writing. And all that flows from one to the other.

I keep thinking about the sleeper, the sleeping ghost

that I almost gave breath to, story to. Perhaps she did awake, maybe she did, real or unreal. Perhaps Cole finished the task for me. I picture her in the apartment, playing with the young boys, the other children of the mirror. Let that be.

Soon, I will move on. Another vehicle, a lift, a stolen car even. Who knows. I may even find a place to settle, but not yet. Not yet.

In these days of chaos, possibilities abound.

I shall leave this book on the nightstand, in between the traveller's bible and the telephone directory. These pages of smoke. They have their own conclusion. I can only hope that some other sweeter device or agency will cast its spell upon them, making them clean, and the world alongside.

Listen now. Whoever you are, with these eyes of yours that move themselves along this line of text; whoever, wherever, whenever. If you can read this sentence, this one fragile sentence, it means you're alive.

>

Only the photograph. The one thing left to me. How it blossoms in my sight. It burns. Or else clouding over, a murmur of scent arises. In scarlet and blue it cradles; in crimson and gold it may scatter and swirl, unfold, dispersing itself. Now, let these colours cascade. Let these whispers awaken; let these sparkles compose, gleam forth, froth and foam, fizzle, burst, enclose and caress themselves, speaking themselves. Now let this tongue emerge from the light that fell once on a garden, on a child's face, on chemicals. Let the picture overflow from itself, spilling itself. It spills over and spells out the word of itself, and then dispelling itself, making a game of itself, a flame of itself, the blossom and bloom and perfume of itself. Only the photograph. This word, this tiny word, almost known. Almost spoken. Louder now, softer. I will wait. Now let me wait.

NEEDLE IN THE GROVE

Jeff Noon

'as fresh and compulsive as anything you'll
read this year'
maxim

if music was a drug, how would you take it? if drugs
were music, how would you listen?

after years of playing bass in lousy two-bit bands, elliot
finally gets his big chance/ he meets a singer, a dj and a
drummer who seem to have everything/ passion, talent,
hypnotic songs, and a whole new way of funky
seduction/ but just as their first dance record is
climbing the charts, one of them disappears/ elliot's
search for the missing band member becomes a wild,
fiercely emotional trip into the dark sould of rhythm/
and in the grooves he discovers a world where the
scratches of the stylus cut the body/ a dj's samples are
melodies of blood/ love is a ghost lost in the boom box/
and the only remix that really matters is the remix of
the heart.

'his best so far . . . this is the most stylistically
ambitious, pushing him beyond the quirky originality
of his earlier novels'
the times

'jeff noon's books are so good they should come with a
government warning'
jockeyslut

'*needle in the groove* is where the mainstream of
literature ought to be in the 21st century . . . seething,
sexualised, chemically enhanced'
the wire

'brilliant . . . lush, loose, rhythmic prose which stutters
and jumps, screeches and splinters all over the page'
city life

0 552 99919 9

BLACK SWAN

AUTOMATED ALICE

Jeff Noon

In the last years of his life, the fantasist, Lewis Carroll, wrote a third Alice book. This mysterious work was never published or even shown to anybody. It has only recently been discovered. Now, at last, the world can read of Automated Alice and her fabulous adventures in the future.

That's not quite true. *Automated Alice* was in reality written by Zenith O'Clock, the writer of wrongs. In the book he sends Alice through a clock's workings. She travels through time, tumbling from the Victorian age to land in 1998, in Manchester, a small town in the North of England.

Oh dear, that's not at all right. This trequel to *Alice in Wonderland* and *Through the Looking Glass* was actually written by Jeff Noon. Zenith O'Clock is only a character invented by Jeff Noon and any resemblance to persons living or dead is purely accidental. What Alice encounters in the automated future is mostly accidental too . . . a series of misadventures, even weirder than your dreams.

'DESTINED FOR CULT STATUS . . . CYPERPUNK AT THE CUTTING EDGE'
Maxim

'CAPTURES CARROLL'S STYLE EFFORTLESSLY . . . A WEIRD ALICE WITH A CONTEMPORARY EDGE'
Mail on Sunday

0 552 99905 7

BLACK SWAN

PIXEL JUICE

Jeff Noon

'NOON IS THE LEWIS CARROLL OF
MANCHESTER'S HOUSING ESTATES . . . THE
COCKTAIL OF ALIENATION, NARCOTICS AND
GADGETRY FIZZES WITH ENERGY'
The Times

From the breakdown zones of the mediasphere and
the margins of dance culture comes a selection of
fifty stories, each one strange, telling, disturbing,
or sometimes just plain weird: urban fairytales,
instructions for lost machines, true confessions,
word-dizzy roller-coasters, product recalls, adverts
for mad gadgets, dub cut prose remixes.
Throughout them all, Jeff Noon delights in the
magical possibilities of language, creating a
wholly new kind of storytelling.

Ideas-per-page rating: dangerously close to the
legal limit.

'SPARKY AND LOOPY, LACED WITH PUNS AND
BLACK WIT . . . FOR NOON, BRILLIANTLY,
TOMORROW IS A BLOW TO THE HEAD'
Mail on Sunday

'NOON REFLECTS THE ENERGY OF THE RAVE
GENERATION: THE HAMMER AND TWIST OF
THE MUSIC, THE LANGUAGE OF THE
COMPUTER GAMES ADDICT AND THE BUZZ
OF TECHNOLOGY'
New Statesman

0 552 99937 7

BLACK SWAN